Solar Kill

The Sand Wars
Book 1

Charles Ingrid

Chapter One

Being a Knight meant he was an elite master of his battle armor—but where in the hell was the transport? What had happened to recall? Jack fought the maddening impulse to scratch inside his armor, as sweat dripped down, and the contacts attached to his bare torso itched impossibly. To scratch now, the way he was hooked up, he'd blow himself away.

Damn. He hated complications beyond his control. Where was that signal? They couldn't have been forgotten, could they? If the pullout had happened, they would have been picked up, wouldn't they?

As sweat trickled down his forehead, he looked around.

Sand. They had been dropped in a vast sea of sand. Everywhere beige and brown and pink dunes rose and fell with a life of their own.

This was what Thrakians did to a living world. And the Knights, trained and honed to fight a "Pure" war destroying only the enemy, not the environment, were all that stood between this planet of Milos and his own home world lined up next in a crescent of destruction that led all the way back to the heart of the Thrakian League. Jack had been galvanized to be here to keep the Thrakian menace from his own homestead.

They'd been lucky here on Milos, so far. Only one of the continents had gone under. Still, it was one too many as far as the lieutenant was concerned. The Dominion Forces were losing the Sand Wars. And he was losing his own private struggle with his faith in his superior officers.

They'd been dropped into nowhere five days ago and had been given the most succinct of orders, gotten a pithy confirmation that morning and nothing since. Routine, he'd been told. Strictly a routine mop-up. You didn't treat Knights that way—not the elite of the infantrymen, the fastest, smartest and most honorable fighters ever trained to wage war.

Jack moved inside the battle suit. The Flexalinks meshed imperceptibly, the holograph that played over him sent the message to the suit and, in turn, the right arm flexed. Only that flex, transmitted and stepped up, could have turned over an armored car. Or blasted it to shreds. He sucked a dry lip in dismay over the reflex, then turned his face inside the helmet to read the display.

The display bathed his face plate in a rosy color and his eyesight flickered briefly to the rearview camera display, checking to see which of the troops ranged at his back. The compass wasn't lying to him. "Five clicks. Sarge, have they got us walking in circles?" His suit crest winked in the sun as he looked to his next in command.

"No, sir." Sarge made a husky noise at the back of his throat. Sarge wore a crest that was a noncommittal comment, a "fuck you" on what he thought of his lineage and his home world, but it made no difference to Storm.

A man who came into the Knights might come from any walk of life and the only criteria was whether he was good enough to use a suit. If he was, and he survived basic training, his past became a sealed record, if that was the way the man wanted it.

Jack wondered if the sergeant was chewing again, even though it was against regulations. His mouth watered. He could do with a bit of gum or stim himself. The sand made him thirsty.

He waved his arm. "All right, everybody spread out. Advance in a line. If the Thraks are here, that'll flush 'em. Keep alert. Watch your rear displays and your flanks."

The com relay crackled as Bilosky's voice came over in sheer panic. "Red field! Lieutenant, I'm showing a fracking red field!"

Storm swiveled his head to the sound, cursed at the obstruction of the face plate, and returned a fraction more slowly so that his cameras could follow the motion. "Check your gauges again, Bilosky. It's a malfunction. And calm down." The last in a deadly quiet.

Bilosky's panic stammered to a halt. "Yes, sir." Then, "Goddammit. Storm—those Milots have pilfered my suit! Every one of my gauges is screwed. I'm showing a red field because I'm running on empty!"

Storm bit his tongue. He chinned the emergency lever at the bottom of the face plate, shutting down the holograph field. Then he pulled his arm out of the sleeve quickly and thumbed the com line switches on his chest patch so that he could talk to Bilosky privately. Voice commands could be intercepted. Toggles put him on a low-power, hard to detect frequency that rarely had been hacked. Without power or action to translate, his suit stumbled to a halt. The Flexalinks shone opalescent in the sun.

"How far can you get?"

Not listening, Bilosky swore again. "Goddamn Milots. Here I am fighting their fracking war for them, and they're pirating my supplies —I ought to—"

"Bilosky!"

"Yes, sir. I've got . . . oh, three clicks to go, maybe. Then I'm just another pile of junk standing on the sand." He turned to look at his superior officer, the black hawk crest rampant on his suit.

Storm considered the dilemma. He had his orders, and knew what his orders told him. Clean out Sector Five, and then stand by to get picked up. The last of Sector Five ranged in front of him. They could ration out the most important refills for Bilosky once they got where they were going. "We'll be picked up by then."

"Or the Thraks will have us picked out."

Storm didn't answer for a moment. He was asking a man with little or no power reserves showing on his gauges to go on into battle, in a suit, in full battle mode. Red didn't come up on the gauges until the suit was down to the last ten percent of its resources. That ten percent would carry him less than an hour in full attack mode. Not that it made any difference to a Knight. Wars were always fought in adversity.

Jack sighed. "We're on a wild goose chase, Bilosky. You'll make it."

"Right, sir." A grim noise. "Better than having my suit crack open like an egg and havin' a berserker pop out, right, lieutenant?"

That sent a cold chill down Storm's back. He didn't like his troopers repeating ghoulish rumors. "Bilosky, I don't want rumors like that bandied around. You hear?"

"Yes, sir." Then reluctantly, "It ain't no rumor, lieutenant. I saw it happen once."

"Forget it!"

"Yes, sir."

"Going back on open lines. And watch your mouth." He traced the movement as the other lumbered back into position. Then, abruptly, Jack dialed in his command line and watched as the minuscule screen lit up, his only link with the warship orbiting far overhead.

The watch master at the console, alerted by the static of their long range com lines, swung around. The navy blue uniform strained over his bullish figure. He looked into the lens, his nostrils flaring. The cleft in his square chin deepened in anger. A laser burn along one side of his hairline gave him a lopsided widow's peak.

"Commander Winton here. You're violating radio silence, soldier. What's the meaning of this? Identify yourself."

"I'm Battalion First Lieutenant," he said. "Where's our pullout? We were dropped in here five days ago."

"You're under orders, lieutenant. Get in there and fight. Any further communication and I'll have you up for court martial."

"Court martial? Is that the best you can do? We're dying down here, commander. And we're dying all alone."

The line and screen went dead with a hiss. Suddenly aware of his own vulnerability, Storm pushed his right arm back into his sleeve and chinned the field power switch back on. His suit made an awkward swagger, then settled into a distance eating stride. Fighting wars would be a hell of a lot easier if he could be sure who the enemy was.

Bilosky and Sarge and who knows who else were talking about berserkers now despite orders. The unease it filled him with he could do without. He squinted through the tinted face plate at the alien sun. Strange worlds, strange people, and even stranger enemies. Right now he'd rather wade through a nest of Thraks than try to wade through the rumors surrounding the Milots and their berserkers.

There was no denying the rumors though. The Milots, who had summoned Dominion forces to fight for them against the Thraks, those same low-tech Milots who ran the repair centers and provided the war backup, were as despicable and treacherous as the Thraks Storm had enlisted to wipe out. And there were too many stories about altered suits. Suits that swallowed a man up and spawned instead some kind of lizard-beast man who was a fighting automaton, a berserker and nothing human.

Rumor had it the Milots were putting eggs into the suits, and the heat and sweat of the suit wearer hatched those eggs, the parasitic creature devouring its host and bursting *forth*—

He told himself that the Milots had a strange sense of humor. What Bilosky thought he'd seen, whatever every trooper who repeated the gossip thought they were talking about, was probably a prank played at a local tavern. Knights always took a certain amount of ribbing from the locals, until seen in action, waging the "Pure" war.

Ahead of him, the dunes wavered, sending up a spray of sand. His intercom blared into sound.

"Thraks at two o'clock, lieutenant!"

Storm set his mouth into a grim smile. Now here was an enemy he could deal with. He eyed his gauges to make sure all his systems were ready, and swung about.

Thraks were insects, in the same way jackals were primates or ordinary sow bugs were crustaceans. Which was to say, they qualified as extremely alien. They were equally at home upright or on all fours, due to the sloping of their backs. Jack set himself, watching them boil up out of the sand from underground nests to launch themselves in a four-footed wave until they got close enough to stand up and take fire. Thraks were vicious creatures with but a single purpose—total destruction—at least, fighting Thraks were. Diplomatic Thraks were as vicious in a more insidious way.

He cocked his finger, setting off a line of fire from his glove weapons that slowed the wave. The line of Thraks wavered and swung away, even as they stood up and slung their rifles around from their backs.

On Milos, they had the slight advantage, having gotten there first and having begun their despicable terraforming. Even a slight advantage to the Thraks was disastrous to the Dominion. Milot was already as good as lost . . . battalions had been wiped out, driven back to the deserts, to make as graceful a retreat as possible. Inflict as many casualties as they could, then pull out. Jack's job, as he understood it, was to make the toll of taking Milos so heavy, so dear, that the Thraks would stop here.

Storm's grim smile never wavered, even as he strode forward, spewing death as he went, watching the gauge detailing how much power he had left. Bodies crunched under his armored boots.

They were mopping up. They were to distract the Thraks and

the cannon long enough to let most of the troop ships, cold ships, pull out, and then they would be picked up. That was the promise. . . .

* * *

And then he realizes he is caught in a dream without end.

He strides through the line, knowing the wings of his men will follow, and seeing that the front is not a front, but an unending wave of Thraks. What was reported as a minor outpost is a major staging area, and he's trapped in it, wading through broken bodies and seared flesh. He sweeps both gloves into action, firing as he walks, using the power boost to vault over newly formed walls of bodies and equipment.

Somewhere along the way, Bilosky lets out a cry and grinds to a halt, out of power. He screams as his suit is slit open with a diamond cutter and the Thraks pull him out. Jack ignores the screams and plows onward. He has no choice now. The pullout site is ahead of him. He has to go through the Thraks if he wants to be rescued. Ahead of him is the dream of cold sleep and the journey home. The dream. . . .

Surrounded by what is left of his troop, and by stragglers from other battalions, he lives long enough to fall into a pit, a pit ringed by Thraks. The Dominion warriors stand back to back for days conserving dwindling power despite the fitful solar re-charges, firing only when absolutely necessary, watching the unending wave of Thrakians above them. And he sees a suit burst open, days after its wearer expired with a horrendous scream, and the armor halted like a useless statue in the pit. He sees the seams pop and an incredible beast plow out, and charge the rim of the pit, taking fully a hundred armed Thrakians with it, even as it bellows. He knows he is dreaming that he has seen a berserker, and tries to ignore the shell-like empty suit left behind in shards, with a defiant crest settling into the sand.

Even as he stands and fires, he thinks of what it is he wants to dream. He wants to dream getting out of there alive, with his men.

That is what he wants most. Then he wants to be able to scratch. And he thinks he hears something inside the suit with him, something whispering at his shoulder, and he knows he's losing it. Aunt Min back home always said that when the Devil wanted you, he began by whispering to you over your shoulder. Storm is scared to turn around. All he wants to do is find his dream of going home. And when the recall comes, he doesn't know if he's hearing what he's hearing or not. Or if he can even be found behind the wall of Thraks.

A sound from without racks his mind. What is he hearing? And then he identifies it. A gigantic metal gate clanks open. A hollowness is suddenly filled, and voices filter through.

". . . no survivors."

"There can't be. This ship has been adrift for seventeen years. All systems are shut down, some kind of massive power failure. Look at them. Frozen solid. Transported out of hell, only to die on the way home. God. Look at these antique cryogenic bays. No wonder they didn't make it."

Jack is still dreaming. He sweats cold tears because he can't wake. He's locked in. The twenty-two years of his life play over and over like a möbius strip. But he senses a stirring.

"One of the bays is illuminated, doctor."

"My god. The auxiliary system is still functioning here. Get the life support in here, and quickly. We might just be able to save this one—"

"But orders—"

"Fuck orders! Imagine finding one of them alive, after all these years. I'm going to do everything to keep him that way."

A tingle of warmth in his icy existence. Is he dreaming or dying?

"If we wake him, do you think he'll be sane? What does a man dream of for seventeen years?"

"He's locked into a debriefing loop. We'll be lucky if he has any mind left at all."

A scraping. Something scratching at his death mask. . . .

"That's enough chatter. Get the coffin open and get ready to plug him in . . . god. Look at his feet. Frostbite. And his hand. He's set the auxiliary system off himself."

"That's impossible. He's in cryogenic suspension."

"When the power failed, he may have come to enough to know there was trouble. He's jammed his right hand against the emergency panel. It's the only thing that saved him. After he's stabilized, check the other coffins. See if any of the dead reacted as well. This man must be a born survivor."

"Look at these suits."

A distracted grunt, then, "We have orders. Destroy them."

"Destroy them? These are relics . . . the black market. . . ."

"You know the orders. Destroy them! Nurse, get your mask on and get ready. The coffin lid comes open now."

* * *

Jack bolted up in his bunk. Dreaming again. Sweat poured off his forehead and into his cupped hands. He took a deep breath, feeling the darkness and the night sway around him. With that deep breath, he began to count down, sending his mind into a hypnotic mode that he'd learned as second nature.

And when he calmed, he told himself, "I'm awake this time. Awake and alive."

As he dropped his trembling hands from his face, he looked at the clock, though he didn't really need to. The graying edges of the room told him it was nearly dawn.

He'd only awakened three times that night. Slowly, but surely, he was getting better. It wasn't that his dreams frightened him. Memories of the Sand Wars weren't pleasant, but he could endure them. No, it was the stuff of dreams themselves. The trap. Being closed off without recourse. Would he awake into reality or be ensnared again?

Jack put out a hand, reaching for the vial of mordil on his nightstand. It came up empty in his palm. He grimaced, then threw the bottle away into the grayness. It clattered in the corner. Black market, the mordil hadn't done much good, anyway, though it had come guaranteed to give sleep without dreams. There was no telling how much the mordil had been stepped on before getting to him. Sometimes it worked, and sometimes it didn't. This night, it hadn't. Not that any of his doctors would have approved. Dreams were necessary, he'd been told, to keep a man sane.

He swung his feet over the edge of the bunk and listened to the sounds of Claron coming awake. The early morning stir and tentative bursts of birdsong swelled in his hearing. It was not a bad place to wake up within. Making his rounds in the virgin green forests of Claron would do more for him than any mordil. Jack stood up and began to get dressed in his serviceable Ranger grays.

Before he left the station, he walked to a locked room and thumbed the door open. It was small, closet-like, and when the storage door swung open releasing pressure, Jack felt the shock, like a physical blow, thump him in the chest.

His battle suit hung in dry dock. Its mother-of-pearl form swayed off the meathook, the stirring of the air in the chamber awakening it. It had the service markings painted on, though fading, and the even more garish personal markings that the twenty-year-old rookie had illustrated for himself. And he looked at the crest, chosen by the innocent young volunteer who could hardly wait to be a full-fledged Knight. Two years later, that rookie would be a veteran lieutenant, abandoned to the Thrakians on Milos.

When the transporter had finally found them, he was the only one left at the bottom of the pit, but it didn't seem to matter, when he boarded the transport cold ship. Only one ship. It left three-quarters full, carrying the only survivors of the Thrakian invasion of Milos. They'd been scraping them off the surface of Milos like so many squashed bugs, all that was left of the Dominion's finest.

He remembered the first time he'd seen his armor since lying down to coldsleep. Nineteen years, three toes and one right little finger later, as he readied to leave the Veteran's Hospital, the nurse had very surreptitiously presented him with a footlocker the night before his discharge. They had shared a lot of nights, lately, and he'd had no suspicion this would be different. But the contents of the footlocker had sent him mentally reeling.

"Don't you like it?"

The Flexalinks winked at him, an obscene pearl from the bottom of the trunk.

"This . . . this is my suit."

"I know that." She had hung onto his elbow, not noticing the tremble that ran through his body.

"They were all supposed to have been destroyed."

She had smiled up at him. "I know. But this one's yours. You survived, and I thought, well, I don't know. I thought you'd like to have your suit, so I hid it."

He should have asked her how she got her hands on it. Why anyone had given her the opportunity to smuggle it away. But he didn't want to ask. Didn't want to know what the payment for a seeming kindness might be. He'd asked too many questions throughout his career as it was.

Jack couldn't force himself to look away. In any other time, from any other war, a Dominion Knight would have given his soul to keep his suit.

But not this time. Not this war.

He stared in horror. He remembered the cold fear it had given him in his dreams to be wearing the suit again. And wondered if the Milots did create berserkers, and if so, *how?* And wondered if the nurse had ever realized what she'd done when she'd saved the suit, hidden it, and then given it to him. She could not have heard the rumors about parasites incubating inside the suits.

A bird trilled outside the compound, reminding him of his new life. He swung the storage door shut. When he could open it and look the battle armor in the face again, emotionlessly, he would know he was well.

Until then, he planned to find the man that had made a coward out of him, and kill the son of a bitch.

Chapter Two

The rehab tech looked down at his clipboard for the twentieth time during the interview, not to review what the screen was telling him, but to hide his face, so that the man sitting across from him couldn't read his expression.

The tech was scared. He'd been scared for the past seven months, when the hospital had discharged this man into his general care at the rehab center. The man was a Knight—an idealist who'd been trained to fight the "Pure" war, and believed in it, had even taken vows accordingly and lived, exercised, breathed by those vows. And the man had been betrayed on Milos, like thousands of his brothers—and was a fracking time bomb because of it.

Who did his superiors think he was, a goddamn saint, that he could rehab a Knight? Thank god, the patient no longer had access to a battle suit, and that the Knights had been disbanded many years ago. Today's armored infantrymen were just so much cannon fodder, and the tech could deal with that. The computer screen blinked at him, reminding the tech that he was supposed to be working on his client's discharge.

"I don't care where you reassign me, just make it somewhere I can be alone. I want to be alone." Storm stared at the wall and watched it form into a comforting hologram. He glared at it until the picture grew hesitant, and then returned to wall.

The rehab tech said blandly, "There aren't too many people as alone as you are." He typed something into his keyboard. "All right. I'll recommend several occupations that go along with your background survey—but I'll tell you this, Storm—you don't want to be alone. And when you realize that, you'll have accomplished what I've been trying to do these past seven months."

He stood up, staring at the stark expression of the sandy-haired man. A forty-one-year-old mind inside a lean, twenty-two-year-old body—both of them harboring the lust for revenge and the killer instinct of millennia-old homo sapiens. He'd been born to fight. The tech shook his head. He'd done what he could.

Jack barely heard the tech leave. His thoughts, waking dreams, boiled over him. Storm stretched out his right hand, tensed it so that the muscles ridged over the back of his hand, muscles that led to the smallest digit and ended abruptly in a scar-smoothed absence instead of the little finger. He rubbed the edge of his hand. That was the finger that had saved his life . . . and plunged him into living hell.

He'd had it explained to him, oh, maybe a hundred times. By the doctor, the nurses, the rehab tech, the computer monitor, and it still made no more sense than it had upon hearing it the first time.

The injuries too old to repair entirely. Maybe he could get his toes back, but he wasn't too keen on the idea of being off his feet for months while transplant nubs healed in place.

He was the sole survivor of the Sand Wars. Oh, there were bound to be a few others—deserters mostly, hidden here and there in the underground strata. But his cold ship was one of only three to have made it off Milos, and the only one to make it past the Thrakian blockade.

That was undoubtedly when it sustained the damage which threw it off course and eventually caused massive system failures. It must have shuddered through an unplanned power surge, hit warp speed, and gone elsewhere until dying. It had drifted then, powerless and off course, lost in the outer lanes for seventeen years. And, inside, only his bay was functioning on auxiliary power. All of the others had gone dark, their occupants as dead as the ship in which they lay.

The doctors had no explanation for it. Somehow, he had roused when the power had gone off—roused enough to jam his right hand against the interior of the bay, pushing the panel that would activate the emergency auxiliary power. The action could have sprung the "coffin" lid and freed him, but instead it jarred the auxiliary power button and he was plunged back into cryogenic sleep. The coincidence had saved his life and lost him his right little finger and three toes to frostbite, a small enough price to pay, his doctors had told him.

If he had been freed, they doubted he could have lived for very long aboard the systems dead ship.

He was heir to the ignominious title of sole survivor of the most disastrous defeat of Dominion Forces since their formation. Jack smiled grimly at this, aware that he was no doubt being monitored from the other side of the wall, beyond the holograph. He wondered what they thought about him—his tense smiles at nothing at all. His inability to sleep a night through without waking, panic-stricken, six or seven times. His determination to stay solo, alone, a survivor.

The Thrakians, he'd been told, had stopped conquering almost as suddenly as they'd started, leaving behind a crescent-shaped path of destruction—once verdant planets turned into seas of sand by war and alien terraforming.

No, not sand. Jack stretched his hands in front of him on the table, aware even as he thought, that the rehab tech was reporting to a superior, and decisions were being made that would determine the course of the rest of his life—or so they thought. Once he was *free*. . . .

Not sand. It looked like sand. Moved through the gloved hands of his battle armor like sand. Flowed. Grit floated on the air when flung. Hot. Dry. Dusty. But not sand, exactly. They knew now that it was filled with microcosms. Tiny organisms that stayed dormant until the Thrakians planted their young, and then went to work.

The Thrakian League had decimated eight solar systems in order to create nests for their grubs. Warm, sand-filled nests. And why they stopped there, no one knew. It certainly wasn't because the Dominion Forces had defeated them at Milos. Nor had they been defeated at the Stand of Dorman's Colony, Storm's home planet.

No, the Thraks simply stopped because they'd wanted to, and for the last fifteen years, there had been uneasy treaty between the League and the Dominion. Uneasy because none of the Dominion scientists could predict when, or if, the swarming would occur again —or how to stop it if it did.

It was already too late for Storm and for Storm's family, long dead, though freshly mourned.

Breaking off his thoughts, Jack looked up at the wall. "Hurry up," he said. "I want to get on with this."

On with what? With saving the universe from the Thrakian menace? He laughed humorlessly at himself and leaned back into the form-fitting chair. It made minor adjustments to his lanky form. He did not sit in a chair so much as he conquered it.

The conference room door sprung aside to admit the rehab tech. He threw a motley looking gray jumpsuit onto the table, where it slid until it halted in front of Storm. He picked it up with his nine fingers and spread it out to read the insignia.

"A Ranger."

"That's right. You've got your wish, Storm. You've been assigned to stay on Claron, one of the Outward Bound planets. Not too much going on there . . . mining and the supportive trade for that. You'll be gathering a data base on the planet itself."

"I'm not a xenobiologist."

"No, but you had some background training in it, before you volunteered." The rehab tech gave a thin smile, matching the sparseness of his brown hair. "The government can't afford a specialist for every backwater planet. But if you want to be alone, that's the place to go. I've ordered a packet of background media for you."

"How soon can I leave?" Storm lowered the suit, curling it toward his chest, a subconscious protective gesture that the rehab tech noted.

"Day after tomorrow."

For the first time in weeks, the veteran smiled, and the happiness reached his washed-out blue eyes.

And in the Claron morning, the echo of that smile touched his eyes again. He threw his pack over the skimmer and lashed it on, listening to the redtails courting in the sky over the compound. Their raucous chatter could only lure another redtail, and that was the way it should be. They swooped overhead toward the forest beyond and disappeared, with a chorus of wild, hysterical giggles.

Storm fit into Claron. He fit better than even his rehab tech could have guessed, and in ways he never could have predicted. The mining syndicates that made up the boomtowns operated within an unwritten code of environmental protection, one that he felt comfortable with. They had a purity to their industry, a code, that perhaps only someone like himself could understand. The plains were filled with obsidite, worth crossing space to pull out, and worth doing it right.

The only trouble he'd had in all his months of work was with a local brewery, Samson's Ale. Claron boomrats had liking for the malt crops, a liking that put them on the list for extinction.

It wasn't that Storm had a thing for boomrats. When he'd first located his compound at the fringe of the Ataract forests, he'd cursed at the skinny little rodents more than once. The thieving, fractious critters stole his supplies and ranged over their territory like packs of bandits, shoulder to shoulder, kits in the middle and scarred veterans to the outside, though they were scarcely big enough to give a predator a decent mouthful.

They walked on their hind legs, to look bigger and more ferocious, Storm thought. And when they'd discovered Samson Breweries' malt fields, they thought they'd walked into paradise. At first it hadn't been necessary to kill them—the boomrats ate themselves to death, unused to the luxury of abundant food. Jack had walked through rows of chewed-off stalks, with bloated boomrats belly-up in the aisles.

That hadn't taken them too long to figure out. Then the crop eating began in earnest and he'd had to go toe to toe with Samson to give the little critters the right to live. Luckily, the sonic fences he'd devised seemed to work all right.

Storm didn't know what niche the boomrats occupied in the ecology of Claron yet, but he knew he'd find out. And he was pleased with himself for saving them for that niche until then.

The dawn fled completely. The mauve horizon of Claron's southern sky hugged the forest and mountain ridge fiercely. He looked out toward the plains, to the mines, and saw the white funnels of their steam stacks. He felt like a little company. In a day or two, after this tour, he might go into Upside, and say hello. A little public relations, and private ones, would go good right about now.

He kicked the starter and swung on, the skimmer shuddering into life beneath him. Its shadow skimmed the dirt clod meadow and took off as he throttled it forward. He'd have to learn to spend more time on the Ataract . . . it was supposed to be the site of his permanent base, but he'd found excuses to keep the compound relatively mobile for several years. He didn't like staring into the eye of Star Gate on the eastern edge, even though that was principally why he was on Claron—why they'd needed a Ranger.

He was little more than a Gatekeeper. Oh, the exobiology work he did was important, but only if colonists started moving in, next to the miners. But it was the Gate—unnatural hole in the fabric of the universes—it was minding the Gate that had put him there.

And so Storm watched it. He watched it with the faint prickling of hair at the back of his neck, as he comprehended just what it was he dealt with, unlike most of the locals. No, Storm knew its powers all too well. Claron had been discovered at the other side of the hole when the Gate had been punched through, and it had taken the energy of a small nova to do it. Star Gates were few and far between, being too expensive and too dangerous to the patterns of the galaxies to use. This one had been a fortuitous accident . . . and would stay that way, as long as he was assigned as Ranger. The Dominion did not want it expanded.

Jack wanted it closed, but knew that wasn't likely to happen either.

He sighed as he brought the skimmer in line with the golden eye. It was a short run from the compound. He measured it off, to be sure it was still anchored. The energy waves radiating from it rippled. He'd set up low level sonic posts to be sure nothing from Claron absentmindedly wandered into it—although the corner of Jack's mouth twitched at the thought of a pack of boomrats wandering into the Gate. He'd like to see the fraction of a second long, wide- eyed expressions on their rodent faces when faced with deep space.

Measurements done, he swung the skimmer about, and turned on his recorder. The morning breeze of the Ataract swept his face, drying the nervous beads of perspiration on his forehead. It was a raw breeze, and spiced, smelling nothing like the planet he'd grown up on. Dorman's Stand had been an agro-planet, with the smell of freshly turned earth and tangy pesticides, and freshly harvested vegetables. He took a deep breath. He'd almost forgotten what Dorman's Stand had smelled like, dampened by the years spent in the stink of his own sweat and lubricants of the battle armor.

Storm brought the skimmer to idle and stalled there, in midair. He felt uneasy. The Ataract was relatively quiet this morning. No boomrats were out. Yet the sun was up.

He rubbed the back of his neck. He felt vaguely on edge, the way he usually did before an assault drop—

Jack swung the skimmer about, and began to patch in his lines to the compound computer. His hand trembled and he cursed as he fumbled over the keys missed by the amputated tenth finger. He looked up, caught a vision of the tree looming in front of him and leaned over, pulling the skimmer around it. But it brought the machine skewing to a halt, trembling in the air, and he caught himself panting.

He took a deep breath and got control of himself. The terminal vibrated under his fingertips, letting him know it had made the connection, and he dropped his gaze to read the board. Everything was fine. There was nothing in this section of the Outward Bounds that wasn't supposed to be there.

Jack laughed at himself. He disconnected the linkage, and returned it to recording. The skimmer coughed once.

Below him, crudely dug out ground rippled in the air discharge from the skimmer. Jack descended and turned the transport off as he recognized the field he'd dug. Small, twisted green shoots of malt edged upward, and he grinned as he crouched down to examine it. He'd conned Samson Breweries out of a sackful of seed, and here was his reward, already pushing up to meet the sun. He tickled a shoot. He hadn't entirely lost his green thumb, he guessed, though only the gods knew what would happen when the boomrats found this patch. He'd grown it for them, though.

A sharp pebble skimmed the air, slashing into his shoulder. Jack yelped with the sting and straightened up, looking around.

The horde of boomrats looked back, shoulder to shoulder, their beady, flint-colored eyes staring, the adults stretched to their utmost height on their skinny hind legs. One of them gripped a stone in his front paw.

"I'll be damned," Jack muttered. He took a step away from the malt patch, and watched as the thirty-strong pack of boomrats shifted warily with him. He pointed. "This is for you, guys—but if you chew it down to the nubs now, you won't have anything left for the winter, or to go to seed for next year."

Scarface, the leader, showed his fangs.

Jack backed up, toward the skimmer. He wasn't worried about one or even two boomrats, but a pack of that size could chew him up a little. He held his hands up in the air even as he wondered if they'd thrown the stone at him. Tool implementation? He'd have to make a note as soon as he got out of here.

As he backed up, Scarface seemed to relax. His tawny body

dropped to all fours and he ran at Storm, and stopped, chittering. His rodent muzzle worked, then he spit something out at the man's booted feet. Then, warily, the boomrat backed up and rejoined his pack.

A shiny green stone, covered with spittle from the creature's mouth pouches, shone up at Storm. He bent over and picked it up, and wiped it off. It was not anything of import, except it was something pretty and shiny. Jack dropped it into this pouch.

"I take it this is a thank you for the malt. You're welcome—but—" Jack hesitated as he swung aboard the skimmer. "Don't do anything rash like taking over the planet, okay? I could be in a lot of trouble for this."

Muzzles and whiskers quivered uncomprehendingly as he kicked the skimmer back into operation and headed for the fringe of the Ataract.

He woke sweating. His pulse pounded in his ears like war drums, and he lay still in the darkness of the room, waiting for his hearing to go back to normal. He wiped the palms of his hands across his T-shirt. As usual, he couldn't remember what he'd been dreaming, just that he'd been suffocating—

Jack swung off the bed. He went to the faintly glowing panel of the computer terminal and activated it. Something was wrong. Not just his life or his psyche, which was always abnormal, but something was wrong with Claron. He feared it.

The screen fired to life under his fingers, but he heard the noise before the tracking came up, and he flinched, looking upward, seeing only the ceiling, but knowing what he heard outside. Blips and streaks across the tracking field confirmed it.

Claron was under siege.

Jack bolted for the doorframe. He looked outside, to the barely lightening sky, and heard the rumble. He cursed, even as his heart took an awkward leap in his chest. The sky over the mines took on a violent, orange glow.

"Holy Knights," Storm muttered and froze, unable to look away.

He was watching a planet burn.

He heard the reentry rumble and knew that the warships were headed his way.

Fumbling, he lunged back at the terminal and transmitted a message along the computer lines. Then he stopped. There was no way of knowing if anyone was there to receive his warning.

Dull thunder spoke overhead. He had no time left. The very air crackled with the heat, the heat of the weaponry being unleashed on unsuspecting, undeserving Claron. He had one chance left. He stripped off his shirt.

Jack pulled open the storage locker and jerked open the seams of the battle armor. He didn't have time to think. The suit hummed faintly as he climbed into it and began the laborious process of sealing up.

He attached only the contacts he had to for operation. He wouldn't have time to fight back—no, all Jack wanted to do was to live. He had one chance to make it. His helmet snapped into place.

The ceiling blew off the compound. Orange light flared in, wrapping around him like a maelstrom. The suit was baffled, but stayed upright. Jack paid no attention as he connected the last of the wires, and the holograph came on, whispering smoothly.

He'd kept it well oiled and powered all these months, in spite of his fear of it. He still feared it, but he feared dying worse.

The firestorm caught up the last of the compound, whipping it up from around him, and Jack stood in the clear. In the orange glow of the burn-off, the golden eye of the Star Gate had turned to an eerie blue. Jack ran toward it, loping easily, the power vault of the suit giving him the ability to move over the terrain even as it charred and buckled under him.

He looked up, once, his sensors dulling the fire, and he caught sight of the tremendous warship cruising overhead, its reentry shields still glowing. He couldn't identify it.

The cannon mouth swung around. Jack ducked his head and put

all his resources into a last leap. He flung his arms forward and jumped, diving headfirst into the blue curtain of the Star Gate.

It wrapped around him, still dormant, hugged him, brought him to a stop. Jack rolled over and looked back out the Gate. Red and orange fire, in sheets, rippled across the verdant tracts of the Ataract forest—over all of Claron. He had only a second to ask himself why, when the energy blacklash hit—and the Star Gate activated, blowing him *through and beyond.*

Chapter Three

There is always a kid in Basic who ignores the drill sarge when he says, "Don't ask." Always. It's a universal law, like gravity. Even when you don't really want to know the answer, there's always some jerk to ask the question.

"What if the drop tubes misfire and instead of going planet side, we get put out beyond the orbit?"

Someone in the back row had snickered, saying quietly, "What if you put your ass in your helmet instead of your head?"

But the D.I. had ignored all of them, his baggy brown eyes sweeping over them with contempt. "Don't ask," he answered. "You don't want to know."

"Yeah, but—what if," the kid persisted. "I mean, your suit's got air —it's insulated and it can pressurize. You got communications, water —you could make it, couldn't you? Until you got picked up? It's battle armor, right, but it could double for a deepspace suit temporarily, right?"

"You don't wanna know," the sarge repeated, wearily.

But this kid that asks these questions, it's also a universal law that he just doesn't shut up until he gets his answer— or fifty laps.

In Storm's case, the kid in Basic got fifty laps. But as he looked out his face plate, doing a slow tumble, he thought . . . *now* I know, Sarge. And the answer is yes . . . your suit'll hold. Not forever. Probably not until you get picked up and especially not if someone is hanging around to shoot holes in it, but yeah—the suit will hold.

Probably longer than your mind will.

And he did another slow roll through black velvet space, praying the tinting on the face plate would block out the starlight, saving his sight for another day. Beyond him, the golden eye of the Star Gate stared back, an unwinking deity which, after having punted him this far, was dormant once again.

He didn't even feel like calculating the time he might have left. The thought was too morbid and, Jack added to himself, he'd probably been on borrowed time since he waded into that pit of Thraks nearly twenty years ago. So much for the borrowed time theory. So what he did do was cautiously, supremely cautiously, for every wave of the suit's limbs sent him veering in another direction, take the time to finish hooking himself up, weapons and all.

His cameras scanned and he saw that he was drifting in open space, but that he might not necessarily drift for eternity—there was a planet within view and, in a few months, he might even drift close enough for its gravity to snag him and pull him down. It went without saying that Jack wouldn't be alive to find out if he was right or not.

He considered his com equipment, wondering if he should put out an SOS. It took little energy, was solar-powered, and up to optimum, so he kicked the chin lever that put out the transmission. Eerily, he couldn't hear it, so he could only assume the suit broadcast what he was telling it to.

Jack spent the rest of his time sweating, hearing things, and being angry. It was the anger that kept him sane . . . and so he fed it, because he didn't like the aching fear of the suit, and he was worried that he was actually hearing what he thought he was. It was a low, scratchy mumbling, just beyond the range of his senses, and he didn't know if he really heard anything or not, like a ghosted-transmission. Just a spidery, whispery kind of noise. It made no difference to him that the suit embraced him like a long-lost lover, that wearing it brought back a kind of easy familiarity, that it nestled him close and kept him alive.

"Sarge, what happens if the Milots got to my suit, too, and put those—those parasites into it and even now I'm hatching them and they'll consume me and I'll be like Bilosky, dead, and then a lizard berserker, like you, Sarge?"

"Ya don't wanna know."

"But, Sarge—what if it's true? What if it happens? What if it's going to happen to me?"

"Don't ask."

"But Sarge—I can feel something tickling the back of my neck!"

"Fifty laps, kid, and then, if you still want to ask a question, ask why some jerk of a commander sent you dirt side to Milos, and then left you there to die? Ask that one."

"Ya don't wanna know why, sergeant," Jack said wearily. He licked his lips for the hundredth time and felt his stomach do an elegant zero-grav flip-flop as the suit rolled over again. "You don't want to know the answer to that one."

"No, but you do, Jack. And you'd better stay alive to ask it, this time. They shut you up with seventeen years of cold sleep and two years of hospitalization and rehab, but they ain't shutting up this time. There's nobody else left to ask the question this time, Jack my boy—and you've already done your fifty laps. And—hell! While you're at it, ask them what happened to Claron!"

His dazed voice echoed inside his plate, and he realized he was still suited up. How long now? How long had he been talking to himself. He shook. Carefully, he withdrew his right hand from his glove, the missing metacarpal bothered him with a ghost of sensation, and he wiped the trickling sweat on his face. Heat dissipation still a problem inside a suit. He grinned without humor. While he had his hand out, he checked the SOS beam. Still on. Had anybody heard him? Somebody had better hear him, because he wanted to live!

The scratchy whispering had stopped. Had he only imagined it? How long had he imagined himself back in Basic? How long had he been tumbling out here?

He spread out. Below him was a canopy of stars. To his two o'clock, the glowing blue ball of a planet which just might snag him in —if he could afford to wait for months. He couldn't. The suit wasn't made for it, and neither was he. And even if he got close enough, who said the planet-holders down below were equipped to pick up a reading on him, and dash out to save him?

He slipped his hand back inside the glove and flexed the fingers. Jack decided to go back to talking to himself. After all, staying angry was as good as staying sane, until he came to the end.

* * *

"Holy shit," Tubs exclaimed, his fat fingers playing over the sensor keyboard of the *Montreal*. He'd been looking for trouble dirt side— they were strikebreakers after all, going in to bust up a planet, but he hadn't expected to sense anything this far out. A mine, perhaps. He waved frantically for Short-Jump to attend him at the screen.

"What is it?"

"I'm tracking the god-damndest piece of space junk I've ever seen."

"A mine?"

"I thought so at first, but don't know now."

Short-Jump frowned and leaned in over Tubs' shoulder.

He was uglier than sin, so ugly it was hard to find a woman who'd look at him twice unless he got a short jump head start, hence his nickname. He wrinkled his spatulate nose. "Hell, that's a suit. Probably deader'n last week's soya rations."

"A scab maybe? Jettisoned out here as a warning?"

"Could be. Strikers c'n be a tough lot." Short-Jump grinned. He relished a good fight. Opinion aboard the *Montreal* used to be that he hoped for a battle injury to give him a free ride into cosmetic surgery. Tubs had given up on that theory long ago. Strikebusters like Short-Jump made enough money to pay for any kind of surgery. He had decided his shipmate just liked to bust heads. "I'll go tell the captain."

Tubs looked back to his screen, his pop eyes still round with amazement. "Shit," he muttered to himself excitedly, as he caught a better view. "That's no deepsuit—that's battle armor!" He began to plot a fix for the tractor beams.

The captain of the *Montreal* watched noncommittally as the tractor beam hung the armor in midair and the hangar doors sealed shut. The Flexalinks glistened like mother-of- pearl in the dingy recesses of the privateer's hold. The suit hung quietly, with no sign of life in it. Captain Marciane scratched his thin thatch of brown and gray hair. He'd never seen battle armor quite like this before—one of the old, elite suits, was his best guess. At his side, Tubs finally babbled to a halt and scuffed his boots on the decking. Marciane realized his men waited for him to do something. He signaled for the transparent bulkhead to open. Still eying that suit cautiously, he stepped into the now pressurized hangar.

"Now that's one oyster I'd hate to shuck," he murmured to himself.

"Shall I go cut it down, captain?" Tubs blurted.

"No. It might be armed." He waved the tractor beam off. It unlocked, dumping the armor five feet to the deck abruptly. It landed with a BOOM that reverberated off the metal walls.

Tubs yelped. "Holy god, captain! If it was armed—"

Marciane silenced him. "Not armed that way. It may be armed against tampering." He walked a little closer, tilting his head back. Whoever had worn the suit had been a tall man. "The men who used to wear these things . . ." his voice trailed off.

"What'll we do with it?" Short-Jump pushed back past the bulkhead into the hangar with them.

"We leave it alone. After we get dirt side, we see what kind of salvage we get from it." Having seen enough of a legend, Marciane turned his back on the armor.

Tubs, a skittish man, but good in his field, gave an odd hop, and grabbed the captain's forearm. "Captain! It moved. I swear it did."

Marciane turned around slowly on one heel. He could see no evidence that the suit had so much as twitched. He grabbed Tubs' torch from his equipment belt and shone the beam into the darkened face plate, and saw nothing. The beam etched dark shadows into the half-empty hold. He lowered the torch. "You guys are all on edge—a fighting edge, and I like that, because that's what I need to break a strike. We'll be doing reentry shortly. Get back to your posts and get ready, because we're going down burning. I want us to be too hot for th' line to handle. Got that?"

"Yes, sir." Tubs' round, usually florid face paled, but he saluted.

Short-Jump just gave him a flat smile from his ugly face. Marciane nodded briskly.

He turned for one last look back at the bulkhead. "Besides," he said to himself. "If there had been someone inside there—he's either dead, or insane by now, anyhow."

A dry, rasping voice followed them. "Would you settle for thirsty?"

The three men froze. Tubs was the first to turn around, but his legs had buckled and dumped him on the deck, where he quivered, his mouth working uselessly. Only his hand twitched into activity, pointing at the suit.

Short-Jump kneed his companion. "Cut it out, for crissakes. It's not a ghost, there's someone in there. Captain, permission to aid the visitor?"

"Granted." Marciane wet his lips as the squat, ugly man waded forward, unafraid, to the death suit.

* * *

Marciane watched the thirsty man gulp down a second glass of water, then motioned for the two of them to be left alone in the tiny galley. The *Montreal* was a refitted freighter, not a passenger ship, and carried few of the amenities. The captain captured a chair and wrapped himself around it, eying the sandy-haired young man with the world-weary eyes. He wore nondescript gray pants, with the many pockets empty sacks, and his torso was bare, except for the tiny crimp marks where contact sensors had been clipped. Those pinches of flesh smoothed out even as they talked.

"What were you doing out there?"

"Dying and praying, mostly." The visitor dried his lips on the back of his hand, and Marciane saw the missing little finger, sliced off neatly at the edge.

"Were you jettisoned? Marooned? Do you know anything about Washington Two?"

The man's head swiveled and he squinted slightly, to look at the tiny view-screen in the galley's wall, as it previewed the upcoming planet. "So that's the name of it. No, can't say as I do."

The two men eyed each other. Marciane rubbed his chin abruptly. He had a feeling there was a lot more to the youth than showed—like the battle armor, for instance. He *knew* it couldn't be Storm's, but it was.

"How long were you out there? Where did you come from?"

"Let me have a look at your bulletin board, and I can give you a pretty good idea of how long I was drifting. As to where I came from . . . captain, I don't want to hedge with you, right now. I've had a look at your setup. You don't want to be telling me too much of your business, either."

Marciane reached out. His fingers drummed the tabletop. "I can't have you sending messages through to Washington Two."

"That's not my business—that's yours."

"All right then. Come with me." The *Montreal* captain was never so aware that, as his visitor shadowed him, the image of the battle armor shadowed him as well.

Tubs' round eyes opened wider as he saw the two men shouldering into the narrow bay of his work station. He craned his neck at them. "Yes, captain—what is it?"

"Storm wants to have a look at our bulletin board. Pull it up."

"Yes, sir."

He brought up the subspace messages. There were a few holos of wanted men, some odd news items here and there, a few personals, and then the brief, startling news flash that the colony planet of Claron had been firestormed forty-eight hours ago, and all survivors evacuated.

Storm's face tightened. "That's your answer, Captain. I've been out here forty-eight hours."

"You're from Claron? Impossible. And who would do a thing like that? Claron's only been open a few years. It's worth next to nothing."

"I don't know. I was rangering there when we got hit. I got to my suit, put it on, and made it to the Gate that opened Claron up. The energy backlash knocked me through."

Marciane made an irritated whistling noise through the gap in his front teeth. "Nobody destroys a planet for nothing."

"No," said Storm softly. "And I intend to find out the real reason. Just set me down dirt side, and I'll be on my way."

Tubs cleared his throat, said nothing to his captain's warning glare, and turned back to his board, shutting down the bulletin board.

Marciane looked to his visitor. "It's going to be a little more complicated than that, son. We're going to be doing a little destroying ourselves."

"Doing what?"

"We're strikebreakers."

Marciane invited Storm back to the galley, where he poured out something a little stronger than water. Faded blue eyes considered the whiskey label on the bottle.

"This is good stuff."

"Tantalos prides itself on its breweries. I saved this for a rare occasion." Marciane poured himself a drink and let it sit while his guest sipped at the mellow amber.

Storm savored the drink, swallowed and then said, carefully, "Where I come from, people drink this kind of stuff over deals."

Marciane, for all his deepspace-toughened hide, flushed a little, then said, "Close."

"What do you want from me?"

"What do you think I want? Your suit, and your expertise in operating it. If it's yours."

"It's mine, all right. But I'm retired."

"So am I . . . into private enterprise. Now, down there, we have Washington Two, in the clutches of strikers who've shut down the spaceport and damn near everything else. I have people paying me who don't want to be shut down. They don't want to be union. They don't want to starve while the unions and the Dominion negotiate over this parcel of space."

"So you're going to kick ass."

"Damn right. I've been invited to the party."

"If the port's closed down, how do you expect to get in? They're going to know you're coming and blow you right out of the sky."

"No." Marciane took his shot glass and sipped the Tantalos whiskey. It fired his throat. He grinned. "I've got a plan."

Storm sat back in his chair. He considered the privateer. "Can I listen without obligation?"

"Yes. You're not going anywhere unless we jettison you. But if you come with us, you can make some credits, and start getting some answers."

Gazes locked and then Storm said slowly, "What makes you think I want to ask questions?"

"You have a planet blasted away under you, and you're not curious as to why? You don't want those renegades hauled up for doing it?" Marciane shook his head. "I know what kind of training the Knights went through. I don't know if that's your dad's suit, or where you inherited it from, but I know you have certain kinds of beliefs, and what happened on Claron violated most of them. What if you find out those were Thrakian ships? Or union ships, softening up the sector."

"What if I do?"

"Then you get the answers and you do what has to be done to stop them. Right? So here's what we do—my sources tell me the strikers have taken over the port, and most of them don't know anything about running it. So, in about three hours, they're going to have a real emergency on their hands."

Storm watched as Marciane refilled both shot glasses. "What kind of an emergency?"

"The *Montreal* is about to have a radiation spill, and we'll be coming in hot, real hot. They'll have to clear the docks and put on their rad suits and follow emergency procedures straight down the line. Most of them won't know shit about what they're doing, but they'll be too scared to think about what it is I'm doing."

"And after we've docked?"

"We come out firing. We'll take out most of the strikers there, because that's where they're concentrated. They've had a stranglehold on shipments for over a month now."

A slow smile played over the edge of Storm's mouth. "And I can guess who's first off the ship, laying down a spray of fire."

"Can you now? Well, who's better equipped to do it than you? And, you'll be well paid in Dominion credits for doing it. Is it a deal?"

Jack took a deep breath. It was, after all, what he'd been trained to do. He held up his corresponding shot glass. "For now."

Marciane had a good crew. The suit was fully charged by the time Jack climbed back into it and sealed it up. As he began to connect the sensors, he braced himself. The *Montreal* was already going down "hot," spewing radioactivity as she went, skewing awkwardly through the sky.

Marciane had an iron fist on the controls, walking a fine line between having a highly responsive ship, and a genuinely out of control vehicle. The radioactivity was genuine enough though, not enough to threaten anyone, just alert the scanning equipment at Washington Two's spaceport.

He sensed the suit come to life around him, embracing him, for one suffocating moment. Storm took a deep breath, pounding the fear out of himself. He'd made it this far, hadn't he?

And he wondered if he could find someone to strip the suit down and flush it out, because it held this stale, brackish scent that was really the smell of his own fear sweated out of his pores and into those of the armor. He felt the lasers come up to power. His wrist tingled, telling him he was now armed and ready.

He'd patched in the *Montreal's* frequency and now heard Marciane calmly telling Washington Two that he didn't care if the spaceport was under restriction, he had an emergency and unless they wanted him to "spill" all over their main city structures, they'd better have an emergency dock opened for him, along with enough manpower to dampen him down once he landed. And he wanted the local hospitals notified to take him and his crew in for rad care once the ship had been shut down.

He'd done his job well. On the open circuitry coming back from Washington Two, Storm recognized the voice of inexperience and raw terror, nearly overridden by the klaxon of the port sensors in the background, bellowing out the radiation crisis.

Marciane didn't have to ask twice. With a thin smile of satisfaction, he put his ship on automatic pilot, suited up, and pulled his own laser rifle out of storage. His men equipped themselves similarly and met him in the corridor near the main lock.

"Now remember . . . we've got the element of surprise for split seconds, and then we've got to have made a big enough dent in their ranks to decimate and demoralize them. Got it?"

The strikebusters nodded back.

"All right. Let's kick ass."

In the hangar, Storm heard him and thinned his lips. The ship rocked as it settled into a bay. There was a clangor as a "can-opener" popped the hangar doors.

Storm turned around, walking through a wall of non-rad foam, appearing out of the suds like a merciless monster, his laser laying down a spray of death that caught the radiation workers in total astonishment.

Within eight minutes, one of the toughest all-planet strikes in the history of the Dominion had been busted and shut down.

Chapter Four

J ack forgot to warn them about his sleeping light, and so he nearly killed Tubs when Tubs came to wake him.

Smashed against the inner door of the sleeping bay's wall, the privateer huffed and puffed under his forearm lock, his face turning a very pale gray, as he gulped for breath, his feet dangling a good six inches above the floor. Then, as Jack awakened and relaxed a little, the privateer slouched under his hold and caught his breath.

"Holy sh-shit, Storm!" He coughed as Jack let him drop back to his feet, and he rubbed his crimson neck. "You coulda killed me."

"I think that was the idea." Storm smiled apologetically. "I don't sleep well."

"Right." Tubs shrugged several times, and tried to recapture his air of bravado. Whatever confidence he'd developed in the fighter had probably just gone out the window. His gaze shifted and wouldn't meet Jack's and he followed the other's thoughts: Marciane was right —this man was a killing weapon. He swallowed, hard.

"What is it you wanted?"

"Ah, th' captain sent me down. He said you wanted to see the approach corridor for Malthen. And . . . the bulletin board's got the latest on Claron. Over twenty-eight thousand dead, with no idea of who's responsible."

That brought Storm abruptly from his half-sleeping state to wide awake. He remembered suddenly just who he was and where he'd come from, and what had been done to him to get him there. The battle armor shadowed his mind for a moment, like a tall soldier looming over him, and he broke off in mid-shudder. "I'm right behind you," he said to Tubs, who hadn't seemed to notice his break in character, and who moved away from him and through the sleeping curtain after giving a nervous jerk of his head.

Barefoot, Storm padded after the man. He'd adjusted quickly to being back in space, back in action—one of the advantages of having a body twenty years younger than his mind. After his performance as a strikebreaker, though, the crew of the *Montreal* had left him strictly alone. They'd never seen anything like the awesome firepower centered in battle armor. In a fleet, maybe, but not from one man. Only Marciane could talk to him without strain in the ensuing days while they returned to the Triad.

Storm had never been to Malthen. One of the three dominating planets called the Triad that made up the Dominion, it was nearly legendary in its wealth and technology. The Emperor himself resided on Malthen, though it was axiomatic that no one person could actually rule a galactic empire. It was easier to set a few boundaries and spend most of the time deciding not to rule. Planets tended to take care of themselves. Running a continent took a fair amount of ability, let alone a planet or a series of them. Even the unions backed off on planetary government. It was enough to muster people.

The Emperor mostly reviewed his computer findings and ruled now and then on whether a planet was free labor or union, and decided if there was an enemy worth fighting on an interplanetary level—the Thraks had been a spectacular example, one the old Emperor's biography would never live down. The Emperor as a ruler was inaccessible except through the layers and layers of bureaucracy comprising the banking and computer information systems of Malthen.

Still and all, Jack knew that meeting the privateers had cut years off his search. The privateers worked for the level of government that did more than sift through information and requests; it acted, though its actions were not beyond review. But finding anybody on Malthen who could do more than channel information was fortune he did not dare turn down or ignore. He might never have such an opportunity again to determine what had happened to the commands on Milos.

He squeezed in beside Tubs in the com room. As the privateer sat down in front of his screens, there was room for the three of them again, Marciane and he standing shoulder to shoulder, though he was a good deal taller than the captain.

The captain smiled. "Sleep well?"

As Jack answered politely, he saw Tubs shiver, and he repressed a smile. "Yes, thank you. Tubs says we're in the Malthen corridor."

"Yes. Bring up the bulletin board, Tubs."

"Yes, sir." His thick fingers played the keys that he knew so well, he'd worn the texturized coating off half of their faces.

Jack fought for composure before turning to read the com screen. There, squeezed in among elections, bounties, union warnings, draft notices, tax bulletins, was the brief blurb on Claron. It was now officially being declared off-limits because of the burn-off and an investigative committee was being formed to review the incident and make recommendations. He found his right hand clenched tightly as he thought of the verdant planet reduced to a char, and made an effort to relax his fist.

Marciane made a cynical noise as the bulletin board switched off. "They'll be years on that one. All right, Tubs. Bring up the duplicate of your screen."

Tubs did nothing other than what he was ordered to, but as he did what the captain said, gave a nervous twitch and Jack the side-eye. Was he wondering why this stranger, this piece of space junk they'd rescued, would be treated like royalty on board the *Montreal*?

Jack had heard whispered discussions at mess. The one called Short-Jump insisted Marciane knew something they didn't. The salt-and-pepper captain who ran a tight ship had cut Jack in handsomely on their operation pay. Tubs had expressed his bewilderment then as he did now. He licked his lips. "Coming up."

Storm took a moment to recognize anything on the circular grid map coming up, then the blips fell slowly into place. He stabbed a finger at an unfamiliar shape moving at the edge of the template. "What's that?"

"Identify, Tubs."

The man squirmed in his chair to see what it was they were looking at, then looked back to his own screen. "That's a warship, captain."

"One of ours?"

"No, sir. Thrakian."

Storm tensed. Marciane couldn't help but feel it, as they nearly rubbed shoulders. His gaze narrowed.

The older man's voice said smoothly, "They're allowed to patrol the outer corridor . . . that's been part of the treaty for the last fifteen years."

He knew then that Marciane had caught him on part of his background. The captain had been slyly questioning him and Storm had avoided most of it, but he couldn't avoid this—the violent reaction to the presence of the Thraks. He said smoothly, "Old prejudices die hard," and then caught the reflection of himself on the com screen—high cheekbones, smooth, tanned skin, a young face—a face which would never have had to consider fighting Thraks. He added, "My father hated Thraks," and hoped he'd covered himself.

"Most of us country boys did the fighting," Marciane said. "Just to keep 'em out of the corridor, and the bureaucrats sue for peace and hand 'em the right. I can't get used to it myself. Your father wasn't wrong in his feelings. It's still a jolt to see them there." He looked at Tubs and cleared his throat. "All right, shut it down. I'm going forward for a drink, care to join me?"

Tubs' expression squeezed tight as he realized the offer was extended to Storm, not to him. He returned to hunching over his screens and well-worn keyboards.

The galley was deserted. In the artificial day and night of the ship, Storm couldn't tell if he should feel tired or fully rested. He just, simply, was. He eased himself into a chair, his knees too high and jutting into the table top. He still wore his ranger trousers and one of Marciane's men had loaned him a spare jump-shirt. He watched as Marciane pulled out the Tantalos whiskey bottle from a sealed niche and splashed the liquid into a cracked but clean plastic mug. Courtesy dictated that he wait until the second mug was likewise filled before he hefted his.

He watched Marciane over the rim of the cup, barely doing more than wetting his lips with the whiskey, though just inhaling the fumes affected him for a split second.

The captain drank deeply and made a satisfied sound. He rocked back in the second chair, and put his boot heels up on a console.

Jack was aware that he eyed the man with caution and flicked his gaze away, wondering what it was the captain was going to ask him.

But when the captain spoke, it wasn't to ask him anything, it was to tell him. "I washed out of the infantry," he said, his voice deepened and mellowed by the whiskey. "I came this close to being approved to be an Elite Knight, then I lost it all, on account of my family. I'd been a farm boy, and had a certain regard for the cycle of things, and the psychotherapists thought I'd make a poor killing machine. So they washed me out, and the closest I got to battle armor was being seventeen and watching it march by me and the other recruits on the parade field, the Flexalinks shining brighter than a baby's first tooth." He laughed softly, a bitter laugh. "Then I learned later that you damned Knights lived by a code and that code was the same thing I'd been washed out for, only I'd had the code before I became a Knight instead of after, and that was the difference.

"That was before Rikor and Milos and Dorman's Stand fell before the Thrakian swarm. If I knew then what I know now, I'd not have been such an unhappy kid. I'd have stayed in ballistics instead of deserting, knowing that the psychs had just kept me out of the worst war fought and lost by mankind in their history." With a sigh, Marciane colored his confession with another gulp of amber Tantalos whiskey.

Storm sipped gingerly at his again, feeling it reach down inside with its glow, knowing that Marciane was not the type of man to open up without reciprocation. He sat there, wondering what of his past he could trade the man, without endangering either of their lives. He'd never been presented as the last survivor of the Sand Wars on Milos . . . when he'd been found, he'd been shuffled quietly from emergency clinic to hospital to rehab center.

All the suits of battle armor on the transport had been destroyed, except for his, which the nurse had unknowingly smuggled to him. He had been allowed to live, but his life had never been celebrated. Jack could not shake the feeling that to know exactly who he was and where he came from would not be healthy for the general public. He caught up the thread of Marciane's voice again, having missed the first word or two.

". . . but try telling that to a green kid. Even the odds of two out of seventy-six were better than no odds at all. Ballistics seemed unimaginative and unimportant after that. Push a button and a sector blows. What is there to that? Blowing up dirt, instead of facing the enemy. So I left."

"You're a deserter?"

"Was. Was. I took the general amnesty six years ago, when Emperor Pepys came in. But I've been a fighter all my life . . . just not in the Dominion forces. I fight in nasty, grimy little wars where you know who the enemy is and you see the look on his face just after you blow away his face plate and he knows you've got him. I like a war where you know who the winners are." He eyed Jack, taking a drink, then asked abruptly. "What's it like to kill a Thrak?"

Without thinking, Jack answered, "Like squashing a bug." Then became aware that a deadly silence had settled into the galley. He hesitated too long to recall his mistake.

Marciane dropped his feet to the floor. Their gazes met and held. Then Jack said quietly, "You didn't hear that. If you value your life, you didn't hear that."

"Maybe I did and maybe I didn't," the captain of the *Montreal* answered. "But it was worth it. I always wondered. They looked like they'd crack and squish real good." He tossed back the last of his drink. "So if I asked you when and where you did it—not how—you got that god-damn suit hanging back there shows me *how*—you wouldn't tell me. Because there's supposed to be a treaty against stomping Thraks. So I won't ask."

For a moment, Jack's mind flipped back to when he was drifting and hallucinating about basic training, and thought, here's a kid who never asked when the sarge said, "Don't ask." He felt an eyebrow arch up, and remained silent.

Marciane put both elbows on the tiny plastic table and leaned forward, his weight making the table shift and the bottle of Tantalos whiskey shimmer. "What are your plans? Will you stay with me, Jack? We could use you."

Storm was careful not to let his emotions play across his face as he answered. "Thanks for the offer, Marciane. You've got a good crew here, but I think my interests lie elsewhere right now. What happened to Claron deserves answers, and I don't feel like waiting around for subcommittees to decide if they should ask the questions."

The middle-aged man sank back a little, and forced a thin smile. "Worth a try, anyway. Guess you heard already that the Emperor's reforming the Knights again. He's starting them up as a personal guard."

The Tantalos whiskey kept Jack from going ice cold. The disbanded Knights being reformed? The shock ran through him. He held his gaze and his voice steady as he looked back to Marciane. "Can't keep much from you, captain."

"No," Marciane said with a sigh, as he poured himself a third helping. "And I appreciate the honesty. Good luck to you when you try for the Guard." He reached out and clicked the battered plastic mugs together. "Here's to the Emperor, and Malthen!"

The third drink reminded Jack that he'd been awakened in the middle of his sleep cycle, and so he left Marciane. As he walked away, he felt the captain's shrewd gaze piercing the area between his shoulder blades, like an itch he couldn't scratch, and he fell into the bunk wondering if he had somehow made a mortal enemy. He promised himself he'd be constantly on his guard on Malthen.

* * *

Jack didn't know how the crew of the *Montreal* rated an appearance at the palace, but he wasn't going to be left behind.

"Now, aren't you happy you dressed for the occasion? You're the guest of honor," Marciane said to him out of the corner of his mouth, as the crew walked onto the elevator platform and began the ascent to the formal welcoming chambers of the palace.

Jack's only answer was an involuntary flinch. He carried his helmet under his arm, feeling as if his head belonged there, too, even as he listened to Tubs' stammering admiration of the rose-pink walls of the immense palace.

The building dwarfed the city structures by virtue of being built on the area's highest hill, its prominence heightened by its color, a rose that he'd never seen in obsidite before, like the inside of a rare seashell. He ground his teeth as the elevator climbed up the outside of one of the wings, carrying them to a grand reception.

Marciane, as they understood it, was now a very big local hero for busting up a very unpopular strike on what had been declared by the Emperor to be a free labor market planet. Below, the crowd cheered and waved and screamed in happiness as their new-found heroes rose above them to claim their just rewards.

Only moments before, their cries had stalled to a deathly silence when Storm had moved forward, geared in the battle armor. Though many were too young to remember the suits, many others were old enough. Although he'd been too far away to hear well, he swore he'd heard the shocked intakes of breath.

He'd had a split second to wonder if he'd made a mistake giving in to Marciane's demands that he wear the suit, and then the voice of the crowd burst forth with a roar that swelled over the crew of the *Montreal*. Then Jack thought that maybe Marciane had been right, that to hide the suit would continue to endanger him. If he and his past were an embarrassment to the Emperor, it would be much easier to remove an unknown than a conspicuous presence. He'd hidden himself away long enough.

Marciane leaned over and flicked an invisible piece of dust off the Flexalinks. He grinned at Jack. "Like a baby's first tooth," he said, then straightened and tilted his head back, watching the rose wall of obsidite shimmer in front of them as the elevator continued inching up.

Short-Jump and Tubs were first off the platform as the elevator halted, and the sliding doors moved out to admit them onto the ballroom floor. The room was jammed with people, and tables, and freestanding bars. Jack smiled broadly.

Short-Jump grinned. "This is gonna be one hell of a party," he said, before wading forward into a swirl of people who did not, for once, shrink away from him. Tubs followed after happily.

A pretty young woman reached for Jack's arm. She was dressed from chin to toe in a shimmering gold veil that did little to hide her form, and she smiled as she recognized the look on his face. "My," she said. "Is it true what they say about what you guys wear inside that stuff?" She was as tall as he was, and as he opened his mouth to reply, she leaned forward on tiptoe and craned her neck to look down inside the suit.

She pouted, as her blue-black hair tickled his nose. "It's only half-true," she announced, and waved her glass of champagne in the air. "Ah well. At least half-naked is a start." She laughed softly. "Don't tell me—you want to join the Emperor's Guard, too. Well, this is as good a place as any to be seen. Now I want you to tell me all about Washington Two and that terrible war." She drew Jack away from the other crew members, and he put up only a token display of resistance, as other laughing, drinking celebrants pressed around them.

The last thing he remembered clearly was the frown on Marciane's face as he disappeared from view. The captain was talking to someone dressed in a relatively somber tone of brown, and they both looked after him, before a glittering veil of gold cut off his sight, and he gave in to the party.

He woke slowly. His head felt swollen and throbbed as though it would burst. Jack cautiously cradled it between his gloved hands. He groaned and rolled over onto his back, squinting at the bright yellow sun. Far away, he saw the shimmer of a rose-pink building hugging the horizon, towering above the city. His tongue felt thick.

"It's a long way from the palace to the gutter," he told himself, as he realized where he was. His right foot felt pinched and numb, and he realized he'd stuck his pay in his boot . . . a stack of Dominion credits that would have choked a Thrak. No wonder he couldn't wiggle his foot.

The hangover surged through his cranium and he put a hand out for balance as he sat up. He stuck it into his helmet, cursed softly, pulled his helmet into his lap, then put his hand where he'd intended it to go, each movement as deliberate and painstaking as he could make it.

His eyes watered and, helpless to dry them, he sat until they quit, and he watched the shadowed alleyway, listening to the throb in his head that threatened to kill him. That had been some party, all right. He didn't remember having been dropped here at all—and probably none of the rest of the crew, who snored around him in sodden heaps, would remember either. Jack smiled ruefully. They'd been wined and dined, and then put out with the rest of the garbage.

Tubs groaned in his sleep. He cradled an empty bottle of champagne to his chest, and a torn piece of sapphire blue veil.

Jack watched him. Then, as his mind and sight cleared, he examined all the other sleepers in the alleyway with him . . . and minded that he didn't see Marciane anywhere. The back of his neck tickled in warning, and Storm got to his feet, even though the sudden rise in pressure threatened to blow the top of his head off.

What had happened to the reverence the captain had held for the Knights, Jack wasn't sure, but it had evaporated, replaced by a sense of bitterness and wariness and— opportunity. Opportunity for what, Storm didn't know, but he knew that Marciane was a soldier of opportunity if nothing else. Something about the suit and his background had led Marciane into an opportunity, and Jack didn't want to be caught with his suit off, when he found out what it was. In the condition he was in, he was definitely vulnerable.

Stepping gingerly around the crew of the *Montreal,* Jack made his way to the mouth of the alleyway and peered out. The shock of what he saw added to the ringing of his ears.

They'd been dumped in what was definitely the underbelly of the city complex. The begrimed and garish buildings were a thin facade over the hellhole he looked out at. The only thing that had saved them from getting their throats cut was undoubtedly the earliness of the hour—and even that wouldn't hold them much longer. Jack hesitated. He couldn't leave Tubs and Short-Jump and the others behind to the mercy of streets that obviously had no mercy.

The hesitation nearly cost him his life. He only saw Marciane out of the corner of his eye when it was almost too late, and then, as he ducked, the slicing blow caught the point of his shoulder, and bounced off the Flexalinks. The power blade hummed nastily as Marciane gathered himself, the knife a blurred blue streak.

Marciane swore, as the alleyway filled with street toughs, hardexpressioned kids who jerked the crew of the *Montreal* to their feet. The hum of power blades cut through the groan of hangovers, as the crew stood up, their faces sagging, and abruptly sobered.

Jack faced down Marciane. "You're ready to sacrifice your crew just to get me?"

"No . . . no, I had a deal with someone. It went wrong. Actually, I helped it. I decided that I already had all the advantages. Hurry up. Give me the suit, Jack—that's all I want. Give me the suit, and you got a free pass to walk out of here. My ex-partners will be here soon."

Jack laughed humorlessly. "Without the suit, I doubt I could get far in this part of town." He gazed past Marciane to the dubious escort. One of the youths grinned and flashed his power blade. The knife hummed, slicers flashing in the morning light.

"Maybe. Maybe not. You could maybe catch a taxi that'd stop for you and that wad of Dominion credits I gave you last night. Course, you'd only have one chance to flash your bank roll—and if he didn't stop, you'd be fair game on the streets." Marciane's dark eyes glittered. "I know you're not hooked or powered up. It's only a matter of time until we get our hands on you and turn the suit upside down and shake it until you fall out."

"Is that so?"

"Yes, that's so. It's only a matter of time."

Jack glimpsed a sudden movement and shifted slightly, to protect his flank better. The buildings leaned in around them. They were close in the alleyway, too close, and it was to both Jack's advantage and disadvantage. "Why just the suit now? Not too long ago, you wanted me in it."

Marciane's face worked, and then he spat to one side. "Because now I know what you've done in it and what you've done to it—to its honor. You're a goddamn vigilante, killing Thraks in spite of the treaty, thinking you're some kind of flaming hero because your *dad* won the right to wear the suit and then packed it away for you. Well, let me tell you something, kid—you're not fit to polish the links or flush out the plumbing in that thing. Real Knights had *honor*."

Jack saw the power blade swing up toward his head before the captain even finished his sentence. He put up his left arm in defense and the knife buzzed off the Flexalinks angrily. He flexed, bumping Marciane back, shoving him off balance. The captain came up, a hand gun filling his fist. Regretfully Jack moved his glove, flexed it, and blasted the man's head off. As the body slumped to the ground, he said mournfully, "Marciane . . . a suit always has reserves. Not enough to fight a war on, but this wasn't a war."

He had a split second before Tubs let out a cry of anguish, and both the crew of the *Montreal* and the hired thugs rushed him. A laser wash flared up the side of his head. Jack cursed and leaned down to pick up his helmet, the side of his face in raw agony. Two punks jumped up and he shook them off, like blobs of grease. Short-Jump moved in with an ugly grin creasing his even uglier face and Jack kicked, sending the hand laser spinning across the alleyway. Beyond, Tubs hesitated.

It gave Jack the momentary advantage he needed. He was hurt too badly to play around with them, and he could tell that Marciane's last swing of the power blade had cut into the suit's seaming. Little crackles ran up and down his bare arms inside the armor in useless surges. If he was going to get out of there, he had, to leave *now*. Using the power vault, he jumped the length of the alley and took off running.

The crew of the *Montreal* was left behind, but the street punks Marciane had hired stuck to his heels like his suit contacts to his bare skin. They harried him as they ran through the near-empty streets, their jeers and signal yells bouncing off begrimed walls. Jack found himself gasping for breath. He hadn't run in the suit since Basic. Though rangering on Claron had toughened him up, he had yet to regain the peak fitness he'd had before seventeen years of cold sleep.

The side of his head throbbed. He must have a nasty second or even third degree burn and his left suit arm dangled all but useless, the circuitry shorting out from Marciane's lucky strike. Maybe not so lucky, for the now-dead captain had known a lot about armor. It was very possible he hadn't just nailed the vulnerable shoulder seam accidentally.

Panting, Jack turned the corner and dove down another street. It wasn't an alleyway, but the buildings leaned so close together that all vehicular traffic was denied access. One of the punks whooped in

triumph. Jack bowled over a storefront owner who was just saun-
tering out his doorway to turn on the neons.

The punks gave up trashing him and stormed the unlucky
merchant instead, yelling as they poured into the building and began
to loot it. Jack kept on going.

The streets had filled and he slowed to a staggering walk. He kept
a tight grip on his helmet as the citizens of the underbelly of Malthen
gave him curious stares and decided he looked lethal enough to leave
alone.

He hailed a taxi, but it swept past him as though he wasn't even
there. Jack turned, and caught his reflection in a store facade. The
laser burn had all but closed his right eye. He was dirty and sweating,
and grime from the gutter covered the Flexalink suit. He looked thor-
oughly untrustworthy. With a grimace, Jack realized that was probably all that was keeping him alive right now. As soon as he showed
his weakness, he'd be pulled down.

A dirty kid in a rag of a jumpsuit brushed against the dangling
left arm. Jack flinched away from the bump, but it was too late. The
kid had marked him as crippled. He disappeared in the crowd, but as
Jack turned around to look for him, he saw the kid reappear, talking
earnestly to an older boy on the corner. His thick black hair stood up
in a brush. The older boy wore quilted body armor and a set of
enamel bracers, and he turned to look at Jack. Their gaze met. The
teenager's lip moved into a jackal's snarl.

Jack immediately reversed directions. He'd been made and his
life was only as good as his ability to keep moving. He made the far
corner and crossed against the traffic. A blazoned wall proclaimed
sleeping cubicles around the corner "with companion" for one
hundred Dominions. Jack pressed against the building, looking for
that stiff brush of black hair following him. It was out of sight at the
moment.

He dipped into the cubicle company's entrance.

"One hundred Dominions or plastic," a heavyset woman droned,
without looking up from her wall screen.

"In my boot," Jack said breathlessly. "Give me a cubicle and when I get stripped down, it's in my boot."

"Fork it over, bud. Do I look like I was born yesterday? In a test tube or something? Show yer money and then you get in. Otherwise, beat it." She waved down the wall of doors to the far end of the alley.

Jack pushed down the narrow corridor. The shoulders of his suit brushed the doors on either side. Someone pushed through a door just as he approached it, and he moaned without meaning to, the collar of the suit rubbing the laser burn with a jagged edge. The man glared at him.

"Get out of the way."

Jack let him pass. He leaned against the bank of cubicles as the dark-haired, naked woman within gave him a leer and then slammed the door shut, saying, "Ask for number 22, honey, if you want more than a look."

At the far end, he saw the brush-haired street punk edge past the woman custodian. The woman leaned out and caught him by the collar. They argued. Jack was done for, at the end of his strength. He leaned forward and pounded on the door, 22.

"Let me in. I've got the money, just let me in."

"Get a key from Dora, honey. I'm no fool," was the muffled response.

Frustrated, Jack went down the row of doors, pounding with his mailed fist on the compartments. Doors began popping open, tarts and customers alike yelling. From his vantage point, he could see the street punk break away from Dora and begin to make his way down the corridor.

Angry at the interruption, a few of the clients shouldered Jack toward the end of the building, where, reeling from a last shove, he nearly bowled over a young girl in her mid-teens, so fresh and young looking that he stopped in shock. She didn't belong in these surroundings. She had mellow brown eyes, so light and golden they were amber colored, and as she looked up at him they filled with pain.

She stamped her foot impatiently, at war with herself over something. The street punk behind her yelled, "Give him over, he's mine!"

The girl looked beyond Jack at the punk, then back to Jack. "Oh, hell," she said. "Get in here, quick!" And she pulled him inside the tiny room, slamming the door in the face of the youth and his muffled curses.

The girl looked at him with a sigh. "You can't stay here. He's going to get help, and when he gets back, they'll strip the suit—and you—for whatever they can salvage."

The top of Jack's head brushed the ceiling. The battle armor dominated the tiny volume of the cubicle. He took a deep, shuddering breath. "I'll leave as soon as he's gone."

"And get past Dora? He'll have her posted." The girl sighed. "Damn! I was havin' a good day doin' the dry hustle. Oh well. Come on. I've got a back way out of here."

She turned around and began to remove a very tacky holo from the end wall. She pressed her fingers against the revealed seams and squeezed through the opening. She looked back. "I don't ask a second time, mister."

"Right," Jack answered.

Chapter Five

He lumbered after her, a clumsy shadow, as she skipped and ducked her way through the underbelly of the city she thought of as the beast. Thinking that way kept her on her toes. It was an animal, with fangs and claws and parasites, and great, raw, running sores where some greater beast had wounded it. And it might bellow at her or look down at her with cunningly slit eyes and snatch her up before she had a chance to even know that the beast had seen her.

For that was Amber's goal in life, to get along with the beast without being seen or noticed until someday when she could somehow run fast enough to escape the city and the great beast that had mauled it.

Of course, her plans and the pains taken for escape would be a lot more successful if she didn't keep picking up strays and extra baggage, like the stray she had trailing behind her now. She'd have to keep him from Rolf . . . yes, Rolf would be furious with her for cutting the day short. Best not to tell Rolf and dig into her private cache for the extra coin and credit it would take to put Rolf off her scent.

Amber paused, aware just before it happened, that the stray

behind her was going to stumble in weariness, and so she caught him up by the elbow just before he toppled. She grunted, but remained unmoved thanks to her wiry strength, balancing the bulk of the man.

He sweated as he rocked back in his boots. The bright pink washing the side of his face did not bead . . . laser burn, and a nasty one at that, Amber thought. She licked her lips in empathetic pain. He'd need ointments and they couldn't hole up just anywhere tonight, else the gutter rats would be drawn by his suffering to gnaw at them, and they'd spend the whole night kicking them off.

Her eyes widened in surprise at that thought. She hadn't considered what she was going to do with this guy past the morning, let alone the evening. If Rolf caught her out of her territory for a night as well, there would be hell to pay.

His eyes of washed-out blue looked a lot older than he did, but who could tell behind the suit he wore? Amber shrugged as he lifted his weight off her shoulders.

"You all right? You've been limping."

"Not hurt," he answered. "I've got money stuffed in my boot. Just my face." He waved at it vaguely.

She could tell he fought to keep from touching his face with the heavy gauntlets of his suit. "Money? Coin? Plastic? Digital?"

"Dominion credits."

The best, most passable currency on Malthen, as of the moment. Amber felt one of her worries leave, and another settle in. How, if she was going to help this stray, could she rob him as well?

She flipped her head, tossing her unruly mass of ash brown hair away from her face. She could feel her brow begin frowning and promptly relaxed the muscles. An unlined face, Rolf had beat into her, can act any age. Wrinkles are a lot easier to add than subtract. She was sixteen, nearly seventeen, and could play an age five years in either direction convincingly.

The man looked at her. He was deeply tanned, but a gray pallor had settled in, except for the sweeping laser burn. "The suit's about powered down," he said. "I've got to get somewhere to rest and recharge."

Amber shook her head. "The way I see it, that's not your first problem, mister. You're in trouble—and your first problem is to get off the streets. I can take you."

He held his helmet under his left arm. It was like watching a man carry around his own head, she thought, her gaze flicking briefly toward it. If worse came to worse, she could always have him put the helmet on to hide the laser wound.

It was a brief enough moment that he looked back, but she knew he was judging her. Irritation flickered through Amber. She disliked judgmental people and yet she knew and worked with the weaknesses of human judgment every day. It was the easiest way to pull a scam . . . simply present your target with an image and let them make the decision.

Amber twitched impatiently. "Come on," she snapped. "I'm a thief, not an assassin. We've both got to get out of here."

"Right," the man said. He moved forward. "That's consoling," his irony-tinged voice drifted after her as Amber pivoted and headed off, her charge in tow once more. She remained aware that the lumbering movement of the suit grew more and more awkward.

She stopped again. "Can't you shed that thing and carry it?"

"Too heavy. Unless you're volunteering? No? In that case, I suggest you find me shelter. I'll pay the going price." '

'Two hundred credits. And I'll need another hundred to get stuff for your face, unless you figure to look like that for the rest of your life."

"A hundred and fifty for the shelter, and fifty for the cream . . . which you probably already have on a shelf at home."

Amber's lips tightened. She looked away from the man, weighing the interest of the now crowded streets. To get to his money, she'd have to shell him first. Too hard to do now, not that she would have any trouble on the street. On the contrary, she'd probably have too much help and end up getting ripped off herself, as soon as she got his boot off.

Plus she didn't like the faint amusement in his eyes as she answered, "All right. A hundred and fifty for the room, but seventy-five for the cream. You're right . . . I've got it at home, but we're not going home. I can't take you there." No way. Rolf would gut him and Disposall the remains. Not that the rescue had ever done her any great favors, but this way she knew she'd get her cut.

"Done. Now let's get out of here. When the suit goes down, we're both in trouble."

"Doesn't it have AI? Move on its own, charge on its own?"

"Not this generation. AI was stripped out of battle armor this sophisticated because it was too easy to hack. It could be corrupted at the manufacturing level, or tapped into dirt side. Every order it gets is from the wearer."

"Better keep you on your feet then!" Amber sneered and jogged away from him. She turned the corner, down a shadowed alleyway and ran right into Plasto-man. The punk leered, and ran the palm of his hand over his bushed hair. He looked mean and pleased.

"Thought you could outrun me, eh, Amber?" He pointed his sharp chin at the dude. "He's mine. I'm going to salvage him."

"You lost him, Plasto. Forget it." But Amber felt her pulse race, and began to sweat behind her knees. Plasto was as bad as Rolf—worse, for Rolf at least telegraphed his moves. Plasto was unpredictable and as psychotic as they came. Worse, he knew Rolf. Even if she shook him off here, sooner or later, he'd be talking to Rolf. He'd be telling her no-necked, hard-eyed boss that she'd been seen working a prime dude, and Rolf would know what she'd done. That is—if Plasto didn't just kill the two of them first.

Amber shied a glance about them. They were deep in the alley. The high walls rising about them were uncaring concrete bunkers. She'd seen Plasto work. If he made a move, it was doubtful that either of them would get a scream off.

Plasto stretched his lips further in a smile and moved a step forward.

The man put a gauntlet palm out. "We can work something out."

Plasto came unglued. "Shut up! I want your *hide!* And when I'm done with this alley whore, I'm going to come get it!"

Amber never saw it coming, but the suit moved past her, and was in front of her when Plasto struck, and the power knife buzzed deep into the armored chest, its wielder laughing maniacally.

She stuffed a hand into her mouth, and turned heel to run, before the suit slumped over, and her scant shield of protection was gone.

But the stray straightened up, and she caught the smell of a burned out motor and Plasto stood up in shock, his smoked knife in his hands. His face turned white under the garish paint as the dude cocked his finger, and blasted him.

Amber's mouth dropped open. She let out a tiny squeak as gray ashes drifted down, featherlike, to fill Plasto's boots. She felt herself sag, and the suit pivoted, its owner catching her by the elbows.

His face was grim, but he said, "Don't give out on me now. Let's get where we're going."

Amber made a soundless answer and stumbled away, steering wide around the cremains that had been Plasto-man, his boots and his smoked power knife all that remained in a pile of ashes. Too bad. She could have used the knife.

* * *

Jack popped the seams and peeled the suit off. He was down to his parachute pants, sweaty and begrimed, the only remnant of his calling as a Ranger on Claron. As he shook himself, he felt a lump in one of the multi-pockets and fished it out. The odd green stone Scarface had spit out for him surfaced in his fingers, nestled in lint. He dropped it back into the pocket grimly.

He could smell last night's booze and today's fear oozing out of his pores. He watched the kid sitting on the bed across the room. Her face was just now regaining its color, and the cocky tilt was coming back to her too-thin, triangular face, absent since he'd burned the street punk right under her nose. He'd used too much power for that, but he felt he had a point to make, as much to the living as to the dead.

The girl, Amber, she called herself, whistled. "You always wear that thing half-bare?"

"Yes." He let it fall into itself, after first looking inside. Nothing there. Never was. Yet, he couldn't help the prickling between his shoulders he always felt when he wore the suit now. He couldn't trust it. He couldn't *not* trust it either.

The girl watched as he collected his bootful of winnings. The corner of her mouth curled as she realized she could have stung him for a lot more money, if only she'd been a little more canny.

Jack picked up the tube of ointment and smoothed it over the fiery ache of his face. "Name's Jack. Jack Storm."

"Already told you my name," she said warily.

He felt the shaking begin. The adrenalin surge had long gone, and now, deprived of the circuitry of the suit, he was at the end of his power. Jack sat down quickly on the plastic hotel table to disguise his weakness. "Where can I get a dry shower?"

Amber shrugged. She wore a spandex skirt, and tank top that emphasized her breasts and thinness. Her shoulders were pointy. Jack found himself wondering just how young/ old she was. A funny expression flickered over her face. "I'm not part of the bargain," she snapped.

"I never thought you were," he said back, but, eerily he had, just for the briefest moment, wondered. "If I can't get a shower, what about a meal? Juice, steak, salad."

She was hungry too, and she nodded. "Let me take care of it. You spread around too much hush money, and they'll know you're in hiding. Another hundred should do it."

That made it one of the most expensive meals he'd ever eaten, but he peeled the credit note off and gave it to her. As the door sealed,

Jack staggered to the bed and collapsed, stretching out. For a little bit of a thing, there was a nice warm hollow where she'd been sitting. The niche was mostly concrete and plastic. It wasn't meant to be comfortable. It was meant for little more than survival.

Jack had no illusions about Malthen, or its darker side. He'd seen the cameras overlooking every street corner and seen the lens caps, blackened out, to thwart the security. There were no rose-colored buildings here. All was dirt-tan except for the territory markings. He felt uneasy and knew he'd have to jury rig the room's circuits to recharge what he could on the suit, and then expose the solars for the rest as soon as he could. Drugs and such he'd worry about later. The important thing was to get the suit up and then repaired so that he could concentrate on his own survival. Once he got his feet under him, then he could afford to ask questions. It would be a long road back to the Emperor's palace.

His tight smile pulled at his face. He touched his cheek carefully. The ointment had immediately calmed down the burn and now he'd have to face the healing and peeling. It shouldn't scar though, as he'd just caught the glance of the beam. He felt a brief mourning for the captain of the *Montreal* as incomprehensible as the little man had been to him. Jack had felt sure that the man had thought he was a veteran but a vigilante? And how had that violated whatever principles Marciane had held?

Storm sighed and turned his thoughts to more pressing matters, like the girl who'd gone after his lunch. He was pretty sure she'd come back . . . if nothing else, to see how many more hundred credit notes she could peel off him before she was done. Jack let the lumpy mattress enfold him. A thief, not an assassin. Wryly counting his blessings, he closed his eyes in sleep.

* * *

Amber sat hugging her knees, watching her charge wolf down the steak she'd brought back. She'd eaten hers already, but it had been a much smaller piece, and she felt more full than she had in a long time. It was a pleasant, warm feeling in the pit of her stomach, but she knew she'd feel sluggish if she ate any more. The man she watched appeared to have no such qualms.

She'd thought he'd been asleep when she'd returned, and had laid the food out quietly on the pock-marked table, but when she'd turned, he'd been sitting up watching her. Amber had let out a shaky breath.

"You sleep light."

"If at all," he'd answered shortly, before sitting down to eat. And now she watched him, thinking that when the laser burn peeled off, he'd be kind of good looking, in a spooky way.

Spooky because she felt that he was in hiding somehow. The age of his eyes didn't match the age of his face. Or maybe that was because of her knowing there was more to him than he would tell or she could guess. She wondered briefly what she would get if she patched into the master program and pulled up his chip number. Probably nothing, or something so blocked by security she'd never be able to access it. Maybe he was a master criminal or spy.

Amber discounted that after a fleeting look at the suit. Whatever the hell it was, it was far from inconspicuous. If Rolf had only taught her one thing, he'd taught her the grace of a chameleon-like existence.

She smiled briefly as she thought of Plasto-man's demise. Maybe her stray was a galactic hero, instead.

Jack looked up. "Want some more?"

She shook her head. She'd cleaned her face somewhere and looked more childlike, and her wide, golden brown eyes appraised him frankly. Then she glanced at the juice. "I'd like some more of that, though."

He poured her a mug and she sipped the sunset-colored juice, savoring the pulp and biting flavors. It had been his money, she hadn't spared it. So what if her stomach sloshed around the rest of the day. She wasn't anticipating out-running any marks.

Jack watched her drink the juice. He could tell she was enjoying it like a rare privilege. He speared the last piece of meat and chewed it quickly.

"Like the city," Amber said.

The non sequitur stopped him. "What is?"

"The city. It chews you up and keeps on chewing, but it never spits you out. You've got to claw your way out if you want out."

Jack swallowed the bite a little prematurely and felt the coarse lump strain as it went down. He dropped his utensils. The salad looked a little brown and wilted, and he couldn't identify all the vegetables. He decided to pass on it and pushed the container away.

Amber's eyes widened. "Those are sun chokes in there."

He smiled. "Be my guest."

She fought the impulse to look around before pinching out a dark, fleshy green leaf and finishing it.

Jack got up and walked over to the suit. He'd straightened it up so that the Flexalinks could lock, bearing their own weight. He examined the shoulder seam. Frayed wires met his examination. He sucked his front teeth in absorption. They'd be easy to strip and reconnect. He was lucky.

All he had to worry about was powering it up.

Amber said softly behind him, "Gonna strip it?"

He whirled. He hadn't heard her come up. She stepped backward quickly in response to whatever it was she read on his face, and he blanked his expression, thinking that she was like the boomrats of Claron. . . scrawny, flighty, ready to flee or scrap, whichever was most expedient. He said carefully, "No, I intend to repair it."

She flopped down on the far corner of the bed to watch, disapproval all over her face.

Jack reached inside the suit to the sealed side pocket containing a probe and a few delicate tools. As he pulled them out, he looked at her. A faint line of concentration was drawn between her brows, as though she listened to something very far away. It was a change from the disapproval.

"What?"

She looked startled. "What what?"

"What are you listening to?"

"I don't know. What is that thing, anyway? You'd be better off without it. Walking through the undercity with that thing on is like driving a Thrakian tank through the palace and wondering if anybody might notice you."

A neat analogy, Jack thought, as he snipped a wire, stripped the fried end and mated it with its connection. "It's the battle armor of a Dominion Knight."

A blankness replaced the air of concentration. Jack smiled wryly as he realized she didn't know what he was talking about. She hadn't even been born until after the Sand Wars. Then something dawned. "A Knight. Like those bodyguards the Emperor is forming?"

"Something like that. They used to be the elite infantrymen, the front line."

"Yeah? How'd they ever move fast enough to keep from getting blasted? You walked around like a pregnant sloth."

He laughed, in spite of himself. "Wait until you see the suit powered up. I can leap tall buildings in a single bound—or something like that."

She picked up the limp gauntlet, examining the fingers.

"And your weapons are built in. All you've got to do is cock your fingers."

"Right. And I wouldn't point that at your face, if I were you. I don't have it totally disarmed."

Thinking of Plasto-man, she dropped the sleeve quickly. "How old is this thing?"

"About twenty-one years, give or take a year. Why?"

She whistled. "Ob-so-lete."

A queer feeling went up the back of his bare torso, but he forced himself to acknowledge that she was probably right. Battle armor had probably been refined by several more generations since he'd gotten the suit. How much better had it gotten?

As he worked, Amber stood up on the bed to peer inside. She

giggled at the catheter tubing and catch bag, and sneered at the toggle switches.

"Old-fashioned but convenient," Jack said, his voice edged with irritation. The girl was making him and the suit feel antiquated.

She brushed her hand across the inside back of the suit, touching the chamois. "What's this?"

"Nothing really. It's easier to wear the connections if you stay bare, but then the back of the suit, especially if you're wearing a field pack, chafes you. So most of the guys patch in a chamois . . . a soft piece of leather or cloth . . . back there. It keeps you from sweating so much and from irritating your skin."

"Most of the guys?" she echoed softly, pulling her hand out.

"Guys who used to wear these things." He pinched together another connection. "Are you supposed to be somewhere?"

Her eyes fluttered. "No. No, I'll take care of that later."

That confirmed Jack's suspicion that she had a pimp somewhere to placate. He set the tools aside. It was warm in the little room and he mopped the back of his hand across his forehead. "How much?"

"I usually make six hundred a day."

"Working or thieving?"

She wrinkled her nose at him.

"I can't have you leaving."

"I know. Don't worry about it. Think you'll be all set up by tomorrow morning?"

"I will if I can get the helmet out in the light. My solars are drained, too."

Amber weighed something mentally, then said, "I'll take care of that."

"And then I'm gone?"

"Right. I'll escort you to the city limits. Getting beyond there is your problem."

Jack had a feeling it would prove a considerable problem, or Amber herself would have pulled out long ago. But he couldn't fault her. She'd done all she'd promised and then some. He said, "That'll be worth six or seven hundred credits to me."

She bristled. "I'm no charity case."

Jack sighed. "Look, would I be alive now if it weren't for you?"

"Probably not."

"Then it's not charity." He recaptured his tools and concentrated on the shoulder seam.

Into the dead silence, Amber said defiantly. "I won't do anything for that."

"I didn't ask you to."

"I don't work! I just do the dry hustle."

"Fine."

There was a rustle as she got off the bed and went to the corner and hefted the helmet. Jack said, "Don't touch anything."

"Right. Just put it in the sun?"

"Preferably. Won't take long . . . maybe a couple of hours, without a power drain on it."

Amber wondered what three hours in broad daylight would do to her, if Rolf found her. She licked her lips, then said, "Well, there's a roof on the top of this building somewhere. I'll be sitting on it. Does this thing play music or anything?"

"No."

With a martyred sigh, she left.

Jack had finished with the suit by the time she returned. She was flushed pink, and he guessed that she didn't spend much time in the sun. She tossed the helmet at him.

"If that wasn't enough, I give up," she said, crossing the room to the drink tray where she tossed off the last of the juice and let out an unselfconscious burp.

He closed the last seam on the inside. He preferred having a tech-valet seal him in, but he could do the job well enough on his own—or he wouldn't have made it through the Gate jump and in deep space. "Hand me the helmet."

She wrinkled her nose. "You're not going out in that!"

"No, but I want to make sure I didn't screw up my own repair work."

She watched him struggle with the helmet as he settled it on and screwed it into place. There was that always disconcerting moment of claustrophobia, then the suit came alive around him as it drew on the power in the helmet solars and recharged.

"There it is."

He felt a welcoming warmth, and looking out at Amber, saw her frown again in that odd kind of concentration. He took the helmet off. "What is it?"

"I don't know . . . but it's almost as if—"

The plastic door shattered before she had a chance to finish, and an immense barrel-chested man stood in the remains of the doorway. "Amber! Get over here!"

She quailed, her wide eyes desperately looking around the room for a way out, her muscles tensed as she poised, ready to run. "He's a mark, Rolf, honestly! I've got him for all night!"

"I told you never to spend more than half an hour with a guy." Rolf's deep-set, dark-as-flint eyes caught sight of the pile of Dominion credits sitting on the bureau. He flushed, and Jack recognized greed when he saw it.

The man was built: heavy in the arms and torso, narrow waist, straight and well-muscled legs. It was only in the neck and face that he showed his brutality, but Jack didn't make the mistake of thinking him stupid. No. Intelligence glittered like a diamond in the depths of those black eyes. And in the next split second, it was overshadowed by the killing instinct.

Chapter Six

Jack moved, as Amber's mouth opened in a silent scream, the cords in her throat straining to mute the sound. Jack hit the pimp and the gun in Rolf's hand spat. Fire sprayed the wall, washing past the suit, and the two of them went sprawling.

Jack didn't have to hit him again. The man went limp under the suit's weight and the hatred in the black eyes disappeared as the eyes rolled back in their sockets. Jack got up slowly.

Amber bent to pick up the helmet which had gone rolling.

"He's not dead," Jack said, by way of explanation, but she shrugged, "I know. We'd better get out of here."

"You're coming with me?"

"No choice." She swept the stack of credits off the desk and stuffed them into the waistband of her skirt.

"Nothing happened between you and me."

"He knows that," she said, toeing the limp form of her boss. "Anybody who ever tried to touch me has ended up dead. Let's get out of here before the Sweepers come."

"Sweepers?"

Her mouth pursed in annoyance. "Local police. Rolf's got 'em on his tab . . . they'll be looking for us to come out. If not, they'll be coming in."

No sooner had she finished when Jack heard the thudding of booted feet coming down the hallway *fast*.

He swept Amber into his arms even as she gave a surprised squeak. There was no sense in going out the front door. He turned and, shoulder first, walked through the wall into the next room. He kept on going until he ran out of walls and looked down at the street, three stories down.

"Hold on."

She was too frightened to do anything else as he jumped.

The suit talked to him as he ran. Jack ignored the soft, subliminal buzzing in his head and the prickling at the back of his neck, and listened instead to the pumping of his heart and the thump of his feet on the broken pavement. Night covered them.

Amber pointed out alleyways and clung to him with her too-thin arms wrapped tightly about his neck, the helmet sandwiched tightly between her body and his chest. She said nothing, her lips pressed together whitely, as he covered as much ground as he could.

He stopped only when his pulse thundered and his heart fluttered painfully in his chest, grinding to a halt underneath a long-dead security camera, its blackened-out lens staring balefully at nothing.

Amber stirred. She dropped to the ground and stood, leaning against the Flexalinks. The links caught the moonlight and shone whitely, reflecting it on her, making her seem paler than ever.

She licked her lips and patted his shoulder. "I guess this thing could come in handy after all."

"You'll have to go back to him."

She shuddered. "Never. I don't want to. Besides, you need me."

"Just to get beyond the city limits."

"And do you know what's out there? Come on . . . you've got no chip. You won't be able to tap into Malthen. You're like a newborn baby here."

Jack stood, looking down at the little wisp of a girl/ woman leaning against him. She was talking about street smart, and he knew he had none in her culture. Even twenty years ago, he hadn't had any . . . Dorman's Stand had been a closely-knit farming planet. The ways of many cities were foreign to him. "Malthen is chip based?" he questioned, thinking. He was fairly certain he knew exactly what she referenced but waited for confirmation.

"Implanted on the wrist, here." Amber made a face. "You need it to buy, sell . . . anytime you want to tap the source."

Exactly what he'd thought it was. Primitive but effective. His gauntleted hand ran over her wrist. He picked up no chip. His arched eyebrows telegraphed his next question to her.

Amber flushed. "Well, of course I haven't got one. I'm underworld. Besides, it's the best thing that ever happened to me. See—I've got no record. No file. Nothing."

"Then how do you get along?"

"Machines are stupid. They don't know the difference between a chip taped to my wrist or one that's been implanted. So, we use counterfeited chips. Stolen. Whatever we can get our hands on. Rolf rotated the stock constantly so that Sweepers couldn't catch on."

"Outside the system."

"Right." She'd caught her breath now and looked up at him. "And so are you, right now. But you don't know how to get around it, make it work for you—I do. And that suit you're wearing—it's like a neon sign."

"Here maybe." Jack's mind flickered to the spaceport. "But not where I came through." He hadn't seen full suits, but he'd seen plenty of armor where they'd disembarked. There was a mercenary underworld on Malthen. The buzzing in his ears grew louder and he shrugged in irritation. Sweat poured down his back, aggravating it despite the chamois. "How do I get to the spaceport?"

"Easy. Let the Sweepers catch up with you, that's where the jail is." Amber tilted her head. "Maybe I could get you through. I don't know."

"Ever tried?"

A gamine grin illuminated her face. "That's not my line of work."

"Right." He reached out and took his helmet from her. "But you're offering to go with me?"

She shrugged. "I can't go back." She pointed down the alley, toward a faint, night-piercing horizon. "It's that way."

It turned out to be much easier than either Jack or Amber imagined. Near the border, he flashed a roll of credits at a taxi. The man practically smoked his vehicle stopping for them. Jack got in the car, carrying Amber with him, and caressing her for benefit of the driver.

He leered at the driver. "Want to go home . . . but, as I'm taking this little bit with me, dampen the sensors, all right? Don't want my chip picked up when we cross."

The driver mirrored his smirk. "That'll cost you, but I can arrange it. We can go back with the shields up, and no one'll know either of you made the trip."

"How much?"

"Two thousand."

He settled for one thousand Dominions, and they made the trip in relative quiet, illegal shields up that sheltered them from surveillance as the taxi buzzed over the borderline. Amber fell asleep in his arms and Jack was taken with an instinct he could only label as maternal as he paid the driver and disembarked.

The driver grinned out the window. "You elite guys are all alike. I remember when I was a kid and that armor stuff was around. Now the Emperor's brought you back. What's the matter? Too hard to follow the code?" The driver eyed Amber's limp form.

He shrugged. "Man's gotta fuck once in a while."

Grin still in place, the driver peeled out, leaving him standing in the shadows of a fourth-rate hotel. It was too close to the pick up and drop off spot to be used, but Jack found a similar place four blocks over. Amber didn't even stir when he raided her waistband for the money to pay for the room.

* * *

Amber woke in strangely filtered light, to the whisper of computer keys, and she frowned. Then she sat bolt upright in the bed and looked at curtains . . . imagine that, real fabric curtains, hanging over a bedroom window. She shuddered and her stomach turned as she remembered Rolf.

She walked into the other room and saw the stray sitting at a computer terminal. He still wore the suit, though the helmet sat on the desk beside him, and he looked as though he'd had very little sleep. His sandy hair stood practically on end, as though he'd run his hand through it several times.

She laid her hand on his shoulder as she walked up, and the emanation running through it shocked the words right out of her. She hadn't felt anything like it before, It was as though there were two Jacks, and one of them was unutterably alien . . .

He turned his face, and she saw the laser burn, festering at the edges, and with a soft cry, touched her fingertips to the edge. He winced and threw his head back, and the whites of his eyes showed, like those of a wild creature. A second passed, and the old, composed expression was back in place.

Amber cleared her throat. "What are you doing? And shouldn't you get out of the suit? There's a dry shower here."

"I'm looking for answers."

"Get any?"

"No."

She grinned and sat down next to his bulk. "I didn't think so. You can't access anything, right?"

He nodded.

"Idiot. That's what I was telling you about yesterday. You don't have a chip."

"And you do?"

Amber fished in her bra and pulled up a tiny sliver.

"Yes." She affixed it to her wrist with skinstic and placed her hand palm down on the Ident screen. The rosy light bathed her skin and then the computer screen came alight. "What are you looking for?"

"Information on volunteering for the Emperor's new guard unit."

Amber bit her lower lip, concentrating intently. Her fingers flew over the keys. "This'll take a while. I've got bureaus to go through to find the right one to talk to. Why don't you peel that thing off and go shower?" Not that she minded the scent of his maleness . . . it was powerful, but nice, compared to Rolf who always managed to smell like a Disposall drain.

"No."

He said it so sharply that her fingers paused and she turned to look at him. Jack shrugged. "If we have to run again, it's too hard to get back into in a hurry."

She looked at him, taking in the flush of his cheeks and the sweat dotting his forehead, despite the cool air of the room. "Okay. If we make it through the next twelve hours, we should be okay, though." She looked back to the screen and became absorbed in her task.

Jack gave over, letting her slide into place at the terminal. She didn't seem to have noticed his violent aversion to taking the suit off just yet. He curled his fingers. Good. He was still in control. He flexed his shoulders and rolled his head about, trying to ease cramping neck muscles. He couldn't face taking the suit off. It had crept into him, into his ability to handle himself and his environment, and it wasn't that he wouldn't, but that he couldn't, take it off just yet.

The tension that knotted his body spread toward his face, pulling at the laser burn, and he winced painfully. They'd left the healing ointment behind. After Amber broke through the layers of bureaucracy for him, he'd have to send her out for more cream. He couldn't risk infection or permanent scarring.

It took her several hours, hunched over the terminal, to find the department they were searching for, and she gratefully let him take over again.

"What'll I do?"

"Just access this number. That'll bring it up on the screen." She reached out, activating it.

"How much of me can he see?"

"For ident purposes when the call is placed, just your left profile. The camera's there, see?"

Profile identification shots were the norm until the call went through. Then the callers could go full face or turn off the view screen if they wished. Jack decided he would turn the screen off, not wanting to reveal the burn. If the Emperor was reforming the guards, he was taking the creme de la creme—no one would interview a scarred outlaw.

Jack placed the call. The screen blurred and then came on, even as he typed in his inquiry.

A stocky man sat at the console, butch-haired graying at the temples, his eyes narrowed into the bird's feet of wrinkles at their corners. But it was the laser burn arching into a widow's peak that caught Jack, a mark as distinctive as a tattoo. "Who's there?" he snapped, even as Jack rocked back in shock. The servos moaned as the view screen camera reacted to follow his movement and record the ident profile.

Jack felt ice cold. It had been twenty-two years, but he recognized the man. It was the man who inhabited his dreams—who'd sent a whole army to its death. Winton. His voice froze in his shock, but his hands clenched the corners of the keyboard. A band of interference rolled across the picture.

Amber shot to her feet, as she recognized the color band going across the screen. "Jeez," she yelped, as she cut off audio. "They've called the World Police. Jack, shut down! They're tracing the call!"

But Jack sat in shock, even as Amber leaned over him and flipped the view screen off. She tore his hands from the keyboard before it could scan for the chip once more, as requested by police authorities at the other end. She knocked him away from the terminal and shut it down. "Don't touch anything!"

She raced to the Disposall, turned it on, and the tap on full, dropped the chip and skinstic down it, and flushed them into the depths of the city's sewer system, even as she wondered what had triggered the World Police and why. Hands shaking, she finally closed the tap. It could have been the chip—or it could have been what Jack had blurted out when the view screen filled. "Milos," he'd said, without even knowing he'd spoken. Whatever that meant, the man at the other end of the call had reacted as though an assassin faced him.

She returned, just as Jack's head went back, and he and the suit sagged into an unconscious bulk on the apartment flooring.

Chapter Seven

Amber froze over the massive body of the fallen man. The Flexalinks winked at her in the half-light of the room. She looked over her shoulder at the now dead terminal. If she'd broken the link in time, they were totally safe. If she hadn't—the police would be there any second, and they would be found. They had no time to run.

Amber flipped a wing of hair away from her face, put her hand up, found her temple wet with sweat. Fear. She tucked the hair behind her ear. First, she'd get him out of the suit, the suit that hummed with a life of its own. Feral. Selfish. Searching. And he'd already told her it didn't have AI. What then?

With nails tearing and fingers that seemed too weak, she scratched and pulled at the sealing seams, from the inside, pushing her hands down through the narrow space between Jack's neck and chest, reaching down inside the suit. The touch of his skin was fire hot. The right seam gave way, and then the left, halfway down. It was enough. She set her heels and tugged, worming Jack's slack body out of the suit inch by inch. More than a dead weight, he seemed impossibly heavy as though—Amber shook her head, as drops of perspiration ran down her face—as though the suit fought to retain him.

Suddenly, he came free, sliding into her arms and knocking her back on her fanny. She wrinkled her nose. He smelled rancid, like the plumbing of an old, decayed building. As long as she was dragging him somewhere, she might as well drag him into the bathroom. She one-quarter filled the tub, impressed at the sight of real water, stripped him and literally rolled him over the tub's edge and into the recessed basin. He'd have to be conscious to get out—he was going to be slippery, now.

Amber went back to the suit and looked at it, lying on the floor. The meshed armor retained most of its shape. She listened for the police and rolled a story around mentally that she might tell, though now she felt a little safer. They should have been here already.

She pulled the suit into the sleeping room, into the shadowy alleyway between bed and wall, on the far side, where a casual observer might not see it. As she left, the suit twitched and the empty sleeve fell over the chest. Amber caught her breath, telling herself it had not moved on its own. Had not. Could not. Already that sentience she had felt was growing dim, was so far away she wondered if she had actually sensed it. Yet, why had Jack insisted on wearing the suit, as if he'd been bonded to it—afraid to go without?

Gooseflesh dotted her bare arms as she returned to the bathroom and washed the man down, then rinsed him carefully. The warm water eased the raging fever of his skin a little, and, once clean, she thought it better to keep him there a while longer. Amber threw a towel in over him, in case he woke and had a sense of modesty.

She disdained sitting on the low toilet and sat on the floor, the cold, embossed plastic tile imprinting her haunches. She crossed her too-thin forearms over her knees. She'd gone too far to go back now.

Rolf would nearly kill her for letting the man come between them. She knew that Rolf could cross the border. He had sources. Sooner or later he would hear of her whereabouts and come after her. She knew that. She'd read it in his thoughts day after day. It was not because of any love they had for one another, or lust either. The only time Rolf had ever tried to rape her, she'd blacked out during the struggle.

But when she'd awakened, she was still intact, and Rolf had a fear and respect for her that he tried to hide, but that had been there all the same. That didn't keep him from beating her . . . he seemed to know more about whatever it was she'd done to protect herself than she had.

And the three other times it had happened, that she'd killed without knowing what she'd done, he had appeared, gentle, solicitous, caring, and taken the bodies away from her. He'd kept her out of trouble, stroked her trembling hand and told her it would be okay.

Amber turned her face away from watching the fevered man in the tub. What kind of monster was she? Rolf told her she killed, but she no more trusted him than the Sweepers. She could remember nothing more than losing control over clients, a terrible, overwhelming fear that this time she wouldn't escape rape, and then—nothing. And worse, she was certain that Rolf could, if pressed, present the evidence of the murders she'd committed. He kept her close with bonds of fear.

In the silence, listening for the police who never came, she bent her face to her forearms and cried a little, tearlessly, for the hopeless future.

She stopped crying when her stomach cramped, hungry for the sparing little bit that she usually ate every day. She thought of a tray beside the computer, a tray with foam containers and crumpled paper napkins, and got up, stiffly, to investigate. When she returned, she was swallowing the last of a sandwich, bread dry on the outside, but the meat and filling still tasty on the inside. She walked in as Jack groaned, and moved, and began to talk in delirium.

Amber touched the laser burn. Infected. She took a handful of credits from her waistband—less than half remained—and she knew she'd have to return to her old thieving ways to keep them going, unless Jack had paid for this room a month in advance. She went downstairs stealthily and waited in the shadows of the lobby where the surveillance camera would only blur past her, and an ill-lit picture at that, until one of the apartment cleaners came by and she called out discreetly.

In moments, she knew where she could buy the medicine she needed, and hurried down the cement streets to find it. Even if she hadn't known they'd passed the border, she would have realized it immediately. Throngs of people did not pass here. The streets were cleaner. The security cameras worked more often than not.

She kept dodging their line of sight agilely, not wanting her images to be transmitted. Merchants or their computer screen counterparts did business from behind metal grills. The credits slipped through her fingers of their own volition as if greased, and she returned to the apartment building quickly. As she walked, she noticed those who sauntered in camera view, either unaware or unafraid.

Jack flinched as she smoothed the ointment on and flailed his arm at her. She ducked aside. She had to pinch his nose shut to spoon in the antibiotic, but it worked. Now she had only to wait. She checked the temperature of the bath. Too cold. Too much discrepancy between his fever, so she ran warmer water into the tub.

It never occurred to her to take what was left of the money and run.

* * *

Jack woke, sopping wet and shivering, his stomach nailed to his backbone in hunger. The girl sat cross-legged on the bathroom floor, and her large golden brown eyes immediately took in his changed state. She was spooning a fantastic smelling stew into her mouth.

"Back again? If we're going to stay here, one of us is going to have to learn to cook. Room service prices are murder."

And as he opened his mouth to protest, she began spooning the stew into him.

When she was done, she gently mopped his mouth with a disposable towel. "There." She sat back. "Burn poisoning. You've been out of it for over a day."

He touched the side of his face. Instead of the slick burn scar, he felt a patch of new skin, already peeled. Its pink tenderness gave gingerly. "And new world germs." He smiled wryly, thinking of how the *Montreal* had bypassed customs when landing on Malthen. He hadn't taken his inoculations before the welcoming ceremony. Served him right.

Amber nodded brusquely as though aware of that, too. She held up his Ranger pants. "I had them laundered."

He realized then that only a towel lay over him, its celluloid fibers gelatinous from being immersed in the water so long. He reached out and snatched the trousers away. "Get out of here."

Amber laughed. "Sure you're strong enough to do it yourself?"

She left as he wadded up the damp towel and threw it at her, the mass sticking to the plastidoor like an immense spit wad. His head whirled as he stood and dried, then dressed himself.

Barefoot, he padded out into the suite. Jack looked around. "Where's the suit?"

"Put away." Amber had spent the time reading and using the wall screen, schedules and films dropped everywhere, carelessly. Then, as he paced through it, a restlessness gnawed at him. He looked carefully at the mess and suddenly it struck him that the whole thing was deliberate . . . part of her cover as a bored hooker.

He scrubbed his hand through his hair. "Where's the suit," he said again, surprised by the petulant sound of his voice.

Amber sat down and crossed her arms. "Sit down, first."

A rage began to build in him. "Tell me where the suit is and quit playing games."

"Me? Raise your voice much louder, and we'll have the Sweepers in here. And, on their tail, the World Police. Is that what you want? Shall we turn on the computer again and try that last access code? Might as well go quickly if we're gonna go at all."

He stared at the girl, wispy bit of nothing from the streets. Her large eyes bored into him, challenging. He forced himself to relax.

She leaned over and put her hand on his knee. He felt a tinge of well-being and the driving ache to have the suit was pushed back a little.

"Jack," she said, "you talked while you were sick. I've never had much education—Rolf taught me—so I don't understand most of what you said, but some of it. And I know that you can't get back into the suit. Not yet. It's . . . it's more than what it's supposed to be, and it wants you, so it can feed off you."

His warmth turned chill. He shook off her hand. "What are you talking about?"

"I'm talking about you and that battle armor. I'm talking about you being burned off Claron, and looking for someone, and fighting Thraks (spit on them), and the rest of the stuff you raved about while I hand-fed you 'biotics."

"But you can't know what you do about the suit."

She stood up and shrugged. "Sometimes I feel things. Like just before they happen, or before someone says something. Rolf told me I had the knack for it."

Psychic, he thought. And he wondered how deep her talent went. He calmed himself and listened.

"The suit, or something inside it, is alive. It's growing. You feed it. It makes you want and need it, like addiction. You can control it, I think, if you know about it."

He wondered if it was the parasite that would metamorphose him into a berserker. Damn! Damn the suit and damn the Milots and Thraks. His hand clenched involuntarily. He'd burn the suit if he could afford to, but not now. "We need the suit."

"I think I can help you control it."

"Why?"

Her gaze met his. "Because you're nice."

Her words rocked him. He hadn't done anything, one way or the other, and, he suddenly realized, on the scale she had to judge by, that probably ranked him as heroic. "You don't owe me anything," he said gruffly. "I owe you."

Anger sparked across Amber's face. "Don't talk like that to me! You need help and I offered it. Well, my job isn't done yet, as I see it. And you've got to help me. I've got to stay out of Rolf's grasp. He's got long arms, that bastard. You've got to help me!"

Storm weighed her plea. Then he knew he had little choice, and didn't want any. She was company. He thought then of the rehab tech who'd warned him he didn't really wish to be alone, estranged from humankind. He looked back at her. "I want to make it into the Emperor's personal guard."

"To kill him?"

"No. But through him, I want to find the man that sent my men and my company to death. And I want to find out why Claron was burned.I want it made green again."

"Terraformed?" Her mouth remained half-open in wonder at his ambition.

"Yes."

"You don't want much, do you?"

It was not a question he intended to answer.

She flicked a finger toward the bedroom, where the suit lay in dusky shadow. "You fought in that?"

He owed her that much, even knowing it might harm her later. "I'm a veteran of the Sand Wars."

Her eyes widened. "The Sand Wars? Nobody survived that. Maybe deserters . . . I've heard of a few who claimed to. But nobody who fought."

"I did."

"Why, you're old enough to be my father."

He grinned wryly. This street kid had a real talent for putting things into perspective.

Chapter Eight

Jack sat in the corner of the bar, his long legs crossed at the ankles and stretched out, maintaining a low profile, a chilled bottle on the table in front of him. Periodically he fed another credit through the slot in the table top and the servo would come by and drop off another beer.

Amber sat in the crook of his arm. The shadows of the corner booth obscured her slightly. She'd cadged new clothes and cosmetics and looked old enough for the role she was playing. It made Jack only slightly nervous to have his arm around someone who'd caused the last three people to touch her intimately drop dead. She'd exchanged her own confidences after he'd told her his.

Amber sighed and tossed her head back, a wing of hair trailing across his bicep before it fell back onto her neckline. "You're going to get a beer belly if we sit around any more bars."

This was the third in as many days. He disposed of the half-empty bottle and ordered a fourth. In all, he'd had maybe a full beer to drink, but as long as he kept ordering, the bartender would let him stay. And he needed to stay, as long as he could observe the underside of Malthen's civilian population at work. Mercenaries had drifted in and out of the bar all day long.

He tickled her neck and said softly, "Just shut up and sit tight."

Amber's mouth thinned in irritation.

A grizzled, lean and frowzy looking man sat at a nearby table. He had containers set up in front of him and Jack noticed that anyone drifting in and out of the bar made it a point to greet him and exchange pleasantries. He had long spindle fingers that scampered spider-like across the tabletop to grasp handshakes or pour drinks. Jack could tell from the man's mannerisms that he was a veteran and so were the men coming out of their way to greet him.

Amber started to say something, but he gripped her kneecap tightly as the veteran and his latest greeter laughed loudly and he caught the drift of their voices.

"... without Marciane."

The grizzled man returned, in a clipped voice, "Served him right. Played both sides against the middle. But he did a lot of work, and that means the rest of us will have to pick up the slack."

The greeter, a young man with scars across the wattle of his neckline, shook his head. "Not for me anymore. I'm trying out for the bodyguard." He picked up a shot glass.

A bitter laugh. "And what makes you think you'll be invited?"

"I've got pull. I'll get an audition."

"Suits take a lot of training. Good coordination and reflexes. You drink and drug too much, Smithers. And look at the risks. Remember what happened to the Knights in the Sand Wars."

The tough kid gave a laugh. "Real funny. You just wish you were young enough to go for it."

"Nothing funny about it. Why do you think the suits were destroyed and the Knights disbanded? Things happened in the Sand Wars nobody could explain. Nobody left to try."

"Maybe. Well, it's good seeing you. Maybe I'll sign up later."

The grizzled man looked after the mercenary and Jack heard him add, "If there's anything left of you."

Amber touched the side of his face. "Jack, what's wrong? You went pale."

"Nothing." He took his arm off the back of the booth. "Let's get out of here."

He hurried her along the streets, both of them taking a pathway that kept them mainly out of camera range. In the apartment, he threw open the closet door, where he'd rigged a stand for the suit, and he sat cross-legged in front of it, his chin in his hands, just staring at the apparition.

It gave him goose bumps. The pull was always there, to put it on, to wear and use it.

Amber sat down next to him. "Jack, what's wrong?"

He shook his head. "I'm damned if I do and damned if I don't."

"Do what?"

"Use the suit. It's the quickest way to the Emperor. Once there, I can locate the man I'm looking for and I can ask the questions nobody seems to want answered. I can cut through the layers of bureaucracy."

"Once you're part of the Guard."

"Right. And from what I've been able to gather this past week, it's not easy to get an audition. You've got to be young, tough, and recommended."

"We'll bribe somebody to recommend you."

"But who?" Jack straightened. "I haven't been able to figure out the grapevine yet. But if I start doing work, I'll get noticed."

Amber spread her fingers out in front of her face and stared at him through them, like a mask. "You don't have to use the suit to get hired."

"No, but it's the most impressive way to guarantee I'll be noticed." A cold chill went down his back. Did he want to be noticed? Or had his survival thus far been purely accidental? "But to wear the suit, I have to be able to control it."

Amber lowered her hand. "I can help, but I'd need to know more. It's weakened a lot since you wore it last. Whatever it is that's growing, it grows in spurts. And I still don't know where it is. It could be anywhere in the suit."

"So I can wear the suit for limited periods of time safely."

"Maybe. I mean, probably. Jack—I don't know what it is. How it grows. What it intends to do. If I did, I might be able to dampen it." She lay back on the floor and stared at the ceiling, the young girl glaring out from under neon makeup. "Maybe you should just blow the thing up."

"No." She turned and looked at him strangely, but said nothing. He added, "It's more of an advantage than a disadvantage right now." He got up and slammed the closet door shut.

Amber rolled over onto her stomach. "If we could find someone..."

He looked down at her. The elaborate mass she'd structured her hair into was already coming down, but she didn't seem to care. He felt a surge of tenderness and squelched it. "There's no one left but me," he said. "Who would you ask?"

"Oh, there're others," she answered loftily. "The question is, where do I find them? Ballard would be the easiest to talk to."

"Others? What do you mean?"

She lifted an eyebrow as he reached down and helped her to her feet. "Jack, you've got to know there are others. Deserters, mostly, before the Thraks wiped everyone out. They won't talk—afraid to, I think, but Rolf has dealt with Ballard. I just never connected what he'd done with the Sand Wars before. But he's got to be one of you, I just know it."

"We can't use him."

"Why not?"

He shook his head. "He connects to Rolf. You'd be found."

"It's worth the risk. What if he knows about the suits?"

"No."

Amber's face pulled into sulky lines, but she walked past him and into the bathroom where she spent an hour vigorously scrubbing off makeup, heedless of the needs of his beer-filled bladder.

They ate sparingly, near the end of Jack's brief wealth. Living illegally, he reflected, cost a good three times what it would have on the other side. When he fell asleep in the bedroom, he could hear Amber moving restlessly on the couch in the other room.

He didn't hear her leave, but he heard her come back. She moved into the bedroom and alongside the bed as stealthily as anybody could. He made a mental note that she could be a dangerous enemy before he said, quietly, "What the hell are you doing?"

She jumped. "Dammit! I found Ballard. Get dressed and follow me, quickly."

"Idiot! I told you to forget about going after him."

"Slag," she returned. "I've already done it and he won't be where he is for long, so hurry."

She fled as he got out of bed and dressed. She waited for him, standing on one foot and then the other, uneasily, chewing on the end of a strand of hair.

As Jack joined her at the door, Amber pressed something cold into his hand. He hefted it. A small, plastic gun.

"It's fully charged," she said.

"But—" Then Jack gave way and put it inside his waistband.

Once outside, Amber took to her heels. It had rained, and the sidewalks were damp and humid smelling, the scent of oil and dirt rising from them. Jack stayed on her heels, knowing that he was seeing Amber at her best—or worst, depending on how you viewed it. She was of the streets and for the streets, and played them to her advantage. Two Sweeper units passed by without turning up even a hint that either of them were out after curfew, her guidance slowing only marginally, she was so sure of herself.

Until they reached a pitch-black section where security cameras had never breached at all, let alone been placed and then decommissioned. Jack knew then, with an uneasy tension along his shoulders, why she'd given him the gun.

She paused at an armored door along a back alley. There were no windows on either side. The door said, "Who passes?"

"I'm a guest."

"ID."

She slipped a card into the key slot. As the door accepted it, Jack had second thoughts about going in.

Then the door said, "There are two of you."

"Both invited!" Amber reached back and, with a chilled hand, grabbed Jack's, as though afraid she'd be swallowed up without him.

There was a very long pause.

Then the door swung open.

"Come on," Amber urged and pulled him through after her.

He expected dark and dingy; he got it. Plastic cubicles with privacy screens lined three wall sides. A bar resided in the middle, holding court to open-air tables, all full, occupants of all genders and alien dressed in worn, comfortable fatigues and laughing and talking loudly.

Holo displays did not show naked dancing companions, but world maps. He recognized two versions of a popular war strategy game, but at least one column reflected a current world struggle. He thought bitterly, briefly, of Milos and Dorman's Stand—had they been illuminated here, with magnetic pins and plastic warships, while the occupants of this bar bet on the outcome of the war?

It was to the largest privacy screen corner she dragged him, a booth intersecting with two of the walls. The holo column in front of it was dark—game over, or did the occupant not like playing? He caught a metallic golden glint as the being in shadow looked up, before Amber sat down in the booth and pulled him in after her.

"Came back, eh?" the man said and pulled a drinking goblet closer to his chest.

"Yes."

"Gutsy move, girl, considering what Rolf is offering for your friend's hide, and you along with him." The man turned to look at Jack, and gold flashed again.

His right eye had been replaced with a gold mesh screen camera — gold, the substance that flesh and blood would accept with the least amount of infection and attention. Jack had seen realistic ocular prosthetics before, but nothing like this. The man not only wanted everyone to know he'd lost an eye, but he wore its replacement like a damn medal.

And that eye, of course, was superior to the original flesh and blood model. It could telescope, contained infrared and night sight, and never needed closing. The man sitting at the booth could see him, and everyone else sitting at the bar, far better than Jack could ever hope to return the observation. Still, he sat with his back to the corner.

Amber made the tiniest of moves and the man's hand caught her almost before she'd begun. Quick reflexes. Was this the man he needed? He had enough years to him.

"What do you want?" the man said. He wore his ringed, black hair cut close, and bushy, and he looked lean and fit, his olive skin tanned darkly. The whites of his nails practically glowed in the dark.

"Ballard," Jack said.

"Why? You a bounty hunter? Sweeper? Police?"

"I'm a friend of Amber's," he said, and looked to the girl. Her eyes were wide and she looked frightened, but not alarmed.

The man laughed. It was a cynical, dry sound, that did not carry beyond the confines of the booth. "What did that cost you?"

"Nothing," Jack lied as Amber made a half-sound and stifled herself. He wanted Ballard. He would play whatever games he had to to find him.

The metallic gold eye focused tightly on him, swept across his plain gray suit to the inside of his wrist. Then the man grinned. "What have I got to lose? With no chip on you, Malthen has no record of you. Can't kill a man who doesn't exist. I'm Ballard."

"Then," Jack said softly, and leaned forward on his elbows, "remember you're in the same kind of trouble."

Ballard's good eye widened. Laugh lines wrinkled about it, and he grinned and released Amber. "Consider me warned." He slipped a card in the ordering slot. "Drink?"

Jack shook his head, but Amber said, shyly, "Hot carob."

Ballard ordered. He waited until the servo brought a beer and the hot mug of drink for the girl. "What is it you want from me?"

"I want to talk to you."

"Talk is cheap. What about? Do you have a job for me?"

"No," said Jack. His hand moved in the dim light, in a brief, two movement gesture. He was rewarded by the clatter of the beer bottle to the table top, where it rocked on its bottom until Ballard shakily rescued it. The man's expression narrowed as Jack said, "I want to talk to you about Milos."

A gray pallor glimmered under Ballard's tan. He pushed Amber away from him, and, voice furred, asked, "Where did you learn that salute?"

"Same place you did—in Basic."

"No. No. There's twenty-five years' difference in our age. And I washed out."

"No, you didn't. The salute is not learned by wash outs. Maybe you ran, later. But you were a Knight just like me."

Ballard chugged half a bottle of beer, and wiped the suds on a trembling hand. "What do you want to know?"

Jack leaned over, quieting his voice even more. "I want to know what you know. And I want to know *why*. There was a general amnesty for deserters six years ago. Why didn't you apply for it?"

Ballard's good eye paced the metallic one as his gaze swept the room. "Couldn't," he said briefly.

"Why?"

"Because of the Sand Wars, dammit! Because of the suits, and the pride and honor of the Knights—everything I fought for! That's why!" Ballard shoved the beer aside. "Because the Sand Wars is a death sentence. If you were there, you know."

"I was there," Jack returned grimly.

"Convince me."

"Ever hear about the troop ships? The coldsleep transports?"

"At war's end? Sure. Most of 'em were blasted by the Thraks as they pulled out of Milos' airspace. Dorman's Stand didn't have enough survivors left to send in a cold ship."

"One stayed intact. It was adrift for seventeen years."

Ballard's breath hissed inward. The two men's gazes locked. Then Ballard said, "I heard rumors about that. But it was a dead ship when it was found."

Jack shook his head. "Not quite. One bay stayed on auxiliary power, holding one man in endless cold sleep dreams. All he suffered was a little insanity and frost-bite. A couple of toes. One finger." He held up his right hand, where the amputation scar glinted in the half-dark. "Me."

"My god. You're the last living true Knight," Ballard said.

Chapter Nine

Rain had come in earnest while they'd talked to Ballard. They walked home through the crust of a near dawn. Jack took deep breaths. For the first time since he'd been on Malthen, he smelled clean air, and he walked clean streets, but it was small comfort after talking to Ballard.

Amber, on the other hand, under the influence of whipped cream and hot carob, had regressed a bit. She took a skipping hop to keep up with his stride. "You're a legend, d' you know that?"

"Thanks," Jack said dryly.

She brushed him with a look from under her wayward hair, then skipped around a puddle, wise enough to leave him alone with further thoughts.

And Ballard had given him a lifetime to think about.

That unblinking golden eye had stared at his hand long after Jack lowered it to the table. Then, Ballard had reached out and touched it, as though to reassure himself. The older man had callused fingers, with skin like leather. Then, Ballard had looked him in the eye.

"Where have you been?" he asked, drawing his glass near him for comfort.

"On Claron. I was a Ranger there."

Sudden understanding wrinkled the other's expression and he leaned forward, out of the dusk and darkness of his booth, exposing his face fully to the half-light of the saloon, a dark-haired angel of truth. "Then I suggest you wake up, Storm. I suggest you really wake up."

The implication of his words echoed in Jack's brain. He stumbled on the broken sidewalk, kicking up a spray of water. Cheap boots. He felt the impact, the bruising stab, clear through the arch of his foot. He felt again the shivery lightning of sudden knowledge, and fear, just as he had when Ballard said, "They destroyed an entire planet trying to get you, you know."

He recoiled. "That's insanity."

"Were the Sand Wars sane? Leaving behind everyone who'd fought in it, including medevac units, to be destroyed because of the embarrassment of fighting an enemy who couldn't be stopped sane? Do you know how I got out? Do you?"

Jack glanced at Amber, who seemed abstractedly involved in her drink, and then remembered a flash of Ballard passing the drink over to her. A powder glinting in the palm of his hand, to sprinkle over the whipping cream. "You've drugged her."

The veteran shrugged. "Nothing unpleasant. She's not listening, and won't remember most of what we've said. That'll be important to you later. If she's important to you."

Amber leaned into the cushiony back of the booth and curled up, cat-like, to play with the cream adorning her drink. Guilelessly, she dipped a finger in it and began licking it off.

Jack wrenched his attention away from her. "I'll take that drink now." He waited until Ballard served him before continuing. "So how did you get out? And where—Milos or Dorman's Stand?"

"I was on Milos. I got out of the hospital and was lifted off by, um, businessmen, who'd heard about the suits and wanted one for a private collector. I'd lost my eye, and was hearing rumors around the hospital. We were going to be left behind, to be gobbled up.

The brass was afraid. Afraid of the Thraks and afraid of the Milots."

Jack curled his fingers so tightly about the glass his scar turned white. "What about the suits?"

Ballard did a double take. His too-full upper lip sneered. "Come on, Storm. The suits that spawned berserkers. Like I said, I ran into some businessmen hoping to capture one for this private menagerie. I offered to sell them mine, provided they transport me out of there. I figured it was the only way I was going to get off Milos alive." He touched the slightly bagged skin below his artificial eye. "That was why I had to have this. Without proper medical attention, I had to settle for this instead of a transplant. Infection, scar tissue, that sort of thing, made it too late for a trans- plant." He smiled and settled back into the twilight of the booth. "I figure it was a good trade-off. There were others who made it off, too. Similar ways or maybe out and out desertion. But there aren't too many of us who admit it. It isn't healthy."

"Why not?"

Ballard's good eye, ink-black, flashed. "Still an idealist? They're killing us off. That's why a general amnesty was offered when the new Emperor came in. It sounded like a good political strategy, but whoever suggested it wanted the rolls."

"Rolls?"

"The scans of those who'd applied. There are damn few of us who served in the Sand Wars left, even those of us who ran. I'd like to get my hands on those printouts myself. They're a death warrant!"

"But they could have killed me. Everyone aboard my transport was dead. What was one more corpse?"

"And who says that the crew who found you followed orders? You didn't exactly get a welcoming committee when you came back."

Jack lapsed into thought as Ballard tipped the last few drops out of his bottle, disposed of it, and signaled for a new one. Amber seemed absorbed in chasing the last drop of cream around her mug. "I don't believe it."

"There's an easy way to check. Go back to the doctors who did that work—" Ballard stabbed a finger at Jack's hand. "Go back and see if they're still alive and well, and happy to see you. You'll find out quick enough."

Jack knew that the suit had been smuggled to him. He'd always wondered how that nurse had managed what had to have been a complicated transaction. What if his whole existence was against someone's express orders? And part of someone else's agenda? Then he was a fool to be walking around openly. If he was open enough, then disposing of him would be dangerous. He'd gone part of the way, he'd have to continue. And Ballard's suggestion had merit. He cleared his throat. "What about the suits?"

The other could not conceal a shudder. "It was real. Didn't you ever see it?"

"I—I'm not sure."

"You would be if you'd seen it. Out on the Sands, you couldn't get out of a suit. You'd be in one for weeks, sometimes. That's all it took. I don't know what the filthy Milots put in them, but it grew. Fed off our sweat and heat. Hatched and infiltrated us . . . until it killed and then consumed us. And then burst out of a suit like it was a god-damn eggshell. Big fracking lizardman—a born killer. Too fast and too mean even for the Thraks to pull down easily. They're some kind of legend on Milos, from what I heard. But even legions of berserkers couldn't stop the Thraks." Ballard spat on the barroom floor. "They deserved to lose Milos."

"Legions? You said legions."

"It was horrible. Whole squads of men lost in the Sands, and then consumed." Ballard grabbed the new delivery of whiskey and, with a shaking hand, poured himself a tall drink. He downed it before he could speak again. "I saw it with my own eyes. Infantrymen, Knights, anyone who wore armor of any kind and had to be suited."

"And so the suits had to be destroyed."

"And the men in them. No telling what they had in their blood-streams, I guess. No telling where the berserkers came from."

"What were the signs?"

"Signs?" Ballard's good eye grew bloodshot. He ran his hand through his coal-black ringlets of hair, and the gold eye stayed impassive. "What do you mean?"

"The possession. What stages did it take? Do you know?"

Ballard grinned without humor. "Still got your suit? Want to know if it's safe? Burn it, boy, while you've got a chance."

"I can't." Jack sat back, forcing a casual expression. "Maybe you didn't see as much as you say you did."

"I saw it!" Ballard crossed himself. "Men would get delirious, start talking to themselves, uncanny to hear. It was like a second person was in the suit with them. Then they'd go off the edge. They were great fighters then, fantastic. They had no fear. Then, the suits would go dead. Some would stagger around aimlessly, but most would just go dead. Then, we thought it was because they'd run out of power, and we couldn't help them. Solars could only carry us so far, y'know?"

"I know."

"Then the suits began to split open. My god." Ballard's speech slowed, then stopped altogether. His good eye dimmed a little, as though he looked into his own past. He shook his head. "Never seen anything like it, before or since."

Jack offered his personal nightmare. "Big creature, lizard, runs on hind legs, tail balancing it, head all jaws, frill that expands. Yellow and green scales."

"You've seen it, too!"

Storm reached over and helped himself to Ballard's bottle. "Thought I was dreaming. Maybe I was."

"No. No, you saw it. Use that suit of yours, maybe you'll be one, too." Ballard laughed. It was too high. "Some idiot bought one, just to see it happen."

"What happened to the collector's suit?"

"Nothing. Couldn't get it to make the transformation I guess.

Maybe he didn't know it had to be full of meat to do it. Or he couldn't get the volunteers."

"Ballard, listen to me." Jack had the feeling that Ballard was drifting from him, disappearing into the oblivion of the alcohol and the darkness of the bar. "How long did it take? How many days?"

"Days? Days for what?"

"For the stages. How many days did it take before you noticed the others changing."

He laughed. "All it took was a war. A lousy, fracking war."

Amber began to stir and sat up restlessly. She blinked and a certain awareness came into her golden brown eyes. She turned on Ballard. "You slag! You drugged me!"

He rolled a shoulder. "What do I care? Tell Jack. He's the last remaining Knight. He's the only one left to care. Avenge us, buddy! They flamed a goddamn planet trying to get you." He coughed. "Two weeks to stage one. Then, maybe a week of delirium. After that, I don't remember. Maybe a couple of days. Maybe hours." He closed his good eye, and pulled his eyelid down over the gold one. Then he leaned over and put his head on the table. A faint snore leaked out.

* * *

Amber began pestering him once they got back to the apartment. "Did he know about the suits? Did he?"

"Yes. But I can't calculate it too closely. After all, like me, the suit's been in cold storage for almost twenty years. But . . . it's coming to life. I think two weeks of constantly wearing it will do me in."

"Then we have to keep you down to hours." She tilted her head. "If we put it in cold storage, too, maybe we can reverse the growth, as well."

"Two steps forward and one step backward?"

"Something like that."

He sat down heavily on the couch. "It's worth a try." He rubbed his face wearily.

"What else did he tell you?"

He looked at the girl, a thin, vulnerable waif. Street smart one minute and totally naive the next. He made a face. "If Ballard had wanted you to know, he wouldn't have drugged you."

"Not Rolf?"

He recognized the fear in her eyes and her voice. "Not Rolf. But something you're better off not knowing." He looked out the window at the tinge of dawn pinking the sky. Soon it would be white-hot again. If he was responsible for Claron . . . then he had to turn it back. It was his duty. Jack clenched his fist.

A coward is not somebody who fears, but somebody who doesn't overcome his fears. Jack looked at the closet door. He could feel the presence of the suit behind it. It seemed lonely somehow. Lonely and ominous. He stood up. "I need my sleep," he announced. "Later today, we're going to get you a decent watch."

"Buy one? I can lift one."

"Buy one," Jack emphasized.

"Why?"

"Because I want to know down to the slightest measurement from now on exactly how long I've worn the suit. And I want you to learn how to read the suit, too, until I get you out of here. I want you to learn to sense the life in it. Anything. Any twitch. Our lives are going to depend on it."

Chapter Ten

"Work?"

    Jack grinned, thinking of the late Marciane and his crew.

"I like to kick ass." At his back, was a long line of men, talking among themselves, taking little or no notice of him. All of them had been waiting since before dawn for the bar to open: it was hiring day.

The grizzled man made a notation without looking up. "Skills?"

This was the hard part. Jack hesitated a second before saying, "I own my own armor. Implanted weapons."

The man looked up then. Surrounded by his bottles of cheer, he looked anything but benevolent. Feral. Alert. Too alert.

Jack scuffed a boot on the tavern floor. "Smithers recommended you," he said. "I—ah—liberated a prototype of the stuff the Emperor ordered for his guard. He said you'd understand."

"You did, and he did," the man said. His was the kind of lean expression that wrinkled vertically, running from mid-cheek to jaw, raying outward from the corners of his mouth. Then he looked back to his printouts. "If you're discreet, I'm discreet. Take this disk.

There's an address on it. I understand they're hiring fellows who like to kick ass."

Jack took the hard disk and shrugged back through the line of men. Today was hiring day, obviously. He'd been in line since midmorning, waiting for the bar to open, so he could get in. He headed down the street to look for Amber. He found her inside a grocery store, trying to glitch the automatic ordering machine.

He grabbed her by the elbow and hauled her outside into the too bright, dusty and smoggy Malthen air.

"Slag it, Jack! I almost had the access code."

"Amber, neither of us can afford to get arrested."

She puffed out her breath in exasperation. "We happen to be out of money. And I, for one, although I don't eat much, I do eat regular. I'm hungry, Jack."

He brushed her errant bangs off her forehead. She'd left her makeup off today and looked about fourteen in the baggy blouse, cut-off knickers, and bow-tied shoes. "I just got a job offer."

Her expression changed instantly. "That's great! When are we going?"

"I. Me. I think this is one interview I'd better go it alone."

She stopped dead in her tracks on the walkway, even as he hailed a taxi skimmer. "I'm the official timer, remember?"

As if he could forget it. But Jack shook his head. "I'm not wearing the armor. Look, Amber. These guys are sometimes legit but often-times not, and they don't like witnesses to their deals. If I go in there, I'll take the job, regardless of whether I like what I hear or not, because if I listen, turn it down and walk away—I'm a liability. Nobody stays in business too long with a lot of liabilities walking around."

"So if they hire you to murder somebody, you'll do it." She sniffed.

"No. But they'll never know I didn't do it. Chances are, if they hired me, they hired somebody else, too. I just won't get in the way. Beside, you don't hire a soldier if you want an assassin."

"What will you get hired for?"

He shrugged. A bright yellow beam headed toward them. He crumpled the last few Dominion credits in his pocket. Enough to get Amber home, if he took a line to get to the address. Maybe enough so she could order lunch from room service. He started to pull his hand out and answer her, as the taxi swerved over and the door opened out.

"Amber!" the driver snarled, snatching at the cuff of her sleeve. She let out a screech and jumped as if she'd been scalded, and bolted.

The driver threw himself out of the taxi, bowling Jack over, and took off after her. He was chunky, and his fat folds danced inside his bright yellow jumpsuit as Jack rolled to his feet and took off after the two of them. Jack panted. The driver he kept in sight, but Amber was nowhere to be seen, though the driver evidently caught a glimpse of her.

Their steps echoed inside the concrete well of buildings. Shadow, then sunlight, blazed across them, and the driver's balding head blossomed with sweat. Jack heard him wheeze as he pulled even, and drove his shoulder into the man's ribcage.

The driver went flying with Jack on top of him. His head slapped the side of the curb and he lay still, sweat bubbling out of his bulbous face.

Jack got up slowly, panting. With any luck, the driver wouldn't remember much when he woke. Unfortunately, the taxi's memory banks would. He turned heel.

"Amber!"

His voice echoed back. The girl was as good as gone. Jack retraced his steps back to the taxi. Its dashboard lay open, gutted. Amber sat on the hood, waiting for him.

She grinned at his expression. "What took you so long?" Then, somberly, "He knows Rolf."

"Then I better get you off the streets." He looked at her. "And fed, too."

The bleak look brightened. "That's a start!"

* * *

The disk took him to an opulent home that was armored like a fortress. Fed into the gates, it led him into a tunnel entrance, where cameras clicked and servos whirled as they moved to keep at least one lens focused on his every move.

Jack ignored them, figuring that anywhere he went to inquire about work was going to have a certain amount of paranoia and security. He would be surprised if it'd been any different. They wouldn't find out anything about him, and he was certain that they had no intention of feeding their observations into the master system. The computer network here was likely to be very one-sided about the exchange of information.

He faced a massive door with three balls balanced overhead. He pushed the hard disk into the slot, where it was promptly swallowed. After a moment's pause, the door swung open.

* * *

"I'm a moneychanger," the woman said. Like its owner, the room was ample and cluttered with antiques and the spoils of a good life. She sat on a form-fitting chair, and her ample form more than fit it. It overflowed, a curve here and a dimpled hollow there. She was sensuous in a way he could not describe, until he realized that the music playing had a subliminal fetch to the tones.

Jack felt ill at ease standing in front of her. When she saw that he had discovered the subliminal message in her musical background, she reached out with bejeweled fingers and turned the sound down. Another tap of a gold and diamond nail, and a second background selection filtered into the air. She waited for Jack to listen to it. In a second or two, he realized that he had a great deal of confidence in her and was inspired by her honesty.

Then he grinned.

"May I suggest we conduct our business without interference?"

She smiled back. The remote brought the music to a sudden halt. "I have my little ways," she said.

"All of them subliminal," he answered. "Why waste them on me?"

She shrugged. It was an odd movement, considering her dimpled and rounded shoulders left little room for her neck. "I'm hiring a crew."

"So I gathered. Moneychangers usually don't fight wars, they finance them."

"That's one way of making money," she said. "Call me Sadie, please."

He nodded. "Jack."

"All right, Jack. I make more money if the money I lend out is repaid. That would be an obvious fact, would it not?"

He nodded again.

She uncrossed her ankles and sat up straight, indignantly. "Well, someone has overlooked his agreement with me."

"And you want your money collected?"

"Precisely."

"And where is it?"

Sadie smiled. Her lips were tattooed a brilliant crimson. Her wise brown eyes crinkled. "The armored satellite of General Gilgenbush."

Jack whistled. Even he had heard tales of the space station of the rogue general. He'd have better luck breaking back into the palace.

"You are afraid, no?"

"I'd be stupid if I wasn't. Who's captaining?"

She moved and reached for a hard disk, similar to the one which had led him to her house. "I had hoped for Marciane, but he's been retired lately. So the man you will be working under is called Tomcat." She waited for a reaction and, getting none, smiled. "I'll pay five thousand Dominions a man, with a half-time bonus for Gilgenbush's balls."

Jack flushed, but asked, "How long will I be gone?"

"As long as it takes."

He mulled that over. Accepting Sadie's job meant that Amber could be alone for some time, and with Rolf hot on her trail . . . he swallowed. "I've had some hard times lately, Madame Sadie. It's going to take a little front money to get my equipment ready—"

She frowned. "That's your problem, soldier."

"I understand that, ma'am. But I thought, since you're in the loan business—"

Her expression softened. "Well, perhaps something could be arranged. What have you got for collateral?"

"Well . . . there's my kid sister. . . . "

"You've arranged for what?" Amber's voice went up with every word until it reached an ear-piercing high.

"Now," Jack said soothingly. "Once you've done it, it won't bother you."

"I won't be frozen like a slab of cold meat!"

"Sadie has her own storage vaults. She has a full bank of people down under there. Think of it this way you won't even know I've been gone. No worries, no wrinkles."

"People actually leave other people for loans?" She pushed her wonderment aside to continue being indignant. "I won't do it!" She shuddered. "I can't do it."

"Rolf will never look for you there."

At those words, she quieted. She pulled her feet up onto the couch, and sat, curled into a ball, very still. Finally, dark lashes fringing her big eyes, she looked up at Jack.

"I have to, don't I?"

He repeated, "Rolf will never look for you there."

"What's it like?"

"Like sleeping. Dreaming. Around and around in circles, dreaming."

She hugged her thin legs close. "I guess if you did it for seventeen years, I can do it for a couple of months."

He felt just a moment of sadness, but he covered it up and smiled, as she reached forward then, grabbed and held out a slice of that ancient Terran delicacy, pizza, and said, apologetically, "I saved you some, and it's even good cold."

It wasn't that good cold—but then, nothing ever was.

Chapter Eleven

J ack noted that Sadie liked to be prepared. In the sterile white prep rooms leading to the cryogenic bays, she had a rabbi, a witch, and a Walker waiting.

Several other groups of people talked quietly and somberly to each other and, in one corner, a husband bid tearful farewell to his wife. As Amber clung, trembling, to his elbow, Jack checked the Walker over. He looked mild and ordinary enough, but the gold cross hanging from his neck was big enough to choke a Thrak. The Walker saw him looking and tucked it inside the neck of his jumpsuit with a peevish expression.

Amber chuckled. "He thinks you're a thief."

Jack shrugged. "You stay out of this."

Eyes widening, she looked up at him. "But a bit of comfort before I get frozen . . ."

"Touch his jewelry and I'll have Madam Sadie leave you in cold sleep."

He felt an answering shudder and the girl said reluctantly, "I was just teasing. Besides, I kind of like Walkers." Jack had only had the briefest exposure to them. Even as a Christian sect, they were rather aggressive, eagerly searching the galaxies for proof that their savior had walked the worlds before them. They paused as a nurse approached.

"Which one of you?"

"Her," Jack said as Amber went suddenly quiet.

The woman frowned. "A bit young for this, isn't she?"

"Talk to your employer about it." But as the hard-faced woman reached for Amber, Jack found himself prying her fingers off his arm. The nurse took a firm grip on her charge and began to march her away.

Amber looked back, her face deadly pale, her eyes like sunken holes. "Jack!"

"I won't leave you alone. When you're prepped, I'll be back in. I'll even hold your hand when you go to sleep." He tightened his jaw, as the door closed behind Amber in mid-sentence, and he wondered if she'd heard him.

* * *

As he gathered his gear and waited for transport, Jack found his jaw still clenched and stretched to relax it. Amber had little to worry about. If he died on this job, his death benefits were enough to cancel the debt and release her from Sadie's vaults, plus give her something to tide her over. Rolf was another matter. . . .

The transport crew bitched as they picked him and his bags up. The case carrying his suit weighed as much as he did, probably, and one of them groused. "What th' hell ya got in here, a body?"

The other puffed, "Most o' you guys carry your own gear."

Jack just smiled thinly as they staggered past him and loaded the rear of the vehicle. He got in the front seat, leaving the second man perching, doubled-over, in the cargo compartment, and ignored their thinly veiled comments about his ego and ancestry as they took him to the spaceport. He knew they'd deal with him soon enough, for they were old hands on Tomcat's crew, and he was subject to "new man" hazing as soon as he set foot in their territory.

As they unloaded, and he watched the ramp carrying the trunk into the bowels of the sleek warship, he spotted the outer accoutrements of the vessel. Stealth equipment, well-hidden, but unmistakable, met his eyes. Stealth in deep space was a very risky venture. Jack wondered briefly where General Gilgenbush had his base, and if the stealth equipment could be used. Not unless there was mass around somewhere to mask their approach.

The two crewmen bowed and said, "Come on aboard."

Jack grinned. "What's Tomcat like, anyway?"

They looked at one another. One, a tall black man whom deep space had burned even darker, smiled widely. "What's th' boss like? Haven't you heard of him, greenie?"

"Heard of him, but never served under him."

The second man, a redhead with a mass of freckles over his pug-nosed face, flashed his teeth. "As long as he keeps you from coming home with your ass in a sling, he's a good commander. Right?"

Jack, though he did not voice it, thought to himself that there were other criteria. He paused on the gangplank, watching a dock across the far side of the bay. Then he ducked his head and entered the ship quickly, knowing he'd seen who he thought he had. Short-Jump, late of the *Montreal,* watching him from across the docking areas, hatred etched into his ugly face.

They gave Jack a cubbyhole for a room, with a sleeping sling tied across it. He reflected wryly that Amber probably had more room in her cryogenic bay. It meant that he had no choice but to leave the suit in its trunk in the shop. He had it bagged there, with a refrigeration unit keeping it cold, causing much eyebrow raising, but if Amber was right and the cold retarded growth, then the eccentricity was worth it.

He saw Tomcat come aboard, his lithe, compact form draped with gushing females crying sorrowfully at his leaving, and knew, with a small smile, why the man was so named. The commander, with silvery blond hair, narrow waist, and broad shoulders, was so good looking that Jack was willing to bet his life that it wasn't the face Tomcat had been born with—or even his second face. Injuries were a common hazard, and cosmetic surgery an expected fringe benefit.

Red-haired and freckled Barney had been standing behind him at the port window when Tomcat shrugged off his ladies. He grinned. "Now you know why we call him Tomcat."

"Never would have guessed it," Jack answered.

Barney's eyes narrowed, wrinkling the bridge of his pug nose. He paused a moment and Jack left him wondering.

But Tomcat earned his respect on the first day out, by calling an orientation meeting for all mercenaries, not in the mess, but in the Shop, where all men were to be stripping down their weapons and readying them for the sortie to come.

It put them all on an equal footing, Jack thought. Not in display to impress anyone, but working shoulder to shoulder, professionals, though each had different talents. Out of the corner of his eye, he watched a thread-slender man with braided blue-black hair take apart and oil each one of his projectile guns, small lethal beauties that could punch a hole through a deep space suit, and, in some cases, even Jack's own armor. Tomcat sat on an empty ammo casing, his torso bare and smeared with soot and glistening with oil, as he worked on his own flamethrower.

Shop had a smell and sound all its own. Sweat and oil, solder and metal, Jack could almost taste it as well. Tools made faint noises as they took apart bolts and stripped wires and reconnected tubings. Cloths silently rubbed lubrication along metal and plastic barrels. Screwdrivers and probes delicately adjusted sightings. There were no heroes in Shop, only mechanics.

Still, Jack sensed the change in atmosphere as he pulled the suit out. He needed a cherry picker for the job. He'd already stripped and re-outfitted the suit, so it hung, glistening, in the light and he remembered what Marciane had said: "Like a baby's first tooth." It twisted on the hook, opalescent, limbs hanging.

Tomcat got up from his seat and came over to look at it. He whistled between his impeccable capped front teeth. "Look at that. Now I've seen armor but nothing like that. Sadie, for once, wasn't exaggerating. Where'd you get it?"

"I lifted it from the labs making the prototypes for the new guard."

The pale yellow eyebrows moved, arching delicately. "No kidding. How long you had it?"

"Couple of years."

"You don't hire out much, do you?"

This wasn't the question. Tomcat was wondering why he hadn't heard of Jack and the suit before. Jack nodded. "It was a personal matter."

"What kind of fighting have you done?"

"I did some strike busting."

Tomcat nodded abruptly, satisfied with Jack's experience.

As Jack looked past the commander, he saw other faces nod quickly back to their jobs at hand. He knew the men of the *Montreal* would have talked about him, but he also knew that mercenaries treated justice as a very personal and private matter. Even if his current crewmates were speculating if Jack had burned Marciane, that was his business. And if the dead man's former crew wanted Jack, that was their business.

Tomcat stuck his hand out. "Welcome aboard. Storm, isn't it?"

"Call me Jack," he answered and took the shake. The man's flesh was cool and firm, and callused across the palm. Tomcat was neither young, nor as pretty as he looked.

They came for him shortly after he'd fallen asleep, in the middle of the night watch. Jack curbed the expression on his face as he saw the black man, Libya, and the redhead, Barney, fill the doorway to his cubby. Barney held a broom.

"You're on watch tonight, Jack," Barney said soberly. He handed Jack the broom.

"No kidding. Sorry, I missed the posting."

"Don't worry about it. It's light duty, Tomcat doesn't post it."

Barney looked around. "It's embarrassing really, but every ship has them, and we have to keep after them."

Jack took the broom. "Has what?"

"Space rats. You're to comb the holds, find the ones you can, and we'll jettison 'em with the waste tomorrow."

Libya said mellowly, "They're fast, quick, and dangerous."

"Dangerous."

"Diseases and they like to chew. With all the wiring on board ship . . ." His voice lowered and he shrugged eloquently.

"Right."

Barney looked at Jack. "The broom should pick them up just fine."

"How's that?"

"We mixed bolts in with food we left out for them. Scavengers will eat anything. The broom's magnetic—it picks up the metallic bolts. Doesn't matter to it if a squirming, ugly space rat has swallowed the bolt or not. Ah—you know the areas to stay out of with the broom, right?"

"Sure," answered Jack solemnly. "Wouldn't want to compromise any electromagnetic fields."

"That's the idea. Okay. We'll start in the rear cargo hold tonight. You're on rotation, so you won't have duty again for five or six more days."

Nodding. Jack followed the two men. As they approached the bulkhead leading to the hold, he asked, "How long's my watch?" and stifled a yawn.

Libya rolled an eye at Barney. The redhead smiled. "We have a quota. We figure, bring in a half a dozen of these babies a watch, and we'll keep the population down."

"Six space rats and I can go back to bed, right?"

"That's right. Just bring your count to me—I'll be in the forward galley, doing a stores report."

"And here's a bag for 'em," added Libya, thrusting a net at him.

"Right." Jack stepped into the twilight of the cargo hold, and the two men swung the bulkhead shut behind them.

As the hold closed, Jack sat down, dropping the broom and sack at his feet. Not that the ship didn't have rats . . . it probably did. Rats seemed to have emigrated almost as far as men had. But Jack knew that the broom was no more metallic than he was and no rat had ever been caught with one. He'd been sent on the greenhorn's legendary wild goose chase.

It pleased him a little, actually. They'd sized him up as a young and innocent straight arrow. Others aboard the ship were probably getting different initiations according to the character assessment made of them. Greedy types were being offered deals too good to be true. Paranoids were being let in on fictitious plots.

He could curl up and sleep until the end of his rest shift, when Barney and Libya would no doubt show up to rescue him, knowing he couldn't possibly have made his quota, hoping he'd be red-eyed from lack of sleep and chasing impossible rats. That, however, would be letting it go a little too easy.

Jack smiled in the dark of the hold, picked up his catch-sack, and stealthily moved forward.

* * *

Barney looked at his cards. He glanced over the tops of them at Libya. "You've got to be bluffing."

The dark man showed his teeth. "Lay 'em down and find out."

Barney shrugged. He did so, and watched Libya rack in another pot. His sole consolation lay in anticipating the look on the greenie's face when they went to get him in the morning, and he had failed to bag his quota of space rats. Barney grunted in happy thought as Libya shuffled and dealt. The tawny-headed young man with washed-out eyes of blue had absorbed all they'd told him with a solemn air, as though knowing they'd told him the absolute truth, and the task was a sacred duty. The happiness turned into a grin. Barney remembered when he'd been put through the space rat chase.

Libya cocked his head alertly. "Someone comin'."

It was far too early for their prey. Barney leaned back in his chair, listening to the plastic back creak. "Probably the commander for his mid-shift drink."

But the figure who loomed in the galley doorway was that of their greenie. He held up a bloodstained broom and bulging sack. "Here you go, Barney." With a wink, he dropped the sack in Barney's lap, upsetting the deck of cards. "I take it initiation's over," he said, and sauntered off.

Barney looked in horror at the sack in his lap. Bulges squirmed and bubbled.

"What is it?" Libya said, getting to his feet.

Barney cautiously opened the mouth to look, and let out a blood-curdling scream. "Oh, my god! It's rats!"

Jack paused in mid-stride, halfway back down the corridor, as the scream reached him. Only then he grinned.

Chapter Twelve

"Let's see what you've got." Tomcat's voice rang confidently in the metal confines of the staging area. "We won't be putting an assault plan together until we know what we have to work with. Targeting is down there. Be sure to aim so that the deflector shields are at the optimum."

Barney sat hunched down close to Jack and he caught the edge of his green-eyed stare.

Other crewmen sat sprinkled amidst the mercenaries. Jack had met most of them in the shop, trading tools and working side by side in casual circumstances, the way Tomcat liked to have his crewmen mix. There was only one superior here. Of necessity, it was Tomcat himself.

Jack watched the men get up one by one and demonstrate their weaponry in the designated area. The air crackled with the smell of explosives and spent cartridges, of energy beams and ozone, of hot metal as the shields were subjected to the firing power.

He sat back, knowing that the shields couldn't hold most of what he could do in the suit, and wondering how to demonstrate it. He wondered if his face showed his disapproval—most of the weapons being used violated the precepts of the "Pure" war—being indiscriminate as to whether a planet was being damaged or the enemy.

Though, he supposed, in its way; the suit could do the same, but no wearer of a suit would. The world, its environs, were sacred; the enemy was not. This was a lesson hard learned long ago on Earth, where the opposite had been true—protect mankind, even your enemy. Dirt was not more valuable than flesh. Unfortunately, humans had learned, it *was*. Dirt, and atmosphere, and water, a closed cycle, infinitely more vulnerable than constantly renewing flesh.

And that was why Jack doubly hated the Thraks and whoever had destroyed Claron.

"Jack. You been chasing space rats again?"

He realized the commander was, and had been, talking to him. In spite of himself, he flushed.

"No, sir. Got my quota the first night, right, Barney?"

It was the redhead's turn to color as Jack stood up. Libya nudged Barney with a low chuckle.

"What can you do for us?"

"It's more a matter of what I can't do. The suit is fully armored, self-contained, weaponry is built in. I can suit up, but I'm afraid the shields in the targeting area aren't sufficient to work with." He grinned. "I don't want to blast a hole in the side of the ship."

Tomcat frowned above the laughter. "I need to have an idea of your capabilities."

"I can give you some idea of the suit's power."

"Firepower is what I want."

In the silence that fell, Jack locked stares with Tomcat. For the first time, he saw the hardness and determination behind the pretty boy face. The man was used to getting what he wanted, even if it wasn't going to be good for him.

He stirred. "How about a computer simulation?"

"Can you do it?"

"I'm not a programmer."

"Barney here is. The two of you can have free use of a terminal while the rest of us work." With that, turning his back on Storm, Tomcat dismissed them. Barney got up with a glare and a heavy sigh.

Barney led him to a terminal. It took him a while to find a suitable graphics and animation simulation program. Resentfully at first, and then with grudging admiration, he worked with Jack.

An hour later he sat back and mopped the sweat off his forehead on the back of his muscled forearm. "You know this thing inside and out," he said.

"Almost." Jack watched the graphic turn on the screen, thinking of the living organism hidden inside the suit. "Almost. Can we feed that to the staging area?"

"No problem."

"Let's get going then."

The room was thick with smoke and the smell of warfare. The men had broken into little groups, going over their weapons and speaking in quiet tones. Tomcat squatted by a harpooner, talking solemnly, and his forehead wrinkled as they came in. "We're almost done."

"I'll wait."

The commander nodded. The harpooner went down to the targets and put his lance three-quarters of the way through a four-inch metal plate. Wryly, Jack made a note not to stand between the man and his enemy. Even the suit couldn't withstand that unless the shields were up.

Barney dimmed the lights and lit up the computer screen. Jack said nothing, but let the computer reveal the suit's capabilities and extrapolate them to the screen. When it was finished, there was dead silence in the bay.

Someone muttered, "Impossible."

"He's a goddamn walking, fracking war."

Tomcat stood with his arms folded across his chest, his compactly muscled body straining the dark blue of his uniform. He ignored the comments drifting into the silence. Then he cleared his throat. "All right. I think we have an idea of our capabilities. I suggest you talk to one another and learn to respect one another's skills. And remember, the man who's fighting with you today may be fighting against you tomorrow. It pays to learn his weak spots as well as his strengths."

As the bay emptied, he signaled Barney to keep Jack at hand. When they were alone, the men looked at one another. "What the hell are you doing here," said Tomcat.

"I signed on as a free mercenary."

"That's not what I meant. You've got enough firepower to take over your own planet."

"I'm not in the war business."

"Somebody should tell your suit."

Jack scuffed his boots uneasily. The metal plates hummed beneath him. Tomcat sighed. "I take it Sadie hasn't seen you perform in person."

"No."

"Anyone else?"

"Marciane," Jack said after a slight hesitation.

The baby blue eyes widened. "Then you're the one responsible."

"I'd say it was self-defense."

Barney scratched his head but kept his silence as Tomcat shifted. He looked back over his shoulder at the computer screen which still displayed a three-dimensional animation of the suit, revolving slowly in midair.

"It's nice to know what our Emperor has in mind for us," Tomcat said dryly.

Jack did not miss the sarcasm in the man's voice.

"With firepower like that, I have to send you in at point."

"I understand."

The commander began to pivot away, then swiveled back. "What do you want out of this, Storm?"

"What do you mean?"

Tomcat jerked a thumb at Barney, who evaporated out the bulkhead, leaving them alone. He leaned back against a rib of the bay.

"This is a relatively small operation. It has to be—send an armada against Gilgenbush, and he'll wipe you out. The only chance we have of succeeding is that he won't know we're coming, and I'm not just talking about the stealth equipment. I'm talking about Sadie. She doesn't send 'pay up or else' notices. Your contract expires, and the money is due. She doesn't even ask once, let alone twice. Gilgenbush has no notice we're on our way, but if he's smart, he'll know because that's the way Sadie operates. And, if the check's in transit, and we cross over . . . that's too bad. We're on comm silence now because that's the only way we can sneak up. If Gilgenbush has paid up, consider the damage we're going to do as 'late charges'." He shifted. "You could have your own ship. Want one? I'll help you get it, provided you partner with me."

Jack shook his head. "Thanks for the offer, but I'm not looking for my own command."

"Then what are you doing here?"

"Is this what happened to Claron? Nobody knew you were coming?"

Tomcat's eyes narrowed. "What are you talking about?"

"You wanted to know what I'm doing here. I've got a couple of reasons, and the burn-off at Claron is one of the foremost."

Tomcat reached out suddenly, lightning fast, and grabbed Jack by the collar of his fatigues. Chin to chin, they glared at one another. Tomcat said slowly, spitting out each word, "I had nothing to do with Claron. Nor did any other free mercenary I know."

Jack didn't let himself blink as the commander released him. "It's a big, wide, galaxy. What about the mercenaries you don't know?"

Tomcat shook his head, violently. "Nobody would do that. Those were civilians . . . innocents, as it were." He looked back to Jack. "What's your interest in Claron?"

"I was there."

The silence stretched. Then Tomcat took a step back. "Working?"

"No. I was in settlement there."

"You're lucky to be alive, then."

"If you call it that."

Tomcat looked back to the screen. He pointed. "What in the hell is a settler doing with *that?*"

Jack shrugged, a ghost of a smile playing over his lips. "One of the mysteries of life, commander, that you'll have to live with. We all have our little secrets."

"Yes, we do. And I have a feeling we haven't even scratched the surface of yours. Just as well. Curiosity doesn't pay in our business. The word on the street is that Claron was union business . . . the miners there weren't, and the union thought they ought to be. The freebooters they hired got too enthusiastic." Tomcat sighed, then. "I still need you on point."

"And I still understand. I want into Gilgenbush's as bad as you do."

"Why?"

"Why not?" Jack clicked the remote, killing the computer screen. As the room darkened, he added, "The suit and I are trying to build a rep."

"I would ask why," said Tomcat slowly, "but I have a feeling I don't want to know the reason. I'll have battle plans worked out by tomorrow."

"Good night, sir," Jack said, and left the commander alone in the bay. Ballard had raged at his naiveté—told him they'd burned an entire planet just to get him. Now Tomcat suggested it was a union matter. But unions didn't lose control like that. And if Ballard was still right—who had enough power to nudge an entire union out of control and point it at a defenseless planet as if it was a weapon? Who the hell was Winton and where was he buried in the Triad bureaucracy?

* * *

Assault morning. Jack sat in the staging area alone, smoking a stim very leisurely, watching the red ash glow briefly in the darkness, before it deadened. The suit hung on the cherry picker, its opalescence catching the briefest glimpses of illumination in the bay, and reflecting back at Jack, as though trying to catch his attention. It had almost a sun-like quality.

Or perhaps that was his imagination, fueled by the stim. He puffed it down to the last centimeters, then ground it out on the deck. Tomcat was creeping up on Gilgenbush's space station from behind the inhospitable planet it orbited. Right now, they were on opposite sides. Soon, the commander would begin piloting toward the space station, using the bulk of the planet to shield him, and then the cloaking device. If all went well, they would be knocking on the rogue general's door before he could possibly expect company.

Which explained to Jack what Tomcat was doing there. As for himself . . . He ran a hand through his hair. If Amber were with him, she'd cluck and smooth it down. If she were with him, he wouldn't be going through this. He had an obligation to her.

But his obligation to himself came first, he guessed. If he survived the assault, he knew word of the suit and himself would go all the way to the Emperor. That was a front door he'd already knocked at once, and been admitted through, but the Emperor hadn't been home, just some of his lesser counterparts. Jack intended to keep knocking until he found the right man home. It had to be Jack who did it—there was no one else.

He stood up. He approached the suit and tentatively reached out to touch the crest on the chest, the crest which could no longer be seen, because Amber had painstakingly painted it out with fingernail polish she'd had that matched the Flexalinks. She'd wanted to strip the crest off entirely, but he hadn't allowed her. He thought of Ballard. He was the last remaining Knight. It was his job to get the word through to the emperor about treachery and betrayal.

"Sir!" Lights went on throughout the bay. It was Barney, anxious and eager in his own battle gear. "I thought I'd find you here, Storm. The commander told me to see if you needed help suiting up."

Jack dropped his hand. "Thanks." He leaned over and stripped off his shirt.

"Boss—you're going bare into that thing?"

He turned around and tossed the shirt to Barney. "The contacts go on bare skin. Besides, if that thing doesn't protect me, a shirt won't help any."

"Guess you're right there." Barney tucked the shirt into his weapons belt and joined Jack as he lowered the suit to its feet.

Inside, the world was muffled. He'd left the com lines on low volume to shut out the nervous chatter of the others. Jack watched the other mercenaries filter into staging, only half seeing them, the other half of his mind occupied with the data Tomcat had shown and discussed with them. Libya came in, complete with bracers made of Endura, an armor combination that left him fleet, mobile, and still well-protected. The black man grinned and saluted Jack. Barney, standing anxiously at his side, saluted back.

At the airlock beyond staging, a team in deep space suits stood ready. Their job was to force a lock open, mate the ship to the space station, and stand back from the breach. If any were going to die, they'd be the first to go. Their job would be easiest if the stealth equipment worked and hardest if they were detected. Of course, the change in air pressure as they blew the lock, then re-pressurized it would give away their presence, but by the time Gilgenbush's men mobilized, Jack would be leading the others in.

Like an onion, Tomcat had described the station lair of the rogue general. They'd have to peel layers away to get at the general himself, but they had to have Gilgenbush to open the vault. If the general refused to cooperate, Sadie herself had ordered Tomcat to bring the man back. Amber would have a new neighbor in the cold vault until someone decided to pay the loan off in order to revive the general.

As Gilgenbush had many enemies, as well as friends, it was only a matter of time until someone paid to thaw him out. Sadie would have her money and her pound of flesh. Tomcat was fairly certain Gilgenbush could not fail to see the reason in her methods.

Barney said something. Jack turned the speakers up to normal, as the nervous crewman repeated, "That's it."

The gentle cushioning jolt of the warship coming to a halt trembled through its length. Jack nodded.

Mercenaries began grinding out smokes and getting to their feet. Tomcat himself appeared. He broadcast. "Get in place, Jack."

Jack and the suit moved out. He wove gracefully through the throng of mercenaries, many of whom couldn't move fast enough to get out of his way. He read the shock and surprise on their faces. They had figured his bulk to be lumbering, awkward, not lithe and graceful.

He stepped into the airlock and waited for the bulkhead to open up. The contacts pinched at his torso and he felt the itching again. Maybe Sarge had been right. Maybe the gel used to anchor the contacts was bothering him. Advice meted out long ago but never forgotten.

Jack twitched involuntarily as he found himself about to turn and tell the sarge that, and caught himself. He stood there, shaking, an adrenaline surge pounding through his bloodstream, waiting for the doors to open, waiting to be unleashed. Any second now . . . soon . . . there . . . NOW!

Jack burst through the airlock tunnel almost before it opened.

His rearview cameras showed the others following, but he barely acknowledged the seeing. His attention was on the corridor ahead. As long as his path led inward, he could use full power, head outward though; he ran a chance of punching a hole through the outer skin of the rotating station.

His missing finger itched. He cocked his glove and took out the first security camera in the tunnel. Coming in, Gilgenbush's men would have to move in blind. His receivers picked up the alarm signal, an oscillating klaxon. The space station systems showed the breach. Too late. He was in and the rest of the mercenaries were on his heels.

Three men appeared in front of him. Jack used the left gauntlet, firing singly, before they could sling their rifles around to fire. They dropped and he vaulted over their bodies, leaving them behind for the others to move. He had but one objective: to clear the tunnels.

He ran, the metal plates resilient under the weight of the suit. A warning light went off and he plowed to a stop. He ducked, missing fire from a sentry unit embedded in the wall. How many of these had he passed without noticing, moving too quickly to be hit, leaving the mercenaries on his heels for targets? Too late to wonder now. He let out a burst of laser fire, frying the control panel.

Back in motion, he took out as many of the automatic weapons as he could. He came to an intersection, did a calculation and took the right hand passage. Layers, upon layers.

The tunnel lights went out, putting any not wearing night-sight goggles at a disadvantage. But Tomcat had prepared his men for that. Jack, with his helmet and suit, scarcely wavered. The intersection looped over and he found himself face to face with Barney and Libya.

They relaxed their weapons.

Jack took a breath. Crimson splashes licked up Barney's boots.

"Where to?"

"Down." Jack took a bearing and pivoted. He watched his screen as it triangulated and gave him a logical presumption. "Secret door, back that way." He retraced his steps. His cameras showed a heat leak, minor, in the panel. Jack kicked the trigger at his left ring finger, traced the panel, found the portal, and wrenched it open. A black hole greeted him and he jumped in, feet first.

He landed, activated the lift and stepped out of the well as the elevator whined upward. Barney and Libya would follow him in a more conventional way. He turned around, and saw a bank of men run in and drop to their knees in defensive firing position. Men and more . . . Thraks, and one or two other aliens he wasn't that familiar with, except that he was sure brain power wasn't among their strong suits.

His heart did a stop beat, then caught again. What the hell were Thraks doing here? He licked his lips even as he dodged back inside the elevator well for cover. He hated Thraks. Inside the suit, he began to shake.

And then it caught him. It sang inside him. He knew a tremendous anger and hatred and it consumed him like the firestorm that had consumed Claron. It commanded him and he reacted. He checked his gauges and cocked his gauntlet for automatic fire.

Jack came out of cover, laying down a spray. Bodies blossomed. They crumpled at the torso, exploded at the head and toppled. His wrist circuit tingled at the expenditure of power.

He caught the Thraks dead center, and didn't even bother to step over their bodies. He waded through them, enjoying the crunch.

He heard war howls as Libya, Barney, and others came through in his wake.

Jack kept firing, driving reinforcements down, down, farther into the tunnels. He followed their line of retreat, letting them lead him into the bowels of Gilgenbush's domain. He lost track of time and damage, hearing Tomcat's voice flickering on and off in his helmet, signaling back when he had time for it, knowing the commander was following him on down. He knew he had to remember the amount of time spent in the suit, but a fierce joy seized him, and he lost track of everything.

* * *

The man sat in the center of his web and watched the monitors. The suited monster plowing through the security of his system had ceased to even blast the cameras as he went through. Resistance was a futile exercise. Gilgenbush watched him plow through well-trained soldiers as if they were practice dummies. He lifted his cigar and took a deep, thoughtful drag. "My men can't stop him."

In the shadows, another man answered, "I can. I've seen the suit operate."

"Then go out and meet him."

"Why? He's exhausting his power. I'll meet him when I have to."

The general, who was general over everything and everyone in his satellite except the other inhabitant in his office, bit into the end of his cigar. He said nothing, knowing this man wouldn't follow his orders anyway. He had other . . . options . . . waiting to meet the battle armor. But Gilgenbush didn't like what he was seeing. He exhaled, filling the air with blue-gray smoke, partially obscuring the closest monitor. He shouldn't have to worry much longer at any rate.

* * *

Jack set off the first booby trap, deep in the center of the satellite, where soldiers had failed the general, and he'd gone to gadgetry. It caught him by surprise, the gas cylinder exploding under his feet, filling the tunnel with white frost.

Jack plowed to a stop as his suit gauges showed an incredible drop in temperature around him. He waited as the face plate cleared. A normal man would have been flash frozen in the tunnel . . . normal men like Barney and Libya and Tomcat, following him inward to Gilgenbush's lair. He caught a shuddering breath, and wondered how long ago it was that he'd ceased to think—to do anything but kill.

He panned the connector tube. Hidden chill points showed him where three more cylinders lay waiting behind plates, like mines. Jack systematically fired them one at a time. He waded through the chilling fog as it affected the suit's temperature, but only momentarily until the suit adjusted itself. A tiny chill remained at the back of his neck.

Jack paused and checked his compass. The bulkhead before him led to a connective link with five arms branching off. The suit and his own senses told him he was making his way steadily to what must be the operative center of the satellite. He needed to continue straight ahead. He stepped into the connective link.

The moment his feet touched, the metal throbbed. The plates beneath him hummed as machinery kicked into gear with a whoosh. Jack hit his hover jets, propelling himself into midair as the link rotated briskly.

The connective tunnel rolled and gyrated, the arms swinging open and shut in front of him in a dizzying array until Jack closed his eyes in sensory vertigo. His hovering suit became the center of the universe, the constant needed to keep him sane.

And he fought with himself, with the bloodsong wild in his ears to keep from bolting, from fighting wildly, to accept the passive inaction of hanging in midair. There was no enemy here, he told himself. Just machinery.

The connective link halted abruptly. His compass rotated erratically. If he had not vaulted into midair and stayed there, he would have been hopelessly disoriented.

Jack began to grin. He kicked the hovers down on low and glided across the intersection into the tunnel opening he'd selected originally, thinking that Gilgenbush had an extremely devious mind.

He'd no sooner stepped into the corridor, than the heat seeking projectile fired, its orange flash arcing like a tracer path from the far end of the tunnel.

Jack froze in place. He checked his gauges and saw the projected trajectory. He held still. The suit shuddered around him as though it knew he was a walking target.

At the last second, he leaned to the right and felt the vibration of the small missile pass him by. It passed because the suit did not even begin to approximate the body temperature of a living target.

It hit the connective link and exploded. The backlash of energy washed around Jack like an inferno. Jack squinted as he turned to look at the damage, and then he grinned fiercely. Gilgenbush was running out of options. He turned and strode purposefully down the corridor.

* * *

"Damn." Gilgenbush snubbed the stub of a cigar out. "He's almost here."

"No tricks left?"

"No."

"Then I suggest surrender."

The general gave the shadowy figure a smoldering look, even as the metal walls of his inner office clanged and began to turn molten under attack.

Jack burst through the final door, melting its center seam and peeling it back. The man behind the desk inside, prepared though he thought he was, reacted strongly, shock and surprise flooding away the stoic preparedness.

"My god," Gilgenbush said. "What did Sadie hire?" He wiped the palm of his hand nervously over his balding skull, ruffling up a fringe of prematurely snow-white hair. His hawk nose jutted out fiercely, shadowing his gaunt and worried eyes. He wore his uniform, the brown fabric setting off the gold braids and epaulets, neckline buttoned severely into a jawline only slightly sagged by age.

"You can't say I didn't warn you," a voice said smoothly.

Jack pivoted to the corner, his blind spot, as the harpooner stepped out. His weapon was loaded, lance head glinting in the office light.

Jack's fierce joy drained away.

Chapter Thirteen

"You made it here before me," Jack said, eying the lance. "But then I guess you must have known where you were going."

The harpooner grinned. Of Asian heritage, he was muscled like a gymnast. He carried the heavy harpoon with an easy grace. "Remember what Tomcat said—the man you work with today may be the man you fight tomorrow." He centered the lance on Jack's stomach. "Or vice versa."

The general made a steeple of his thick fingers. "No, Khan, you're wrong. This man is not the Owner of the Dragon, though I can clearly see why you might have thought he was. This man is another law unto himself. You did well to tell me about him."

"What's he talking about?"

They looked at Jack. "Another mercenary," Gilgenbush said shortly. "If you live and stay in the business, you'll meet him sooner or later."

Khan took the safety off the harpoon gun. "I wouldn't worry about it."

Gilgenbush said, "You're sure the suit's repairable?"

"That should be your least concern," the harpooner told the rogue general.

Gilgenbush made a diffident movement.

Jack realized then that he had the luxury of not being seen that well inside the helmet. He would not be telegraphing his movements. "I take it that you've reached a financial agreement."

The white-haired general smiled, very thinly. "The madam does charge an outrageous interest. Khan's proposal leaves me a great deal more money. He tells me that once you've been taken out, my men can mop up the rest of the detail rather quickly."

"I wouldn't count on that if I were you."

Khan snapped, "We're wasting time."

"Right." Gilgenbush got to his feet. "Take him out."

Jack moved before the harpoon left the gun, reaching out and grasping the shaft in his gauntlets, and bending the deadly lance into a hook. Khan gasped, dropped his weapon and turned heel to run, but Jack caught him by the scruff of the neck.

"If you'd been with me," Jack said grimly, "like the others, you'd have seen how fast I can move." He jammed the butt of the spear into the wall and hung Khan from his own hook, while Gilgenbush stood transfixed by the side of his ornate desk. The general held up his hands.

"I know when I've been beaten. Why don't I just give you the location of the vault. I doubt you'll have any trouble opening it."

"Why don't you just walk with me anyway, general. Your men might get the idea that this battle is over."

Gilgenbush smiled that thin smile of his. It was a pale line under his outstanding nose. "Well put. This way, then." He pressed a button and a panel opened, while Jack broadcast to Tomcat that the quarry had been taken.

Tomcat sounded out of breath, and busy, but congratulated him. "We'll be there in a minute. Blazes, Storm—you plowed right through them. I'm still wading through bodies back here."

He felt a moment of panic, because he didn't remember killing more than three or four men and a few Thraks. But he remembered the fierce joy that had gripped him, and now he heard the buzzing in his ears, the awakening song of whatever it was that possessed the suit and fought to influence him. Which of them had been in control?

As Jack followed the old man in the brown and gold uniform, he was afraid he knew the answer.

* * *

"Sadie was so pleased she let me out two days early," Amber crowed. She squeezed his arm again.

Jack looked down at her, faintly quizzical and unexpectedly pleased at Amber's joy in seeing him, though he disliked the influence Madame Sadie had had on the girl.

No . . . not girl. Not any more. He didn't know if it had been the weeks away, or Sadie's work, but Amber had finally crossed the nebulous border from girl into young woman. His nerves tingled at the discovery.

Amber laughed. "You still look surprised."

"I am. I was expecting to find you in hypothermia." He reached out to ruffle her hair as he would have once, and drew his hand back. She'd spent too much time on the arrangement to mess it up. One of the differences between a girl and a woman was her reaction to having her hair mussed. He swallowed instead and gently regained control of his right arm.

"So what's this bonus you got?"

"A new apartment. Nicer section of town, not too far from here."

A subtle expression filtered through her happiness. Then she said, "Farther away from Rolf."

"That's one advantage." Sadie had a taxi waiting for them, and one of her men was standing guard by the small pile of Amber's belongings. She looked around as the guard returned to Sadie's fortress. "Where's the suit?"

"In storage."

"Did refrigeration help?"

He took her by the elbow and seated her in the vehicle.

"I think it did more good for you than for the suit."

She waited until he settled and then said, "It wasn't so bad. I thought it would be awful on account of . . ." Her voice faded off.

"Why? On account of what?"

Very small voice. "The way you act. You have coldsleep nightmares."

"I have different reasons," Jack said reluctantly. He fed a hard disk to the autodriver.

"I know." Amber folded her hands in her lap. "Still . . ." She brightened. "Madame Sadie told us to come back any time. I think she likes you."

"Right." Jack looked out the taxi window. The streets here were infinitely brighter, houses instead of buildings crowding the curb. And trees. He'd forgotten how much he missed them. Every square meter of free space was planted with grass and shrubs, and trees. In the back, where the houses reigned, flowers flourished under the Malthen sun.

But it was the trees he watched as they boldly leaned over the curb and waved their branches over his roadway.

Amber seemed to sense his mood and lapsed into silence herself, though he caught her nibbling at her newly polished nails, a brilliant gold, thanks to Madame Sadie. She looked into her side mirror and saw a squat, ugly man ducking beyond the boundary of Madame Sadie's house. There was no doubt in her mind that he was a mercenary because of the jumpsuit he wore, and the ever present weapons belt, but he was so ugly, she gave a little shudder. She thought of telling Jack, took a look at his bemused expression, and changed her mind. He hadn't been one of Rolf's contacts, and so she didn't worry.

* * *

He dreams again.

He walks through the enemy, gauntlets up, spewing death, and the bodies fall before him, exoskeletons crackling under the weight of his passage. And as he walks, he sings a bloodsong, and the killing satisfies him. But then, inside, he quails a little as he begins to recognize the faces of his enemies, and they're not made of exoskeleton, but flesh. Sarge, Bilosky, Marciane, other men whose names he does not remember, but their faces are not alien as they roll over in crimson death.

He holds his gauntlet up a moment, ceasing fire, but it drops into position again of its own accord, despite what he wants. He cannot control the spew of firepower even when his own face appears in front of him and he kills himself, but he plows through the ranks and he does not, cannot, scream until he shoots the girl and then she screams, and his own echoes it, finally.

Jack sat up in the bed. He found himself panting, his heart pounding desperately in his chest. He covered his face with his hands, awake again, this time thankfully.

The darkness split as the door opened, and Amber slipped in, not turning on his light, but leaving the hall light on, shining like a beacon through the doorframe.

"Jack?"

"I'm okay. Just go back to bed."

She hesitated, a bath towel wrapped around her, hiding her nightgown and the frail body that was just beginning to curve with a woman's shape. Then she sat down at the far corner of the bed. "It's not all right. *I* don't have dreams like this. I thought I might, but I don't. You've been waking up seven, eight times a night."

"It'll be all right."

"It's *not*. You shouldn't have hired out for Sadie, I know it."

He wiped his face, and surprisingly, found it dry. But he couldn't wipe away the blood splattered image of that last death, and now she sat, looking at him with worried accusation. "Go back to bed."

She crossed her legs. "No."

"Then I will." He threw himself back down on the mattress,

tugged at the wrinkled bedding underneath him and rolled to his side, trying to ignore her. The golden brown eyes burned holes into him. Jack finally sat up. "Amber, it's all right. Go back to bed."

"Would it help if you told me what you dreamed about?"

"No," he said firmly. "Usually I don't dream and even if I did tell, it wouldn't help."

"Then what will?"

He remembered Claron. "Mordil," he told her. "Can you find some?"

Her nose wrinkled. "That's bad stuff. You don't want that."

"It's what will help."

"I think you need a rehab tech."

"I've had one." He stopped as Amber's face wrinkled all over and she began to sniffle. He reached forward then, and tugged her over, keeping the blankets bunched up between them, but hugging her as well as he could.

He smoothed her sleep-tangled hair and looked out into the hallway, his sight homing in on the beacon of light. "Listen. I'll tell you what they told me. Cold sleep for military transports is different than storage or medical cold sleep. The government takes advantage of the time and programs in a debriefing suggestion. Brain waves, though minimal, are read. Then they have a record of every participant's memory of the action. It saves time later and it's usually helpful. You wake up purged, more or less."

The sniffling quieted, but he could tell from the movement of her shoulders that she was still crying softly, while listening to him. "My transport was damaged by Thraks as it left Milos. Most of the support systems went down, we went off course and were lost—you know that. And you know my bay was knocked into auxiliary power and so I survived. Seventeen years, I survived. But all of those years, I dreamed."

Amber hiccoughed and interrupted. "But I dreamed too, at Madame Sadie's, and they weren't all bad dreams. Some were nice. I even remembered when I was little and my mother was still there."

"But I was programmed into the debriefing loop—all I could dream was the war. Over and over again."

"The same thing?"

"Yes . . . and no. The mind still creates. Facts get stretched, bloated. Sometimes the detail is exact, and sometimes the mind is creating new out of old, until I wasn't sure what I'd gone through and what I'd imagined. But always the Sand Wars."

She shuddered. "And then what?"

"And then when they picked me up, it ended. But I still had problems. I wake up. They told me that was my mind's reaction to all those years when I couldn't wake up. And I forgot."

"Forgot what? The war?"

"No. I forgot most of what I'd ever been before the war. My family. My life."

Amber pulled back from him and stared at him in the twilight. "You don't remember your family?"

"Not much. Sometimes, a momentary picture. They died on Dorman's Stand when the Thraks took it, but they died inside me a long time before that."

"How sad!" She started to reach for him, but he caught her hand in midair.

"I didn't tell you that for pity."

"And I wasn't giving you 'pity'." Her lips curled at his rejection. She pulled her hand back and said, "I can probably find the mordil, if I have to.

"Good." He watched as she flounced off the bed. "We'll be going through this off and on, as long as I do work."

She grinned then, illuminated in the doorway, her hand on the handle before shutting it behind her. "I guess I won't mind," she said, "since you said 'we'."

* * *

Jack sat cross-legged on the living room floor, a tarp spread out in front of him, and the suit supine on the tarp. The tarp was a precaution to keep the floor clean if he decided to do some tinkering. No sense in upsetting the landlady. Sadie had done a lot for them. He frowned. There ought to be a way of isolating the organism and flushing it out of the system. He considered taking everything out he didn't absolutely have to have for it to function . . . the repair kit, the chamois . . . He hated to take the chamois out, though—damn suit itched enough even with the soft cloth at his back.

The phone rang, interrupting his intense concentration. "Hello," he called. It went onto speaker automatically, and he caught Amber's breathless tones.

"What is it?"

"I'm in trouble, Jack. Someone's following me and I can't shake him."

"Where are you?"

"Picking up the mordil." She gave him the location. "What's he look like?"

She quickly described Short-Jump to him. He grimaced, knowing that the vengeful mercenary had now tied Amber to him and possibly brought Rolf in on it as well.

"Does he know you're on to him?"

She made a rude noise. "I'm better than that!"

"You used to be good enough not to get followed."

A sigh. "There is that."

"Stay there. I'll get you out."

"But Jack—"

"Why did you call if you didn't want help?" He cut the connection before she could argue back. He got up, looking wistfully at the suit, repulsed and attracted by it. He was invulnerable in the suit. And conspicuous as hell walking down a city street.

He walked past the suit and, instead, tucked the small plastic hand gun into his upper right thigh pants pocket where it scarcely bulged. He walked down to the line to catch a public car headed toward where Amber was trapped.

She looked scared as he walked into the corner drug shop. He thought for a moment that the independent, street-smart kid had fled, replaced by a scared, clinging girl-woman, but then Amber straightened and he saw the old determination.

"I didn't call you for help," she lectured him as he joined her at the counter. "I just wanted you to know what I was up to."

"Too late now. Get the mordil?"

"Yeah. He insisted on patching into the doctor's master system to verify the prescription." She sucked her even, white front teeth. "Good thing I put the entry in this morning."

"What's the best way out of here?"

"The front. Unless you want to go in back with the pharmacist." She grinned, suddenly. "He's been hinting at me." The thought made him, already angry at Short-Jump, angrier at everybody in general. He took her by the elbow. "We'll go out the front. If Short-Jump wants me, he'll try to take me there." She nodded as he added, "You hit the deck."

They stepped onto the sidewalk. Laser fire streaked past Jack's face and he shoved Amber to one side, but she let out a tiny squeak and clung to his arm. As Jack swung around, he saw the man who'd frozen her in terror.

His instincts were right—Rolf awaited them as well. He and three of his men closed the semicircle with Short-Jump. Jack reacted blindly. He pulled the gun and snapped off three quick shots, pivoting before his targets fell. Short-Jump hit him in the chest with a stunner. Jolted, he pitched back into Amber, feeling his muscles let go as he sagged to the concrete, unable to help himself, though he was still conscious. Short-Jump's face flared in surprise.

Amber whirled on Rolf, her face snarling. "Don't you touch him!"

"I don't want him, little one. Just you," said Rolf calmly.

His hard black eyes glittered as he looked down at Jack, who rolled helplessly on the pavement, trying to collect himself. The man was dressed well, his brown hair combed in wings, silk shirt drawn tightly over his bulging biceps, his waspish waist cinched into expensive pants. He drew back a boot tip and kicked Jack lightly in the ribs. "He won't be bothering you any more." With a proprietary gesture, he reached for Amber. "Our deal's finished," he told Short-Jump.

"I won't go with you!" Amber stood, cornered, over Jack's body.

Rolf shook his head. "I thought I taught you never to get involved in your work," he commented and reached again, this time determined not to be denied.

Jack shook his head. Pins and needles flared painfully through his body, but even as he jerked uncontrollably, he knew he had the stunner beat—he should be limply unconscious, and he was gaining control back in flashes. But not soon enough to protect Amber from Rolf, as the man reached out and grabbed her, jerking her from her protective stance over his body.

Amber let out a sound and even Jack felt the flare of energy. His brain seemed to explode with the pain she radiated.

Rolf made a small grunt and collapsed to the sidewalk, to his knees, expensive pants splitting at the thigh seam. He clutched his head. "Don't, Amber! Don't do it!" he ground out. Then he sagged into himself and fell over on the sidewalk. A thin trickle of blood seeped from one hairy, flared nostril.

Jack regained control and caught Amber as she collapsed. He staggered to his feet, as Short-Jump unfroze from the spectacle in time to face him, his arms full of Amber.

"Shit," the mercenary said. His beady eyes had widened in shock. "I've never seen anything like this." He looked down at the pimp's body and they watched Rolf's chest heave in and out in tortured breath. "What did she do to him?"

"Nothing. He had a heart attack. Let us past, Short-Jump."

The ugly man's face twisted as he spat out. "You killed Marciane."

"Kill or be killed. You know what he did to us. He let all of us be drugged and then dumped out there, just to get me and my suit. He let all of you be dumped—just to get me."

"Th' captain had his faults." Short-Jump brought his stunner up again, but he looked as though he'd lost faith in it.

"That won't work on me," Jack told him. "It didn't the first time and it won't this time." Though, truthfully, as his knees began to quiver, he wondered if Short-Jump hadn't won after all.

His opponent wavered. "Holy shit," he said again. "I never seen a man beat a stunner before."

"I've got good reflexes. Let me by, Short-Jump! You know I killed Marciane in self-defense, and it was his own greed brought him to it."

"Aye," said the man suddenly, with a heavy sigh, as he dropped the stunner. "I know it. We're quits, Storm, though I can't vouch for the rest of the crew. But I just want you to remember, it wasn't the greed. The suit drove him crazy. He thought you dishonored it. It was in him like a woman, a lover, something he wanted and could never have and could never forget—that's why he did what he did."

Jack shifted Amber's weight in his arms and smiled at the poet hidden in the rough, homely man. "I think I understand." He brushed past Short-Jump and began to run down the street as a crowd started to gather, and Rolf let out an anguished groan.

* * *

Amber moaned and her eyelids flickered. Her skin began to show a little color again, as he took the dampened cloth off her face. She sat up.

"How are you feeling?"

She turned away from him and violently vomited off the side of the bed. He'd thrown the blanket there when he'd laid her down. She grabbed the washcloth from Jack and pressed it tightly to her mouth. Unhappily, Jack gathered the blanket up and took it into the bathroom, where he fed it to the Disposall.

Amber called out faintly, "I'm sorry."

"Forget it. Next time, give me a warning."

"I will."

He came back in, drying his hands. As she looked up at him, the whites of her eyes showed again, and he grabbed her by the shoulders, afraid she was going under again.

Unshed tears sparkled brightly in her eyes. "What is it?"

"I killed him!"

"No, he was alive when we left."

"He was?" Amber unknowingly wrung the washcloth between her hands. "I tried to . . . then I found out what I was doing and I—I tried to undo it."

Jack helped her sit back and bolstered her up with a pillow. "Just what was it you did?" His own head still throbbed. He'd thought of taking the mordil for the ache, but wanted to be awake when Amber came around.

"But I could have." She shook her head. "All the time I thought Rolf had killed those men, and told me I'd done it, and then planted the evidence so I'd be framed. I was so sure . . . I'd blacked out every time. I knew . . . I knew I couldn't have killed them. Not actually. I thought he'd lied to me."

"Amber, what was it you did?" he repeated wearily.

She looked at him fully. "Jack, I pushed at him with my mind. I thought that I wanted him dead. And then he began to die. Oh, frack it!" She slapped her fist into the mattress. "I can kill with my mind! No wonder he doesn't want to let me go. What has he done to me?"

"I don't know. But I do know where you'll be safe." Jack left the room abruptly and went to the small screen computer terminal. He fed in enough credits to activate it and began typing out the access code when Amber staggered over to stand, leaning on his shoulder.

The video scrambled as the call began to go through channels.

"Jack, don't do this. They were going to come looking for us last time."

"They didn't know who was calling last time."

She placed a trembling hand on his shoulder. "And who's going to be calling this time?"

"The last remaining true Knight, to quote Ballard." The computer paused to query him, and his fingers stayed over the keys, hesitating a second. Then, just as he should have responded, the screen flared to life, and Jack found himself face to face with the officer who'd denied his men the right to life on Milos.

The man frowned. "Turn your screen on and identify yourself. This is a restricted access channel."

Jack opened his mouth, but Amber started, and she reached over and hit the cutoff button rapidly, shutting the system down.

"What the hell?"

Her face had paled again, but she stood firm under his outrage. "Didn't you seen that band of interference across the top of the screen? They were setting up tracers again. We don't want the World Police here. You don't want to see the Triad here."

"But this is the Dominion. . . ."

"Don't be so green! There's more corruption here than anywhere." Amber perched on the desk top. She shook her head. "You must have been a farm boy before you went into the infantry. I don't know who or what that access code leads to, but it's no recruiting office! Any slag can tell that."

He flushed and pushed himself away from the terminal. "So it takes a guttersnipe to protect me from myself."

"Yeah—and it takes a white knight in shining armor to protect me from myself," Amber bandied back. "Heaven help us both."

Chapter Fourteen

"I don't think you should use the suit this time," Amber stated, with a slight frown. She nibbled at a cuticle while waiting for Jack's reply.

He paused in mid-struggle to open the seams as it lay on the floor of the apartment. "That's what they hired me for. Blame Sadie, not me. The recommendation came from her, and we can use the money."

She knelt by the suit. "I'm not trying to blame anyone. But I can feel the vibrations without even touching it, and they're strong. Jack, why didn't you tell me the refrigeration didn't work at all?"

"Because I wasn't sure."

"Well, be sure now." She set her shoulders, and a stubborn expression clouded her triangular face. "Besides, I don't want to do that any more."

Jack felt exasperation nudging at him and sat back on his heels. "I didn't ask you to kill it."

"I couldn't anyway—I can't get a grip on it." She tossed her head back and angry blue eyes locked with her amber-brown ones. "I don't want to do *that*."

He flipped a sleeve over, angrily, and it flopped into the chest of the suit, as though it beat itself. *"That,"* he said, "is something you were born with. You can't shut it out."

"I can try."

"You'd be better off learning how to control it."

"That's the thing with you, isn't it? Control. You want to control yourself, the suit, and now me."

He didn't respond and she grew uneasy in the silence that stretched out, until Jack finally said, softly, "I can't do it without you."

"I know." She looked away, toward the panorama window. It looked out on a part of Malthen she had never thought she'd be privileged to see, home with a park that stretched along the street. Small, but green, and bursting with life. She sighed gustily. "I *know.*"

"How do I start?"

"First you're going to have to let me work with it." Reluctantly, she laid her hands across the Flexalinks. Her eyes flew wide open. "God, it's strong now! Life, death, life . . . it sings, Jack."

"I know," he said. He sat back, and watched her.

"But it's gibberish. I mean, it doesn't sing right." She frowned. The tiny line of concentration etched itself into her smooth forehead. "What could it be?"

"DNA, maybe; like whale song. Who knows? If it's regenerating, maybe that has something to do with it."

"A mystery," she said faintly as she let herself sink into it.

Jack watched uneasily, alertly, wondering if the bloodlust he'd felt in battle could be heard in that song. The frown faded, to be replaced by an expression of happiness, and she smoothed her hands back and forth across the links. She whispered, "I could never kill this."

He reached out and grabbed up her hand, suddenly afraid. Amber snapped back to attention. "It's strong."

"Too strong for you?"

"No, but . . . I'll have to teach you some meditation exercises."

"I know a few already."

"Good, that'll help. That song—t really draws you in. It catches at me." Amber moved back, but remained kneeling. "Do you really think it helped you kill all those people?"

"I don't know. I only know I don't remember most of what happened."

"I don't think it was the suit."

He didn't want to think otherwise. She looked at his face and shrugged. "We all know man's the most vicious killer in the skies."

"Except for Thraks."

She responded to the impatience in his voice by adding, "I want to do one last thing, and then I'll work with you." Leaning forward, she placed her palms on the suit again, and closed her eyes.

When she opened them, Jack asked, "What was that for?"

"Well, I put a . . . a repulsion on it. I don't think it'll be able to break through. You know what? I don't think it knows it exists yet."

"What?"

She tossed a long strand of hair off her shoulder. "Well, it's hard to explain, but I don't think it knows it's an it yet. It's like a baby, y'know? All they want to do is eat and sleep and piddle on everybody, and they make a lot of noise about it, but if you try to 'feel' them, they don't know they're an it."

"No self-recognition."

"I guess that's it. Okay. Stretch out on the floor behind the suit and close your eyes and do what I tell you."

* * *

Jack breathed deep and tried to shut out the furor of the staging area around him as some fifty men equipped and readied for the drop. He didn't have the qualms this time that he had had working for Tomcat as to whether he did right or wrong. He was helping the tax collector for this region "collect," but he also did not have the same confidence in his commander.

Truthfully, Wayne was a self-righteous prig, and Jack had yet to decide if he was a tax collector because of his personality or had acquired his personality in order to rationalize his job. But, because of his abrasive nature, Wayne had failed to pull the men together or coordinate what they were about to do.

Nor were they exactly sneaking up on their target. On the contrary, Wayne was determined to make an example of this seizure. The show of force he'd attempted to orchestrate would not surprise anyone.

Jack hated to walk up and knock on the front door that way.

He spewed his breath out, unable to do the exercises Amber had taught him. The suit pressed around him tightly. He made a slight adjustment on the humidity/temperature control as his breath steamed the inside of the faceplate. The being that shared the suit with him had finally come awake. Even Jack could feel it now . . . a wispy, breathless nothing that swept over him like an intuitive feeling or an ill wind. Now and then it would quest, or at least, he thought he could feel the query in the touch. Most often, it made him uneasy, on demand, as though there was something he should be providing and wasn't.

"The drop tubes are ready."

Jack looked up and saw the others making their way to the tubes. They were dropping in shifts—Jack, as usual, would be in the forefront. The five other men in line for his tube moved to make way for him. Jack shrugged, making sure his field pack and parachute were secure before he climbed into the tube.

They shut the hatch after him, and Jack was in darkness, except for the faint glow from his instrument panels. His heart missed a beat. He was always nervous in the drop tubes. Always. It would never change. Sarge had told him not to worry, that it was part of his job and his makeup, and that's what made him a good soldier, a good Knight. Jack licked his lips and felt his skin quiver. The contacts shook.

A probing thought touched him. *Who?*

"Us," he thought back, before he realized what he'd done. Then he snapped to, and the fear that had just gently pricked at him before sent him rigid. It had realized itself, but what in the hell was communicating with him?

The tube flared, and with an awful force, he was slung into space. No time to think further. He drifted, weightless, floating above the blue and white marbleized planet, then through the low cloud layer. The chute popped, pulling him roughly into awareness that he'd been launched safely and now approached the target city.

Wayne expected them to seize an entire city. Jack looked down, half-expecting to see tracers etching their white fingers toward him and his fellow assaulters. But no one was shooting at them. With a jolt he felt clear to his molars, he landed feet first, and ran forward, turned, and gathered the chute to him, so he could shrug off the pack. Others landed about him. Some wore only jumpsuits, disposable oxygen masks and weapon belts, others were equipped nearly as heavily as he was.

Wayne shrilled in their ears. "Go get those bastards! I want that writ served—I expect you to shove it up their noses! I want that city!"

On the local frequency, Jack heard someone mutter, "I'll shove it up their asses if that'll shut him up any faster."

The corner of Jack's mouth quirked. He checked his compass for position, but it wasn't necessary—the line of mercenaries dropping into formation told him which way they were headed. The terrain was mildly broken.

As he walked, dirt clods puffed up from his boots, and sweet grass twisted under his steps. It was semi-arid land, and the trees twisting upward had sparse, parched leaves, and shaggy bark that sloughed off even as they passed because it was the dry season. As they rounded a knoll, Jack caught sight of the walled city Wayne expected them to seize.

It was little more than a settlement built up around a main water evaporator operation. Little wonder—to the farmers in the area, the project meant life itself. From that nucleus, it had collected traders, bars, stores and so forth. Then, as though aware it had blossomed into a city, it had wrapped an enormous metal wall about itself, protecting the water rights, no doubt.

Jack eyed the wall. With a short run and a power vault, he'd be over. But he might be the only man to scale it that quickly. Wayne had told them to blast the main gates. He hadn't seemed to care how many lives it might take to accomplish that maneuver.

They approached the city unchallenged, and it wasn't until they drew near, that Jack could see the weapons his sensors were picking up. Hand-held, most of them, and relatively short-range. Their owners perched on top of the wall and glared down at the invaders, unaware, perhaps, of the excellent targets they themselves made against the skyline until somebody barked an order at them, and they all flattened.

Jack felt grateful for that someone on the other side of the wall. He also had a feeling he was about to dislike this whole operation. He squinted as the sun reflected off the wall, dazzling him.

"Serve the writ!" Wayne shrilled in his headset.

The com line screen was already on as they came to the gates. A picture of a tan, lean, silver-haired man focused in. Even as he said, "What is it you want?" a khaki-clad mercenary stepped forward with laser rifle cradled in his arm.

"I'll serve his fracking writ," he ground out. He etched the writ into the metal wall, writing until the barrel of his laser rifle turned crimson, looked at it critically, and then finished the job.

Wayne, catching the gist of what was happening, began to scream maniacally. "Not like that! Into his hand! Storm, where the hell are you? I want that writ placed in his hand."

"You'll have it," Jack said complacently. He faced the com line screen. "We're representatives of the Dominion Treasury. We'd like to talk to your city administrator, mayor, or whatever de facto head you've chosen to represent you."

The silver-haired man who had been looking askance at the metal gate, now turned back, scowling. "You're talking to him. What are you, a walking bucket of bolts? I won't talk to you. Get someone made of flesh and blood in front of me.

Jack took the sunscreen shield off his face plate. "You've got him," he said. leaning forward.

The man's eyes widened, then narrowed. "Good god," he muttered. He looked over his shoulder at someone out of range, then looked back. "I've got a Temporary Restraining Order. Tell that to that bastard, Wayne. Can he hear through you?"

Jack pulled a hand out of his gauntlet and sleeve and thumbed his interior switches. He said, "Now, he can. Repeat what you've just said."

The flat image grimaced, then said, "Forget it, Wayne. We've got an injunction. We've got a Temporary Restraining Order. Call off your dogs."

The mercenaries around Jack began to laugh. They lowered their weapons and went into at ease stances.

Jack's headset fairly vibrated with Wayne's response. The man on the com line waited until he was finished, then said, "Same to you, Wayne. Come get me if you want me . . . and watch us sue the pants off you and your department. We'll have free water for the next two generations!" The com line went blank.

Around him, the men began muttering darkly. Wayne spat out, "Go get him."

"He's got a restraining order," Jack said.

"I don't give a good goddamn what he says he's got. It's a forgery. A mistake. I want that writ served and the city seized."

Jack began to back up, wondering how in the hell he was going to get off-planet if he pissed off his ride back. But it might be worth it.

Wayne began offering outrageous bonuses to anyone who would go in. The mercenaries looked at one another. A few brought their weapons back up to firing level as the headset continued to crackle with the tax collector's venom. The mercenaries started to fan out, when Jack's cameras caught sight of a considerable amount of action on a nearby rooftop. He focused it in. "Holy shit—that's a well blaster they've got aimed at us."

He, and others, thought twice about how poorly defended the city appeared to be. Anything that could blast through layers of rock strata would cut through flesh like a hot knife through butter. He patched in to Wayne, saying, "We can have a first class slaughter here, on both sides, unless you listen to reason."

"I'll make sure your writ is served, but there has to be another way to do this." From the static on the line, Jack was fairly certain the call was being monitored. "Look, Wayne," he persisted, "if the man's injunction is the right stuff, your ass is on the line, as well as ours."

A short silence, then, "I can be reasonable if they can."

The gates began to swing open slowly, and the com line came back on. The tanned man smiled grimly from the screen.

"I know you want your pound of flesh, Wayne—so tell you what. Our champion against yours. You win, I'll pay the taxes and then we'll straighten it out in court. We win . . . and you pull back your troops until after the hearing. Agreed?"

A sputter on the wires, and then Wayne said, "Agreed." Sotto voce, he said, "Go get 'em, Jack."

Jack abruptly chinned off the com line. His heart sank a little, suddenly wanting absolutely no part of this. He knew he was right when he heard the gasps of his comrades, as they moved back from the gate.

"It's the Dragon!"

He pivoted quickly, and saw the monstrous mauve-tinted suit coming out toward him.

It was such a shock to see another suit of battle armor that his knees went weak, and he felt his thoughts jumble abruptly, as though the world had spun to a stop. And the other inside his suit, feeling the barriers go down, took a stab at his mind. *Me? Us?* came the alien thought and Jack started, just like a wild creature, inside the battle armor.

An incredible lust for blood and mayhem seized Jack. Before he could salute the other fighter or signal readiness for combat, he lunged, gauntlets curled.

He seized the Dragon's suit and threw it three man-lengths away, shuddering with the effort as the suit hit, dust blossoming from the meteoric impact. Jack shook his head, trying to shake off the alien thrust inside his mind. He circled the Dragon suit, waiting for movement—for attack. No longer a soldier, he'd become a predator.

The warrior in the Dragon battle armor rolled over slowly. Jack bared his teeth in feral joy.

Us? Me? jabbed the alien mind, and his right arm went up, gauntlet facing the sky, as the warrior known as Dragon sheered off a close range spurt of fire. Jack spun on his left heel, and felt the wash of heat . . . and a wave of fear generated by the discovery that the "other" could trigger the suit circuitry. He mentally wrestled with his suit's co-inhabitant even as he dropped to his knee and fired, left-handed, at the face plate of the other man.

White frost obscured the plate instantly, a little trick picked up from Gilgenbush's satellite, blinding the other fighter.

That quick, he had him. Jack ground his teeth, fighting himself as much as he fought the man in the Dragon battle armor. Better to be done now, while he still had some control, for his ears buzzed, and his nerves quivered, ready to kill—not capture.

He jumped, overtaking the downed warrior and drew back his foot, to grind down the outside power packs, disabling the antiquated suit.

It was then that his own suit decided to sit down. As Jack's ass hit the ground, he saw the other mercenaries running to give the two fighters a wide berth, and another lash of energy sizzled the air where his head had been but a second ago.

"Shit," Jack said, and tried to wrestle control of his suit back. The song of fierce joy echoed in his brain, and nervous sweat trickled down his bare back, as he rolled over on the dirt road and literally crawled out of range. He tried to project an image of himself, in the suit, fired to a char, unless he recovered usage of it. As he got to his feet, he triggered the power vault.

He curved in midair, into a graceful somersault, and landed on his feet. He was so shocked by the sudden return of his control that he never saw the blow coming that knocked him off his feet. He slammed into the ground and lay gasping for breath, watching helplessly through the fishbowl as the Owner of the Dragon jumped on his chest, and wrenched Jack's helmet off abruptly.

The dry air of the world hit him and Jack gasped, as it sucked all excess moisture from him almost instantly. The other mind went absolutely quiet, as he lay still, pinioned under the Dragon suit.

The man reached in and pulled a wire out, and the suit went dead. He then took his own helmet off and grinned, saying, "Everything has its weak spot."

Jack gaped up at the man . . . the tanned and silver- haired face from the com line.

The Owner of the Dragon ran his gauntlet through his hair, getting it away from dark, humorous, brown eyes. "They elected me mayor," he said.

"In that case," Jack answered, reaching into his inside tool pouch. "I have this writ to serve you with," and put the disk into his hands. "Who the hell are you?"

Sadness flickered but an instant in the other's eyes. "I'm the last survivor of Dorman's Stand. Who the hell are you?"

Chapter Fifteen

"And then what happened?" Amber looked at him avidly, the slice of pizza hanging from her fingers, where it had frozen a sentence or two ago.

"Then he helped me out of the suit and rewired it." Jack watched as the slice continued to its final destination on the tabletop and Amber winced.

"You said his suit was really old. Did you find out how he got it?"

"Yes." Jack trailed a string of cheese into his mouth and lied. "His grandfather was a veteran and the suit's been passed down. He let me open it up . . . some things have really changed." But not, he thought, the code of honor of a Knight. The Owner of the Dragon, whoever he was, had told Jack more than he'd ever told anybody, knowing that they were both bound by the armor he wore. He wondered vaguely if Ballard would know who the Dragon really was.

Amber swallowed quickly and looked up. "Do you think you know where 'it' is? I mean, could you tell in the difference between the suits?"

He shook his head.

"Well, if *it* kept the suit from moving right, you've got trouble."

147

"I know." He sighed. Sand War memories flooded him . . . of a suit moving herky-jerky, a scream of death, and then grinding to a stop. But it couldn't be that much alive . . . he couldn't even see it. And the intoxication of the contact, the sheer adrenaline pumping invincibility of it was like a drug . . . a drug that had done far more good for him than anything he'd gotten since being awakened from cold sleep.

Amber touched his arm. "What are you thinking?"

Jack started. "I'm not sure," he answered slowly. "Ballard told me, and I remember, the last stages before the berserkers emerged. According to that, *I'm* in the last stages. But I can't be. Nothing is assimilating me. At least, nothing physical. It's as though we've just been touching minds and the—the thing—is just learning to think. Either we're wrong or—"

"Or what?"

"Nothing." But as Jack reached for his dinner, he wondered if he'd been looking in the right place . . . what if the creature were inside him . . . in his bloodstream or some such, the parasite Ballard thought it had to be. He shuddered.

Amber delicately polished off two more slices, then wiped her mouth and said, "Well, it sounds like he's a good guy. I guess I'll give you this, then." She held out a thin piece of paper, a subspace message. "It came yesterday, before you got home."

It was from the Dragon and it said, succinctly, "Meet me at the Rusty Bolt," and gave a time and day.

"What does he want from you?"

Jack crumpled the note. "I'm not sure. We talked about a lot of things. I don't think there's anything he could say here on Malthen he couldn't say there. Maybe he has work for me."

Amber watched him. "Are you going?"

"Yes, I think so. I'll bring you along this time, if you want."

Amber hesitated as if uncertain, but she forced a smile. "Okay." She hesitated, then swallowed the rest of her doubts. "I *have* to go along. The Rusty Bolt is one of Rolf's favorite hangouts. I know the ins and outs of that dive like the lines on the palm of my hand. You're going to need me."

The Rusty Bolt was a quiet riot of neon, shaded obsidite sliced wafer thin as a facade over the concrete walls with rusted out bits and pieces of ancient robots and cyborgs tacked around. It had a certain flavor to it, aided greatly by booths with privacy curtains. Almost anything could happen at the Rusty Bolt—and did. The Dragon had picked early morning for the meet, and the bar was practically empty. Jack approved though Amber was still yawning as she trailed him inside.

"Nobody here," he said, glancing around. He'd developed the mercenary habit of not sitting or standing with his back to the door.

Amber looked around too, seeing things Jack did not, like the hidden surveillance cameras playing images to rooms in the back. Most of them looked out of commission, but one or two seemed in use. She swallowed uneasily and took Jack by the elbow. "Let's go this way." Surreptitiously, she guided him out of view of most of the cameras. Fat Fred, who owned the Rusty Bolt, played both ends against the middle—while cameras seemed to cover every angle, there was still a pathway through the bar, if one knew where to step and turn.

Amber telegraphed her nervousness to Jack, but before he could say anything, the curtain covering the corner booth parted suddenly, and she let out a tiny squeak.

Jack grinned as he recognized the elegant silver hair of the Dragon's tanned face, dominated by those humorous brown eyes. Laughing eyes.

Amber, turning up her face, met the look in them, but she wasn't consoled. "What in hell is he laughing at?"

Jack felt her stiffen. "This is Amber," he said, pulling her forward.

The Dragon appraised her. "I thought you told me she was just a street kid. She's come a long way."

Amber curled her lip. "What kind of name is the Owner of the Dragon? Don't you have a real one?"

"Amber!"

The Dragon laughed and drew them into the booth. He dropped the privacy curtain, quelling the glare of the neon, and pulled his laugh into a broad smile. "Says what's on her mind, doesn't she?"

"Not by half," Amber spat out. She sat sideways in the booth, looking out through the tiny crack between the curtain and the booth. If she really said what was on her mind, Jack wouldn't be sitting here so calmly.

The Dragon evidently decided to ignore Amber. He offered Jack a drink. He waved it away, saying, "What's on your mind?"

"Work, if you want it."

"What kind of work? Is it on the bulletin?"

"No, and it won't be."

Jack sat back in the booth, mulling over the implications of a secret recruitment. "Why me?" he asked finally, comfortable in the knowledge that the Dragon waited for him to think it over.

"I want quality. I also like conscience."

"To do what?"

"Let's call it strike-busting." The Dragon lifted his glass and the brown eyes continued to smile at him over the rim.

Jack felt a wave of uneasiness. What else could it be called? He felt Amber stir at his side. She looked back over her shoulder, a golden-eyed, hostile stare at both of them. What was happening here? Why did he feel it was all beyond his control? "If you want conscience," he said slowly, "you don't need a suit."

"That's right—I don't need a suit. I need what's inside of it," the Dragon answered. He did not seem impatient, but his strong fingers tapped the table gently.

"You want me specifically?"

"I can't think of a better man to have at my side." Jack felt the tension in Amber's wiry form, and tried to ignore it. "You're doing more than the recruiting?"

"I'm running the operation. Premium pay, good living quarters—"

"You sound like you're talking long term employment."

"Could be."

Jack felt Amber go absolutely rigid. He put a hand out to soothe her, but kept his attention on the Dragon. "I don't want to leave Amber . . . and I like to know who I'm working for."

"Amber can go with you, but you'll have to keep her out of trouble with the rest of the troops."

Jack said, "Amber can take care of herself."

"All right, then. As for your employer, he prefers to remain absolutely confidential."

"But you know who it is?"

"I do." The Dragon nodded. He sat back in the booth, putting his left arm across the back, at ease. "I gathered when we talked last, you had the Emperor's guard in mind. I can guarantee you this is one of the better, and faster, ways to meet that goal."

Jack thought. "I don't like breaking union work," he said. "I've done it, but I don't like it."

"I can't tell you the nature of your employer," the Dragon said. He shrugged. "All I can tell you is that you won't be ashamed."

"This is bad timing. I have some people I've been tracking down." He hadn't told the Dragon who he was, but knew the other had done some accurate guessing of his own. "I don't like being taken away from it."

The Dragon shrugged. "The kind of money I'm offering will let you access a lot of systems."

Amber said softly, "Jack, give me the gun."

Preoccupied, he answered, "Later," and leaned forward on the table. "How long term and how much money?"

"For you, five thousand credits a thirty day cycle. Plus living quarters. Board is up to you, since you've got Amber. Besides," and the Dragon grinned, "you might not like the local fare."

Amber pitched to her feet. "God, Jack," she hissed. "Give me the gun and get out of here!"

The Dragon and Jack reacted simultaneously, getting to their feet. Jack then saw Rolf at the front door, looking around, two very big and very nasty looking creatures at his elbows.

"Company," remarked the Dragon. "Looking for you?"

"Yes."

Amber tugged at his pockets. Jack smacked her hand. "No guns. There's a back way out of here?"

"Yes," she said. "But—"

"No buts," the Dragon countered. "You two get out of here. I'll cover you, if you still want the job."

Amber opened her mouth to protest, and Jack squelched her, saying, "We'll take it."

"Spaceport tonight then, Dock 42. I'll have IDs for you."

He pulled a very nasty, needle-nosed gun out of a hidden pocket. "Go for it."

Jack threw open the privacy curtain and bolted, dragging Amber behind, until she dug in her heels and snapped. "This way, you slag idiot!"

He responded by throwing her over his shoulder and going out the way she pointed, the air crackling with laser fire behind them. A projectile hit an antique helmet next to the eave of the back door. It spun around and then hit the floor at their heels with a metallic clang as he slammed the door shut after them.

"Got any more bright ideas?" Amber sneered as the bright white-hot light dazzled them momentarily.

"Yeah," said Jack, grabbing her hand and pulling her into a run. "I suggest you pack."

Chapter Sixteen

"Welcome to Otterville," Amber said. She wiped a finger along the doorframe and her lip curled. "Everything is moldy!" She took a few mincing steps into their assigned quarters, her gratitude over being off ship not extending to her new home.

"It's not Otterville and Dragon says things will shape up once we move in and use the moisture absorber on a regular basis." Jack dropped his armful of crates in the living room and moved to a room-wide window. "Look at that view!" The platform house was relatively isolated on a beautiful curve of a wide, slow-moving river.

Amber's nose stayed wrinkled. "It looks like a bowl of spinach, stems and all!"

"That, Amber dear, is a tropical rain forest, and a pretty thick one at that."

"Right, and out the back window, you have a view of swampburg."

Jack sighed. "You know, you could have stayed with Sadie."

"Could is the wrong choice. Should is the operative word here. She wasn't even going to put me in cold storage— said she wanted the company. I could be trying on new clothes, jewels . . ." Amber kicked the door shut. She sat down on a crate and folded her arms defensively. Jack couldn't help but notice the curves she didn't used to have. She sighed. "I'm sorry. I'm glad I'm here, but this place is . . . is . . ."

"Not Malthen. Look, the clouds will clear up and then, I promise you, you're going to see a sapphire blue sky, rivers with honest to god water in them, not concrete, green trees and grass. . . ."

"Until the next rainstorm, which is, if I remember our media package correctly, twice a day until the rainy season. Then we're in for it—we're bound to get wet."

Jack stopped in mid-protest as a knock sounded on the door, and two aggrieved loaders brought in the trunk containing the suit. They dropped it with a resounding thud, accepted a Dominion credit for a tip, and left.

The room vibrated another second or two longer, and Amber looked with alarm at the floor. "This thing is on stilts. I hope we can keep our asses out of the swamp."

He pointed a finger at her. "And that's another thing. You're getting too grown up for guttersnipe language."

Amber sniffed. "Censorship is everywhere. Well," and she plucked at her blouse which was growing limper by the second, threatening to plaster itself intimately to her skin. "Let's find that water sucker and turn it on before I mildew."

The air grew more bearable as the moisture absorber *whirred* into smooth operation. Amber got up and sauntered through the rest of their quarters. She came back, her face lit up with excitement. "It's a palace, I swear, a fracking palace!" Then, "I know, I know. I forgot. I mean, the place is a bloody castle."

"It's all ours?" Jack had sized the place up from the outside and figured it, at the very least, to be a duplex. But to find out the spacious stilt home was all theirs was a real surprise. He followed her. Four bedrooms, two bathrooms ("a tub . . . a real tub," squealed Amber), a large study with a wet bar, kitchen, living room and dining room. Jack hadn't seen anything like it for years.

Amber swung on the door-frame leading to her bathroom, the one with the tub as well as a shower. "I think I could learn to like it here."

A laughing hiss answered them from the front door, where a sleek, sable-coated humanoid lounged against the doorjamb. Caramel brown spots, the color of Amber's eyes, mottled the sable fur. His only concession to clothing, was a shiny, water repellent, bright yellow pair of shorts, bulging with seamed pockets full of various implements, and with a sable tail neatly hanging out the back. He straightened as Jack covered the distance to the front door, and he snapped a salute with a dark-skinned hand that was almost a paw—but not quite.

"Welcome to Fishburg," the otter-man said, with another laughing hiss. "I am Skal." He moved his whiskers flat against his cheeks, and his short, well-rounded ears flattened also, as though he waited for approval.

"Commander Skal," Jack said, somewhat relieved at vaguely recognizing the name, and reached for the being's hand. "I'm pleased to meet you."

The otter-man twitched his whiskers after appraising Jack momentarily. "And I you, Commander Storm. A fitting name for a being stationed here, what?" And the Fisher laughed. His very large, luminescent eyes strayed to Amber. "And greetings to your mate, also."

"I'm not—"

"Quite used to being here," Jack finished up smoothly. "Commander, please come in. I haven't raided the kitchen yet, but I'm sure I can find something to drink."

Skal moved inside and shut the door gently. Both ears and whiskers came forward and he looked alert. "I think," he said softly, sibilantly, "You'll find the foodkeeper well stocked with the local beer. A rin base, but enjoyable." He grinned, wrinkling his lips and showing jaws full of sharp teeth. "I put them there."

The beer was tangy, a clouded white instead of the mellow brown he was used to, but it tasted good all the same. Jack knew he had found civilization again, a planet where they understood the secret of proper fermenting. The Fisher Skal curled in his chair rather than sat, and Amber copied him, her body equally as sinuous as his. Jack sat, dwarfing the chair carved for other uses than sitting. He flexed his bulky shoulders.

The Fisher looked at him with glistening eyes, the amenities satisfied. "The Dragon recommended I look you up as soon as possible."

Jack held up a hand. He looked at Amber. "I suggest," he said to her, "you select your room and begin unpacking."

The girl made a face at him and left the kitchen.

The Fisher watched her go with interest. "You do not let your mate formulate strategy with you?" he commented.

Jack said nothing, and the being's whiskers twitched, although whether in amusement or embarrassment, Jack couldn't tell. "When can I expect to hear from the Dragon myself?"

This time, he was sure he saw amusement. Skal wiped the palm of his hand along the side of his face, rather like a man stroking a mustache. "We are a backward world," he said, "and things move rather slowly here. We should have the com lines in by tomorrow evening. They were supposed to be in yesterday, but . . ." and he shrugged eloquently, the gesture sending muscles rippling.

Jack looked up. The house seemed to be run totally on electricity. The foodkeeper was refrigerating more than adequately, and the moisture-absorber worked admirably. "What's the power like?"

"Reliable. Our reactor keeps this area well provided for, although downriver. . . ." Again, that supple and incredible shrug. Jack blinked, thinking that he had once known a belly-dancer who would kill for muscles like that.

Jack brought himself back to the business at hand. "Reactor?" He hadn't expected that.

"A breeder reactor. Effective, if crude."

Jack swore. "Crude? Shit, I thought those things were outlawed. Who built that thing? And who let him?"

"You did, and we did," said the Fisher mildly. "Don't worry, Commander. Things will change in the future. In the meantime, our de-tox and dumping program is operating quite well." He reached into one of his many pockets and withdrew something. "There is a custom among my people. I would like to gift you with this ceremonial knife." Hilt first, he gave the knife to Jack, its handle made of exquisitely carved ivory.

Jack took it carefully. "It's handsome," he said.

"Thank you." The Fisher seemed to be waiting. Although Jack couldn't remember the tapes mentioning it, he guessed the next step was reciprocation. Jack had little on him he could give. "My effects have been delayed in shipping," he said carefully.

"Another time perhaps."

"Assuredly. In the meantime, is there anything I can do for you?"

The sable face glittered with excitement. Skal forced himself to speak slowly as he answered. "I have heard much about the battle armor. Perhaps a look?"

"No problem. In fact, I could use your help. I need to uncrate it and put it on its rack."

"The armor is heavy?"

"Awkward, when it's not powered. It's in that big trunk." Jack got up from the table, and the Fisher followed him to the living room.

The two of them got it out, with very little struggle; the humanoid was extremely strong, for all his lithe shape. He watched the Flex-alinks shine as the suit hung from its frame.

"It is very beautiful," the Fisher said, his eyes very round and glowing.

"And deadly. The weapons are recessed. Some in the gauntlets, here," and Jack showed him the right sleeve.

The Fisher refrained from stroking it, although he put out a hand tentatively, and then drew it back. He looked outside as though weighing something mentally. "I must pardon myself. It's getting late, and I have other appointments. Perhaps another time?"

"Anytime, Commander Skal."

"You honor me," the other returned, with a flick both of his whiskers and his tail. "But one last thing . . . in a marshy world such as ours, don't you think this might be an inconvenience?"

"I don't plan on wearing it all that much," Jack answered seriously. "But it has capabilities I haven't even touched on."

Skal stroked the whiskers on the side of his cheek again. "I'm sure." He bowed. "Enjoy our gift, Commander Storm. I hope to meet with you again, soon." He flowed to the door and down the ladder, to the river where a sleek powerboat awaited him.

Amber joined Jack as the powerboat sped from sight. "I like him," she said, even as the sky turned charcoal and rumbled threateningly.

"I do, too," Jack answered, turning the knife over in his hands. "Let's finish the unpacking."

The storm broke. It rumbled and flashed and poured so loudly, they barely heard the pounding on the door long minutes later.

Jack opened it. A very rotund Fisher stood there, dressed in a jumpsuit, and the Dragon stood next to him, both bowing their heads against the deluge. Jack grabbed them and pulled them in.

Jack threw spare blankets over them, and watched them steam, as Amber left to bring out two more beers.

"What's up? We've been trying to get you on the com for hours. We finally decided to come over and see if there's a problem," the Dragon said. Then, his brown eyes twinkling, he added, "Pardon me. This is Commander Poonum. He's from the northern provinces and isn't used to this much rain."

"Commander," Jack nodded to the miserable Fisher. His black and gray striped pelt was almost dry already, but the jumpsuit hung, sopping. He looked back to the Dragon, who finished an appreciative pull on the beer. "What com? I was told it wouldn't be in until tomorrow."

Poonum's black eyes flashed. "It was installed yesterday!"

Amber stuck her head in the room. She delicately held out a piece of cable, snipped at both ends. "Is this supposed to be like this?"

"Damn," the Dragon said. He got to his feet and took the cable from her. "This is part of the com line. No wonder we couldn't reach you."

"It doesn't matter," Jack returned. "We've been welcomed already."

"Who?"

Jack looked closely at the Dragon, then said, "By a Commander Skal."

Poonum let out a sound that was between a curse and a bark, and collapsed back into his chair, both hands wrapped firmly around the bottle of beer.

The Dragon smiled grimly. "Well, Jack. It appears the rebellion forces got to you first." He reached out and obtained the greeting gift the Fisher had left.

He turned the ceremonial knife over and over in his hand, then looked up at Jack. "Well, if nothing else, it appears that they consider you a formidable and honorable enemy." The Dragon glanced briefly at Poonum, whom Amber was trying to console by custom-tailoring his jumpsuit with a rear exit for his thick tail. The Commander was a far cry from Skal . . . short, rotund, and trying to fit into the mold of the Dominion, though it was clear the jumpsuit and boots made him miserable.

There was a sharp squeak, and then Poonum said, aggrievedly, "Watch out where you stick that thing!"

"Sorry," muttered Amber. She flashed a look at Jack, trying not to laugh, and re-applied her scissors.

Jack took the knife back. "That's not the only consideration. I must have remembered his name from the briefing— but how did they know who I was, when I was hitting dirt side—"

"Swampside," interrupted Amber.

"And where I was staying, and how they knew about the battle armor."

"They knew about the suit?" The air became charged with tension suddenly, and even Poonum drew to attention, irritably waving Amber away.

"He asked to look at it."

"And you showed him?"

Jack shrugged. "There was no reason not to."

The Dragon slumped against the table. "Our surprise weapon just went down the tubes." He clenched his fist. "Damn. I wish I knew where the leak was. Skal knew all the right buttons to push. How did he leave?"

"Powerboat, down river."

The Dragon waved at Amber. "Don't bother unpacking. We'll have you moved tonight."

"No," said Jack and Amber together.

The Dragon looked at him. "But he knows where you are. For security reasons, I must insist you move."

"He found out before, he'll find out again. Besides, if I stay here, I'll know to expect him again—and he'll know that I'm expecting him again."

The Dragon let out a low whistle, and a grin replaced his tense expression. "All right, Jack. We'll play it your way. But Amber—"

"Amber can take care of herself. Believe me," Jack said, as the girl tensed behind him.

"Good enough. We'll leave you for the night." The Dragon paused, temporarily distracted by the sight of the very rotund otter-man trying to pull his tail out through the hole Amber had made for him. "I'll send a skimmer by tomorrow morning for briefing."

"Done." Jack said good-bye to the commander as well, and shut the door behind them.

Amber waited until the sound of a motor cut through the rain, then asked, "What's wrong?"

"Nothing."

"Something's wrong. I can tell by the look on your face— and the way I feel."

He squeezed out a smile. "Nothing's wrong that I can put a finger on. Let's see if there's anything besides beer in that foodkeeper." He moved past her.

Amber looked out the dark, unshuttered window. "It's still raining," she said mournfully.

"Wait until tomorrow."

She followed him into the kitchen which had been brightened by Skal's appearance, and dampened by the Dragon's and Poonum's. She took a towel and mopped up the wet spots, then looked at the ceiling to see if it was holding under the steady drum of rain.

"You're not upset about giving away your secret weapon?" she asked, as she plopped down wearily at the table. The storm-darkened sky had given way to a night far blacker than she had ever seen, she who'd grown up in the underbelly of a beast that never really slept, amid the glow of neons that rarely went off. Malthen dimmed but never went out.

"No," he said, taking down two packs from a cupboard. He sniffed at the contents before following the preparation instructions. "No . . . in fact, Skal's visit will probably work to my advantage. He left with the distinct impression that I could never manage the suit in the swamp."

Amber flashed a grin. "You'd sink up to your ass, huh."

"Something like that. I've never had to use it on terrain like Fishburg, but I went through something like it as part of basic training. I know how to handle it. And, there's something else that Skal is undoubtedly not prepared for— I can go native, if I have to."

Her grin grew wider. "You'll run around in nothing but shiny yellow shorts?"

"And a weapons belt. If that's what it takes." The heater sounded. He pulled out the steaming pouches and set one on a plate in front of her. "Now eat up. It's past your bedtime."

Amber cast a look at the dark window. "How ever can you tell?" she muttered, before grabbing a fork and digging in.

Chapter Seventeen

"You're a real shit," Sadie said. She glared at the man stalking the room in front of her, narrowly brushing past her art treasures and antiques, every step taking him closer and closer to disaster. She watched, knowing that he was trying to unnerve her, and hating herself because he was succeeding.

"All you have to do is tell me where they are."

"I won't do that."

Rolf pivoted on one heel. He smiled slowly, revealing teeth ground to a slight point on one side, from years of chewing on that side of his mouth, and clenching his teeth even when he slept. He wore tight white pants of the smoothest leather, and royal blue boots that matched his royal blue shirt. Sadie found it only slightly disconcerting that he seemed to have no neck.

"I got in here once," he said. "You won't be able to keep me out. I'll get in again—and again. And worse, you know what I told you is true. I may not be big enough to ruin you, but I can cause a serious crimp in the cash flow of your smaller loans. A very serious crimp."

Sadie swallowed.

He touched fingertips gingerly to a healing bruise above his right eyebrow. "I won't hurt either of them. Amber's my girl—I just want her back. She's dangerous. Right now she's in the hands of someone who has no idea of her potential or her training, and that can be deadly. It's for their own good."

Sadie'd heard enough half-truths in her time to know it when she heard another one. She drew herself up in her chaise, lavender-flowered gown quivering with the effort. "Get out, Rolf."

He twisted suddenly, his elbow striking a vase, sending it crashing to the ground. He looked at the shards. "You shouldn't startle a person like that, madam. So sorry."

"It was nothing." Sadie looked at the vase in sorrow. Her first lover had forged it from a priceless Ming. It contained great sentimental value—and his ashes—but little else. Still, she'd been extremely fond of both. "I won't tell you."

"Ah, but that's where you're wrong. You will tell me. You'll tell me because I know you don't want trouble. You and I," he checked the cuffs of his shirt sleeves, tugging them into place, brushing off the gray ash from the vase, "don't need trouble."

"No," said Sadie, sensing a change in the flow of negotiations, "we don't."

"I understand you've done some business with a General Gilgenbush."

Her eyelids narrowed. "Perhaps."

"Strictly legitimate, of course, but the dear man doesn't know where your base of operations is, as he dealt with one of your banking satellites. I'm told he would very much like to know where you're situated so that he can—ah— pay his compliments in person."

"Malthen is neutral territory. Gilgenbush would never be so stupid."

Rolf looked up, his black eyes glittering like onyx. "There are clandestine operations, and then there are clandestine operations."

She made a decision and sat back. "If, of course, he were given my address."

"Correct."

"Which he will not be if I—"

"—give me the information I need," finished Rolf
smoothly.

"They're off-world."

"I know that."

Sadie examined one gold and diamond nail. It needed buffing,
she realized. "You don't intend to harm them."

"Of course not."

"All right then. The Owner of the Dragon has taken them. You'll
have to trace down the flight pattern . . . Dock 42. That's all the information I have."

Rolf nodded, saying, "That's all I need. Good day, madam."

"Show yourself out," Sadie said. She waited until the boot steps
faded, and the heavy doors clanged shut. Once, there was a time
when she would have taken the bastard to bed, then chewed him up
and spit him out later. Her advisors were right . . . she was growing
soft. She touched the com button.

* * *

Jack headed the skimmer toward the island, watching the lights of the
base come on as the pending storm set off the dimmers. He had used
those lights as a beacon more than once the past few days. The island
had been a hilltop, then a high peninsula and now, with the storms
growing more and more frequent, the only high ground for quite a
way with the exception of the palatial city, where mercenaries were
strictly persona non grata.

The sky was a dark, glowing blue, but the boil of clouds as dark as
pitch marred the horizon and blew in as the wind rose. Their platform house on the riverbank was now surrounded by water, which,
Amber said, in some ways was better—at least she didn't have to
worry about marsh lizards scampering up the stilt legs, and dinner
was certainly easier to catch now.

Jack wouldn't have been worried either, except that he knew that, even for a watery world, this amount of rain in this territory was abnormal. And *that* bothered him. The rainy season, in all its glory, could not account for half the amount of rainfall they'd had just since Jack had arrived.

A tree branch whipped across the windshield of the skimmer, snapped under the burden of the wind and rain and caromed off the side fender. Jack fought the skimmer steering and righted the vehicle. He turned the wipers on, as all of a sudden, the blue sky was swallowed by the maw of the storm, and the rain came pelting down.

The skimmer buffeted over the waterway which had once been dry land, and Jack saw a disturbance down on the shoreline. Some of Poonum's men, well-dressed in Dominion jumpsuits, looked to be harassing an older Fisher, forcibly beaching him and his old powerboat.

Jack nosed the skimmer down and stepped out, feeling the slick, chilled rain hitting his bare chest. He'd done as he'd threatened to— gone native, at least until he could reach operations and be assured of staying reasonably dry. His uniform and battle armor stayed in the skimmer. He wore thongs which kept the silt-like mud from between his toes and afforded him some hold on the slippery ground, in addition to the dark blue shorts and weapons belt.

Poonum's men growled in surprise, twisted around and saluted when they saw Jack approach. The older Fisher, dressed in a drab kilt of lizard skin, frowned, wrinkling his grayed muzzle. He was a deep russet, with whiskers of red-blond, and lively dark eyes that showed surprise at the amount of respect Jack commanded from Poonum's men, regardless of his manner of dress.

The rain slowed a moment.

"What's going on here?"

"Appropriating the boat, sir," the bigger of the two said, so burly his neck fur and muscles bulged out of the khaki jumpsuit. His whiskers twitched in a manner which told Jack, after several weeks of study, that the Fisher was extremely irritated.

"At ease, soldier," he said. "Appropriating it for what?"

"The war effort. We need every mode of transportation, and," he drew his lips back at the old Fisher, "we don't want to leave the enemy with anything he can use."

"What enemy?"

"This enemy, sir." The burly Fisher stood tall, his sable pelt glistening in the storm twilight, his light colored whiskers fairly twitching with his emotions. His second, a skinny, sloppy-looking Fisher, said nothing, but trembled in his shadow. "And, he's trespassing. Commander Poonum says that no unauthorized personnel is to be allowed to approach."

Jack looked at the elder Fisher, who huddled in the bottom of his boat, looking for all the world as if he was trying to hug the wooden frame to himself. A few sacks of what might be rin, the local equivalent of rice, took up the hull of the boat. "What's your business here, elder?" Jack asked.

"Selling rin, your honor," the Fisher quavered. "Business is slow downriver. I thought the eminences here would appreciate the stores." Liquid brown eyes glanced resentfully at his kin. "It's too bad I was mistaken."

Jack had had trouble getting rin. He reached over and poked the sacks. Grains of rin moved under his inspection inside the fabric bags. "Have you been up to the base?"

The blond whiskers flattened. "No, your honor. These two—" and the Fisher broke into native speech which Jack roughly translated as 'jerks'—"stopped me. They think my rin is poisoned." He spat over the side of the boat, dangerously near the high gloss surface of their boots.

The bulgy one said, "Orders, sir," to Jack's questioning glance.

In the days Jack had worked with the Fisher commander, Poonum'd been nothing if not paranoid. He sighed. The soldiers had been doing their job, though he suspected they had been harassing the old Fisher with more enthusiasm than the job called for.

As Jack looked at the three of them, three blunt-nosed alien faces looked back and he reminded himself that he couldn't tell by looking at them who was the enemy and who was not. "Is your rin poisoned?"

"No, your honor," the elder returned. A quiver ran down the back of his pelt.

"Then I'll buy it. What would you consider a fair price? Five Dominions a bag?"

The elder moistened his lips as Poonum's two men shifted uneasily, and Jack guessed for the first time their game. They had been planning to confiscate the rin for themselves. Four big sacks loaded the boat, and he said, "A bag each for my alert sentries here, and two for my command. A deal?"

"A deal, your honor but not for Dominions. Have you flake?"

Jack smiled, then curbed it. The elder was asking for gold flake, no fool he, to take plastic Dominions in an environment which might or might not accept his money. "Yes, a little."

The elder made the facial grimace Jack had grown to interpret as a smile. "My wife and I have humble needs. A little is all we ask. Ten flakes?"

That seemed high to Jack, who seldom carried more than twenty leaves, or flakes as the natives called them, at any one time. "Eight flakes," he responded, "and keep your boat."

The burly Fisher positively quivered with agitation as the elder bowed so low his whiskers touched the rin sacks. "Your honor! For so generous an offer, I must tell you I will only take seven flakes. And thank you! Thank you!"

The two soldiers waited until the old man had unloaded the rin sacks and then kicked his ancient engine into service, and disappeared down river, as a new curtain of rain swept in, obscuring him. Then the big soldier turned on Jack.

"What'd you do that for?"

"How'd you expect him to get home?"

"Swim."

Man and Fisher squared off, then the soldier seemed to realize who he was facing. He saluted reluctantly, and the two troopers slogged off along the shoreline, continuing their patrol, shouldering their share of the rin. Jack got back into the skimmer and checked the onboard monitors. Not that he didn't believe the old Fisher's gratitude, but he would have made a damn good diversion. The monitor showed no other activity in the area, however. Jack pitched the rin sacks into the back seat, brushing the suit's sleeve.

Hi, Jack! We kill today?

"Not today," Jack said absently. He put the skimmer into gear as the rain swept back in around him, and the lights of the base shone like a yellow-gold beacon marking his way.

The suit's talking didn't bother him as much as it used to when it first began to happen. Amber and Jack had come to the conclusion that the damp and warmth of Fishburg had nurtured the being inside the suit into full consciousness. It hadn't taken the suit long to identify Jack. Jack's skin still crawled when they "talked" though, even with Amber's help as a bridge between Jack's mind and that of the alien presence. She'd assured him the suit could be kept harmless as long as Jack repulsed it.

Sooner or later, though, he knew the killing urge would become impossible to repress. It was a drug he needed to function while he wore it. He was on borrowed time. Would he be able to keep the suit repressed when he had to wear it into battle?

Jack felt the hair on the back of his neck prickle.

Chapter Eighteen

The hangar door to the base opened as he pressed the transmitter, and his eyes were dazzled for a moment by the bright lights. The Dragon was there waiting for him when the door opened.

"Trouble?"

"Just bad weather." Jack reached back and threw the ten pound bag of rin into Dragon's solar plexus and grinned as his boss staggered back along the dock. "Getting soft?"

"Hell no! What is this stuff?"

"Rin. A local farmer was trying to peddle it to stores when some of Poonum's overzealous Fishers tried to confiscate it."

"What did you do?"

"Me? Like a total innocent, I asked him how much he wanted for it, bought it, and split it three ways."

Dragon laughed and shouldered his sack. As they walked along the bay to the inner offices, he asked, "Do you think he was with the rebellion?"

Jack shrugged. "Might have been. If he was, the rebellion is seven flakes richer." He halted long enough to put both feet into his jumpsuit, straighten and zip up. He carried his boots in his hand as he padded after the Dragon. "If he wasn't, I got good PR on both sides."

"Well, thanks for thinking of me. I can use it."

"Anytime. Ah—have the chemist look at it before you take it home. There was some question about whether or not it had been poisoned." Jack ducked over to put on his shoes, and the flying bag of rin missed him by a good hand's width.

"We've got trouble here." The Dragon's tanned face, undiminished by weeks of bad weather, looked deadly serious as he leaned over the wall map and, attached a marker on the transparent screen.

"How much trouble?" Jack looked at the map. Overlays showed the lay of the land, and he soon recognized the downriver region.

"When Dominion engineers came in and built a reactor here, they stayed to work on some other projects at the request of Shining Fur-grinning tooth." That was the name of the religious-political head that Poonum served. The Fisher's actual name was totally unpronounceable and nearly untranslatable. Jack had long since gathered that this Fisher ruled the entire planet—whether or not anyone else wanted him to.

Jack stabbed a fingertip at the map. "Like this? That's the dam, isn't it?"

"Yes . . . and downriver, where the rebellion is centered, is suffering. The rain runoff from the floodgates has kept it from being totally disastrous, but a little drought goes a long way in these provinces. Not to mention the strain the dam is beginning to show upriver, where some of the smaller villages are getting completely washed out."

Jack scratched his head. "Must have seemed like a good idea at the time," he said, before tapping the downriver regions. "Were they rebelling before or after the dam was built?"

The Dragon smiled. "Near as we can tell, they've been in rebellion the last three generations."

"Oh."

This was the first serious talk they'd had since Jack arrived. The Dragon had had Jack touring with Poonum, learning a little of the language, and drilling the troops. As a result, Jack was now extremely familiar with the weather patterns, the burgeoning river which seemed to be the major highway of this continent, and much of the local geography. Jack had been very busy, but he hadn't really been briefed on the true situation here.

"I take it we've dropped the pretense of calling it a strike."

The Dragon nodded.

"Then you realize we could be in violation of Dominion law here. If the ruling power is using us to stay on top, in spite of the mandate of his own subjects, we have no right to treat with him. The Dominion only recognizes the popular government."

The Dragon lowered his hand and moved away from the wall map. "We're not working for the Dominion."

"No, but we've still got the dictates of the Emperor to consider."

Dragon perched on the corner of a desk. He tapped the desktop with a rigid finger. "Jack, you're treading on some dangerous ground here. We're working at the behest of a private employer."

"And if that employer is wrong?"

The Dragon shrugged. He was as lean and fit as ever, inside his silvery uniform that reflected the sleekness of his silver hair. "That's not for us to worry about."

"Treason is for everybody to worry about."

"Not you!"

Jack straightened. "You said you wanted to hire a man of conscience."

"Conscience be damned. This is a military operation."

"If it's a rebellion, it's not that simple. We're not supposed to interfere."

"And strike-busting isn't interference?"

Jack made a small movement, aware that the Dragon was coiled, like a deadly snake ready to strike. "It's not my job to argue politics or economic sanctions with you. It's just that I—I don't think we're in the right here. I don't think that Shining Fur-grinning tooth has the right to declare himself ruler here, and be supported by the Dominion, if he's not wanted."

"And what is it that makes you think he's not wanted?" All humor had fled the brown eyes watching him closely.

Jack dared to turn his back and eyed the wall screen map. He shrugged. "A voice or two in the local pub. That old Fisher out on the river whose hide I just saved. Maybe it was Skal's attitude when I got here. I don't know."

"Well, if you don't know, I suggest you don't wonder. We have trouble downriver and you're going to have to go in there and chill it down."

"With Poonum's men?"

"No. With the suit."

Jack spun around. He said nothing, but his pulse sped up. He had no wish to reveal to the Dragon his fear of his own battle armor. "You want a show of force?"

"I want them to know downriver what we can do—if we have to. There are silos there, of grain and rin. The rumor is that the locals have been tapping them, in spite of government protection, and His Highness wants to avoid food riots. There's a very good possibility that the rin you bought today came from those silos—and was intended as part of a set up to tweak our noses."

Jack started to say something, then snapped his mouth tight. The Dragon raised a gray eyebrow, challenging him to finish the statement, but Jack shook his head.

"You leave tomorrow morning."

"By boat or skimmer?"

"You can take your skimmer. And, Jack, don't go native on this one. That's not the kind of statement we want to make. But don't avoid them either. Keep your ears open, and let me know what you hear."

"Even if it's not something you want to hear?"

"Especially," said the Dragon, getting up. The tenseness

sloughed away with the graceful movement as he stretched. "Make sure Amber knows how to contact us if there are any problems."

Jack nodded. He left the war room and listened to the dull roar of thunder, muffled by the massive building. If it kept raining, they might wish this place had been built on stilts as well.

* * *

"You can't take the suit."

"It's my orders."

Amber sat, cross-legged on the floor, on top of a small, hand-woven rug they'd bought from the natives. It was a beige and brown design of interlocking circles and she liked to use it for her meditation. She traced one of the circles now, not looking at Jack as she spoke. "It would be a slaughter. None of the Fishers use armor."

"I won't fire on anybody if I don't have to. The suit's just for making an impression."

"Skal wasn't that impressed by it."

She had a point there, but he wasn't going to concede it to her. "Skal has never seen the suit in full operation—and besides, he's a rebel commander. He's in hiding. No one's seen him since he approached us."

Amber looked up. Her long hair framed her face and, not for the first time since they'd arrived, Jack felt the stirrings of emotions he didn't want to have. Not toward Amber, anyway. He swallowed.

"What did you call Skal?" Amber asked.

"I called him a natural leader," Jack said, turning away from her gaze. He buffed the Flexalinks exterior with a soft cloth, admiring the opalescent gleam.

"Maybe he's the one you should be taking orders from."

"I signed a contract, Amber."

She made a disdainful noise. Then added; "It's not like a religious oath or something. You'd think you were a Walker and this was your life's mission."

"My work is my life's mission. Have you forgotten why we're even here?"

"No, but maybe you have."

They glared at one another. Jack dropped his polishing cloth. "I came to build a rep with the suit."

"But that's only part of it! You came because somewhere along the way, you want to find out who ordered all your men stranded on Milos, and who ordered Claron burned off. You came because someone dirtied the "Pure" war, and you want to find out who it was, and make them pay. That's why we're here, Jack—and if it looks like the Dragon is walking the same streets as that someone, then, I don't know about you, but I don't want any part of it!" She pushed herself up off the rug and stomped into her bedroom. A door slamming echoed her footsteps.

Jack kicked the suit. The Flexalinks shimmered and, almost instantaneously, he heard, *Hi, Jack! Going to wear me?*

"Oh, fine," he groaned. Now the suit was awake. Amber must have shut down all her dampers, out of spite. "No," he said. "I'm not going to wear you."

Why not?

It was like arguing with a three year old. "Because I don't want to."

Silence ensued, but he caught a mental wave of unhappiness. He picked the polishing cloth up and went back to work on the Flexalinks. He stopped. "Can you feel it when I do this?"

There was a dip in consciousness, as though he'd tripped over a black hole in the midst of a thought, then *I can if you want me to.* Another pause. *Do you want me to?*

"Not now," Jack answered absently. He stopped again. "Do you know where you are?"

Everywhere came the answer in a blinding flash.

"No, I mean, inside the suit."

Not inside. Around you. Use the suit and I am all around you. A wave of pleasure.

Jack shook his head. It was hopeless trying to deal with the beast. Amber hadn't been able to pinpoint it any more than he had. The suit began humming that strange song of its own fashioning. "What are you doing?"

A wave of surprise. *Growing.*

He stopped polishing. It knew when it was growing now. "What are you?"

Thoughtfulness. Then *I don't know. I—* A very long pause, during which Jack almost felt something raking his own mind and thoughts. Then, a moment of satisfaction. *I'm Bogie.*

"Bogie?"

Yes. Unidentified object.

Jack smiled, in spite of himself. "Right. Okay, you're Bogie."

We're going somewhere?

"Definitely." He gathered the suit in a hug and carried it to the door. The skimmer was tied to the veranda, and Jack loaded the armor with suitable huffs, puffs and grunts, intended to let Amber know that he could use her help. The sky had cleared. Overhead, the evening showed a canopy of stars, none of which he recognized, all of which he appreciated.

He walked back into the house to get his duffel bag. Amber peered around the corner of the hall.

"Were you going to leave without saying goodbye to me?"

"Not if I could help it." He paused. "I need you to put the restraints back on the suit."

Her eyelashes lowered, then she looked back up at him. "All right. I still don't think it's dangerous—"

"I'll be the judge of that." He stopped at her sigh. "Look, Amber, the suit has a whole different reaction when I'm fighting in it. Call it blood lust, whatever. And the berserker that's growing is a mindless, fighting beast. The suit is treacherous and to treat it any differently can be fatal for me—and possibly you."

"Then get rid of it."

"I can't . . . not just yet. When I make the guard, I'll get a new one."

She wrinkled her nose. "You just don't want to get rid of it. You won't admit it, but you're kind of fond of it, just like you got fond of me, and you won't admit that either."

Jack hefted his duffel bag. "Yeah, I guess I'm just good at picking up strays." He regretted the words the minute they were spoken. Amber's head snapped back and her face flushed as though she'd been slapped. She brushed past him without a sound, heading for the skimmer, and leaned into the back where the suit lay.

She put her hands on it for a few minutes, then backed out. "That should keep it quiet for you," she said woodenly. "By the way, if you're interested, it's named itself now. Calls itself 'Bogie'."

"I know," Jack said after her retreating form, but the slam of the front door cut off his voice. He threw the duffel into the skimmer, climbed in, gunned it savagely and took off in a roar.

He entered his room in the inn apprehensively, all too aware of the suspicious stares he received in the sparsely populated tavern below. Downriver was dry, for this part of the continent, dry, and its soil was brittle. Jack vaguely remembered from long ago days on Dorman's Stand what a worry it was not to have the rains or the wells available for irrigation. Crops and animals both withered, the life sucked out of them. He paused after stepping into the room, trying to gather that memory that had all but been permanently wiped out by seventeen years of cold sleep, tried and failed, as it slipped beyond his grasp again.

"Have a beer," a pleased voice suggested from the shadows. "It may help ease the cares of the world."

Jack dropped the suit. Even before the sinuous form stood up and moved into his line of sight, he knew who it was.

Skal grinned at him, whiskers flicking. A beam of starlight from the skylight glanced off the lethal-looking blaster in his hand.

Chapter Nineteen

"You have me at a disadvantage," said Jack, moving slightly into a patch of darkness in the room.

Skal flipped his tail. "With your pants down, eh?" he said with a laughing hiss. He put his gun away. "I wasn't sure it would be you, after all."

"That would have been a surprise."

The Fisher stroked his whiskers against his right cheek. "It's good to see you again, commander. You can come out of the dark now. In case you haven't experienced it yet, we Fishers have excellent night vision." He extended his now-empty hand.

Jack shook it. "I'm told you're the enemy."

Skal gave a body-long Fisher shrug. "Perhaps it depends on the point of view. Come in, sit down. I have some stew and cold beer—the imported stuff—waiting for you." He indicated a small table, set with bottles and a clay crock which let off a savory smell. Bowls and wooden spoons awaited.

Jack tilted his head. "Sounds good." He settled down and let Skal serve him, taking care to keep his profile clear of the smallish window and his back to the wall of his room, rather than the door.

Skal noticed and let out a barking laugh. "Once a mercenary, always a mercenary, eh? Not an ordinary dinner guest."

"Neither are you."

"No." Skal held out a beer after opening it expertly. "Here's to honorable adversaries."

Jack took it with pleasure, the beer still chilled and the stew, judging from the steam wafting up from the chunks of real meat, still hot. He took a long draught from the bottle, savoring the flavor of beer from off-world. It wasn't Samson's, but it was an excellent brew.

Skal put his feet up on the wooden seat of an extra chair. "I think," he mused, tilting his chin up, "I will invite breweries for industry when I take over."

Jack nearly choked. He wiped the foam off his lips. "I didn't hear that," he answered.

"Of course you did." Skal eyed him. He turned up the lamplight on the wall sconce behind him. The oily wick flared a little, and the room brightened. "You surprise me, Jack Storm. I had gathered, from our first meeting, that you had blood like the icy waters of our northern continents."

Skal hadn't known, then, Jack thought, that he'd been mistaken. Jack sat back and took another pull while he thought of an answer. He decided no answer was the best one, and sat with what he hoped was an enigmatic expression.

The Fisher's whiskers flicked, once, barely. Jack took that for an edge in the conversation. He leaned forward on his elbows. "You must remember, Skal, that I'm considered a formidable fighter, with or without my battle armor. But, like all fighters, I prefer not to begin the conflict, but to see if it will be inevitably carried to me."

Skal pushed a little away from the table. "Shining Fur- grinning tooth has done that already," he said. "By inviting off-worlders to help him elevate his leadership so that no flood of unrest can possibly wash it away. But he's a fool Fisher."

Jack took a bite of stew, determined to have something of a hot meal while he could. He chewed slowly, letting the juices fill his mouth. Amber was only a slightly better cook than himself, and that wasn't saying a lot. "This is good."

Skal nodded. "My eldest litter mate will thank you for the compliment." He relaxed a little and took up his own spoon. "I take it you're not into politics."

"Not really. I'm generally not into rebellions either."

"Then perhaps I can convince you that my side has some merit to it."

"All sides have merit," Jack answered, "even if it is only to subjugate and thereby avoid dying. Not much merit, but some."

Skal chewed his meal with much relish, flashing his sharp, white, teeth. "What would it take, then, commander?"

"Nothing you could provide me with. I would need to find the motivation on my own and," Jack scraped the bowl for a last bite, "I'm not going to be looking."

Skal said nothing to that, but his whiskers and face moved in a Fisher grin.

In companionable silence, they finished their meal. Skal pushed back. "What is it you're here for? The silos?"

"I've been told the drought here is bad enough that the silos might be attacked."

"Possibly, but not probably. Why don't you come downstairs with me and have something a little stronger to drink? Meet the locals."

Jack hesitated, then stood up. "All right."

Downstairs was nearly deserted. Perhaps three Fisher groups were scattered throughout the massive tavern. Wooden tables gleamed in the glow of lamplight. No electricity here.

innkeeper waddled over, an ebony Fisher, with grizzled gray at his hands, feet, and muzzle. His thighs were bowed, and his tail thick and sleek. He wore a shirt as well as shorts, with a heavy, oilcloth apron over a slightly round stomach. "Lads!" he said in the local dialect, and then switched over. "What can I do for you?"

Skal pushed out a quarter flake. "Two draws of your finest, laid down in the cellar."

"Ah," the innkeeper said. "If your eldest sister didna work here, Skal, ye wouldn't know I had sech hid. Ah, well, ye paid for it—ye'll get it." He strolled off.

Jack could feel curious stares at his back, but ignored them. "Quiet tonight," he commented.

"Most nights, now. Fisherfolk are moving out of the flatlands and up into the mountains. River water there—and it's harder to collect taxes that way."

"Did the dam do this?"

Skal shook his head. "It didn't help, but the heavy rain upriver is our doing."

"What?"

Lamplight glowed in the Fisher's orbs as the being considered him. "You're no fool, Jack. You heard me the first time."

"You can't control the weather. You haven't the technology, and even if you did, it would be too damned expensive for you. Look at the toll here. And displacing moisture centers could cost you the ecology of the whole continent." Jack had to force himself to keep his voice level. He felt that everyone in the room was listening to the two of them.

"We haven't displaced anything, except a cloud or two from downriver. We've just concentrated it all upriver."

"But how?"

Skal leaned over, mischief gleaming in his face. "Magic, Jack. By magic."

Jack choked back a disbelieving laugh as the innkeeper leaned over in front of them and set down two exquisite cups brimming with liquor. The smell alone was enough to put off any thought of an argument.

Skal lifted his cup. The gold-rimmed porcelain was so fine, the shadow of his fingers showed through, darkening the liquor. "As one of your philosophers said long ago, 'the truth will set you free.'"

"Another one also said that candy was dandy, but liquor was quicker," Jack returned, sipping cautiously at the ambrosia. It fired his throat and settled into a comfortable, banked warmth in his stomach. It was mellow and very slightly sweet, and totally unique to the Fisher world.

"And what is candy?" asked Skal.

"Never mind."

They sat in companionable silence a moment longer, then Jack said, "What do you mean by magic?"

"Magic. I'm not a mystic, and even if I was, I wouldn't tell you the secret, but I can tell you, it works. One look at our parched flatlands will tell you that it works."

"It could be coincidence."

Skal shook his head emphatically.

"It can't be done by magic."

"Perhaps you have another name for it." Skal wrinkled his brow in thought. "Chants, or prayer, I think, would cover it."

Jack thought that would cover about anything, including wishful thinking. He picked up his cup, looking at the exquisite workmanship. The anomaly pricked his curiosity. Just how backward were these innocent-seeming marshworld folk, anyhow? They distilled a liquor that compared favorably with any he'd ever tasted, and someone, somewhere, had discovered the secrets of porcelain, and they used mind-power to control the weather. "What do you hope to gain?"

"That," the Fisher said, his large eyes twinkling, "I expect you to find out for yourself, worthy adversary."

They had another cup of the innkeeper's finest, then staggered back to Jack's room, where Skal left him to make his own way into bed. The Fisher first shuffled through Jack's duffel while he watched bemused. Skal seemed pleased to find the ceremonial knife, and displeased not to find what he was looking for.

"Where is it, Jack?"

"Where is what?"

"The control for your robot there."

Jack sat up and swung his feet to the floor, feeling a pleasant *whir* in his brain. "There's no control. It's not a robot. It's battle armor."

Skal made a movement with his whiskers and eyebrows that Jack had learned to interpret as a frown. "It's inefficient."

"Insult me all you want, but not my suit!" Jack found the bemusing haze of the alcohol slipping away from him, all too soon, like the effects of a stunner. He stayed relatively limp to allow the Fisher to think he still had an advantage over him.

Skal balanced on the fronts of his supple feet. He hooked a thumb in his weapons belt. "I don't know how much I can believe you."

"Same here. With your wild stories about Elders using magic on the weather. . . ."

The Fisher's eyes fairly glowed. He held out his hand. "Come with me, then, and I'll show you. And wear the armor."

"The armor?"

"The Elders must see it. Yes, that's the only way to do it. You've got to come with me and wear your suit."

"And if I don't want to?"

"Of course you do!"

Jack stood up carefully, feeling a last farewell rush of alcoholic haze numb him to his toes and then disappear. "I've got the grain silos to check on in the morning, and a guard to arrange before there's a riot."

Skal shrugged a sinuous Fisher shrug. "Don't worry about it, my friend—the rin is all gone. Has been for days."

Somehow Jack wasn't surprised. "What about the riot activity?"

Another ripple of pelt and muscle. "A little intelligence misplaced—I was hoping they would send you into my embrace. And they did! Come on, Jack—what have you got to lose?"

It wasn't a question of what he had to lose so much as what he suspected Skal had to gain, but he nodded. "Where are we going?"

"To the hill country."

"And we're hiking over the dried-out mud flats to get there?" Not only was he worried about the terrain, but also about the displaced fauna which might be out looking for meals.

"I've appropriated a skimmer." Skal drew his lips back in a smile.

"I'll bet you have. All right. I'll send back word."

Skal reached out and caught his wrist. "That's something I strongly suggest you do not do. If worse comes to worse, you can always claim you were taken."

Jack felt his eyebrow arch, but he said nothing. He walked over to the suit and prepared it for the journey. Bogie's questing mind failed to come to life at his touch and, though he'd asked Amber to squelch it, he felt a brief sorrow.

The mauve edges of dawn were curling back as the skimmer shot over the crackled and dried mud flats. A layer of flashing-bugs hovered over the barely moist ground, their golden flashes flickering on and off. Above them was a layer of butterflies, multicolored, their wings frail against the morning breeze. Still higher flew dragonflies and birds, dipping now and then for a butterfly or flash-bug breakfast.

The blue-gray haze of night was soon burned off by the yellow sun. Skal rode his skimmer as though it were a wild creature, as it bumped and hydroplaned off thermals. He turned and grinned at Jack.

There was no windshield or hood, and the wind tore through Jack's sandy hair. He wore goggles and paid attention to keeping his mouth shut, though the layers of bugs were below him. He squinted against the dawn. It wasn't burning bright as Malthen's had been, or even the dawns across the sands of Milos, but bright enough.

They hit an air pocket and the skimmer bucked across it. An empty sleeve brushed eerily at his arm as though the suit reached for comfort. As the ride smoothed out, there was a dull rumble.

Jack looked up. The cloud layer overhead was high, but already growing thick and. dark and moving upriver. There was little wind here. What pushed them?

What indeed?

Chapter Twenty

"There is no one man wise enough to rule us," the Elder Fisher said.

Jack blinked in the dim light of the immense cavern. Minerals glowed in the walls, catching the sparkle of tiny tallow candles set in niches about the cave, drip marks flowing down, showing that similar candles had melted away in the same niche, for generations.

He sat awkwardly, enfolded in his suit and helmet, as Skal had insisted, and his pearly form dwarfed those of the Fishers sitting on either side of him. He wanted to shift from hip to hip, or shrug his shoulders, but knew that such a movement would annihilate the beings closest to him. Fisher muzzles turned to him, then, and he realized he was expected to make an answer to the statement he had just heard. He began to clear his throat, when a one-armed Fisher cleared his own with an angry growl.

"And you, old shit, would leave decision-making to a circle of Elders such as ourselves, who do little other than chant about the rain and argue over everything else. A village, let alone a planet, cannot be ruled this way." He waved his stump of a shoulder. He was raven black, except for the silver that tipped his muzzle and ears, and chunky for a Fisher.

"And who here is to believe you are taking the side of Shining Fur-grinning tooth?" A Fisher of a rare, almost pure cream color spoke, a female, Jack believed her to be. She wore an apron as well as the shorts.

"You know me better than that, Mist-off-the-waters," the one-armed Fisher said. He looked to her and made a tiny nod with his head, a movement Jack was beginning to recognize meant respect. "But there must be one authority to take action."

"One man backed by a council, then."

"Perhaps."

"Bah!" growled the first Elder, and the hackles along his russet back bristled. "No one man can feel what all Fishers feel."

Jack fought the urge to shift again. He looked to Skal, who lounged impassively across from him, the candlelight sending a glow to his light spots, giving him the look of an ancient leopard. Though Skal appeared at ease, he had the look in his eyes of one absorbing every word, every nuance.

Skal stirred then, as if feeling Jack's eyes on him. "I brought a guest, not for him to hear you argue politics, but for you to show him the magic you can do."

Every Fisher eye, bright and luminescent as the moon, narrowed at his words. Jack felt his back grow cold inside the suit.

"This is a thing," Mist said, "that we consider sacred. Even talk of it is not allowed. You know this, Skal."

He inclined his head and kept it down. "These aren't ordinary times," he responded.

"Indeed? And why not? We parched our own rin fields, sending our villages to the hills to survive. Why? Because we wish to show our snarls to our Emperor?"

Skal shrugged. His pelt rippled, then settled, as Mist's tone echoed away in the cavern.

One-arm moved his stump. "You're both less than turds in the water, if you continue to argue in front of this outsider. You would show him all of our flaws and none of our strengths."

Jack spoke then, "I'm not here in an official capacity."

"You represent no one other than yourself?"

Jack nodded.

One-arm showed his teeth in a pleased grin. "Good! That's the way it should be."

"Politics again, you old freak," a russet-coated Fisher in the shadows of the circle spoke out. "The stranger's ears will be filled with our feuds when he leaves."

"And why shouldn't they be?"

"Because," Skal said quietly, "he is our enemy."

An abrupt silence fell in the cavern, broken only by the flaring of a candle as its drippings caught fire, flared up, then sizzled out.

Cream-colored Mist, her eyes a midnight blue, looked to Jack. "Is this true?"

"I'm paid to serve Commander Poonum—and it's my understanding he's the commander in chief for Shining Fur- grinning tooth."

Someone hissed. Another said, in broken phrasings, "Enemy of some of us, allies of others."

Jack blinked. What would allies of the Fisher emperor be doing in this group? He began to grasp that the politics of the situation was rapidly growing beyond his reach.

Skal held up the ceremonial knife. "Yet, even for an enemy, he has honor. And, I made him wear what soldiers of his own emperor wear, so that all of us can understand what we face if we allow a full-blown war to begin."

It dawned on Jack that Skal had brought him here for a demonstration. He shrank within the suit. The Owner of the Dragon would be furious with him for getting trapped into this. He imagined Amber saying, "Jack, you're too damned gullible."

A droplet of sweat squirmed its way down his torso, leaving behind a trail that itched where he could not reach. For a fleeting second, he had a panic-stricken sense of deja vu—this was Milos, all over again, with the natives they were supposed to aid and defend hav- ing ideas and wars of their own.

It was worse than Milos, because the enemy he would be fighting had become human to him; these Fishers were not despicable Thrakian bugs that crunched satisfyingly under his boots. Skal was as much a comrade in arms as Dragon. How could Jack destroy him?

And it was the same as Milos because Jack knew this was a no-win situation. No wonder he worked for a private employer. If the Emperor heard about this, he'd wash his hands of the whole affair, and Jack stood a good chance of disappearing again, lest he become a public embarrassment. If this became too much of a fiasco for a private employer, he'd simply become a battle casualty.

No, not again!

He would not let himself be buried alive again. He realized that Skal had said something else to him, and that all the Fishers were staring, waiting for a response. He shoved himself to his feet. "This is not what I came for."

To a murmur of disappointment and anger, Skal held up his hand. "No, my guest is right. He is from another world. He scoffed when I said that you had driven all the rain upriver. This is my pride gift I ask."

Mist-off-the-waters looked at Skal. Her whiskers trembled. Then she put her head back and began to sing, eerily, almost a howl, a primeval sound that sent ice-cold chills through Jack, even though he was buffered by the suit's sound system.

The twelve other Elders in the circle joined in. Some sang, one barked in accompanying cadence, and several chanted, paused, then chanted again.

Jack felt the sound beating at his ears. The suit wasn't pressurized or carrying an air supply against an alien environment, he was breathing off the vents. It muffled his hearing. He could feel pressure building up, as though he was making a drop from an assault tube, or climbing rapidly in altitude. Then, suddenly, he heard the distinctive rumble of thunder.

Jack swung to the mouth of the cavern, so far away, he could barely see its opening. He left the circle and walked toward it. Skal bounced to his feet and stood in front of him, as though he would block Jack's passage, but he paused, then let Storm pass.

When he reached the outside, he stood on the side of the mountain crag. The skimmer flashed a glint of sunlight at him. Mountain grasses, thin and wiry, tossed as a building wind ruffled through them. Trees below rustled.

Jack looked through his topside camera, and scanned the heavy skies overhead. What had been blindingly sapphire blue when he entered the cavern was now charcoal—and the high, boiling clouds were headed upriver. It was impossible, but his cameras scanned it in the distance, and his gauges told him there had been a drastic change in the barometric pressure.

He had no explanation for what they'd done, or at least none that he could accept. If Amber had been with him, maybe. . . .

He scanned Skal at his back. "I see it," he said, "but I don't understand it."

"Some things are beyond knowing," Skal answered. "I don't understand how you can be here, on my world, yet you are. And why have you no tail?"

Jack smiled, in spite of himself. He turned to reenter the cavern. "You brought me here to show them the suit, didn't you?"

A Fisher shrug. "I wanted to see what it can do." '

'Why?"

"I've heard stories. I have been trying to convince my people that, if we wish to win this war, we must make a single, sweeping gesture. Otherwise, you and others like you will chew us up." Skal pointed into the dark recesses of the cavern. "They don't believe you can."

"And if I show them I can?"

"Then I will have convinced them of what we must do to win."

Or, Jack thought, convinced them to surrender to the inevitable.

He hesitated. "You once laughed at my suit. You didn't seem to think it would work in the swamps and marshes."

"And I don't think it will," Skal answered.

"Then it won't be a true test."

The big brown eyes, so like an animal's, with very little white, widened. "Do you intend to convince me, too?"

"If I can."

Skal paused, then said, "There's a mire not far from here. It's fed by mountain springs. We use it to protect the entrance to this cavern on the far side. It's not big, but it will engulf a man easily enough."

"That's all it takes."

He grinned. "I look forward to seeing you waddle in mud. Please, come back inside. The Elders are waiting."

The chant had stopped. Mist-off-the-waters had her arms curled lightly about her knees. The others reclined. A sweet-smelling smoke filled the air and Jack. saw a pipe being passed around. It didn't surprise him somehow.

"I saw the storm moving," he said, simply.

One-arm grunted. "It is only a small spate. Little enough effort."

"But how do you do it?"

The Fisher folk froze, and Jack realized then what a stupid thing he'd said. He waved a gauntlet. "I beg your pardon. I had forgotten this . . . thing . . . is sacred."

Skal sat down cross-legged in his vacant spot in the circle, just in time to accept the pipe. "I would ask more for Jack."

"What?"

"Mist-off-the-waters, read the smoke for him." Skal gave him a crooked grin and passed the pipe by.

The ivory female frowned, then inclined her head with the faintest ruffling of her whiskers. "All right then." Her bluish black eyes slit with concentration. She looked up suddenly then, the glow of candles making bright suns in her eyes. "You are far older than you look. Almost twice your years have you spent, but in dreams . . . dreams of war."

Jack started. The helmet protected him from showing his emotion, but inside his suit, he began to tremble.

"I see flames. Everything is flames." Mist shook her head. "What a terrible world it must have been . . . no, wait. That was its end."

One-arm muttered, "Like the *skahala* says he will make for our world."

"Ssssh." The Elder was roundly hissed silent and he bowed his head in embarrassment, though Jack couldn't tell if it was because he had interrupted Mist or because he'd spoken the name of one of their evil gods.

Mist pointed at him. "You have a duty, born out of the sands and now tempered by flame. Do not forsake it, no matter where you go." She paused. "And there is another—"

Jack could not bear to hear more. "Thank you, Elder, your reading is true, but allow me some secrets. As Skal would remind you, he is my enemy."

Mist nodded. She got to her feet. "And, now, we will see how you move."

Skal guided him through the mountain to the far side. A slit opened into a bowl-shaped valley. The mire lay in front, with only a very small path marked with tiny white pebbles to the side. Jack saw the narrow pathway only because he was looking for it, saw it, and realized that he might not be able to traverse it in the suit, anyway.

It was not an open pit of muck. Deceptive wisps of grass grew from it, the ground in spots even looked quite firm. But because he'd been told it was there, he knew it was, and identified it. He made a note, in case the future decreed that he come by this way again.

The Elders ringed the pathway and watched him expectantly. The storm breeze, still building, ruffled their sleek pelts. A few of them, he saw with surprise, had balding patches. Mist moved gracefully, but one or two of the older males had stiff joints and needed help getting from stepping stone to stepping stone. As Jack watched them, he thought of them less and less as alien or strange to him. He shook himself inside the suit. One of the contacts gave him a nasty pinch.

Skal stood on the far side, waiting for him.

"Well, old boy," Jack said to himself, "here we go." Bogie didn't answer, though Jack felt that it was listening somehow. Jack flexed his knees. He put the power vault onto hover and stepped out over the muck.

Skal sucked his breath in, his tail arching in avid fascination, as Jack moved into the bog. The Fishers, evidently, expected him to sink rapidly, but on hover setting, as long as his jets didn't clog, the suit more than buoyed him.

He strode quickly toward Skal. The commander stood between him and the throat of the valley. Beyond that, he could see a cool green vale, with silvery trees that wept in the wind, a demi-paradise in a world he'd once referred to as the mother of all swamps. Only Skal blocked his passage to it.

Jack chinned the power vault and literally blew himself out of the mire, over Skal's head and onto the edge of the valley turf. He landed with a deep bow, straightened, and twisted to face them.

"I was trained," he said, "to fight a war in a way so that the earth, the land and all its environs, would be damaged as little as possible. We call that fighting the 'Pure' war."

"Makes sense," grumbled One-arm. "What purpose is it to gain a swamp if you've polluted it."

"That's something of the idea. Our critics say that we've forgotten the worth of a soul. Maybe there's something to that, too, but if the flesh is stupid enough to war upon other flesh, then the world ought not to be destroyed so that a different flesh can someday be born there and, perhaps, in a wiser way, rule the world again. Anyway, I'm not a . . . I'm not an Elder. I'm just a soldier. What I'm going to do now is against my training, but it will show you the kind of damage I can do, if ordered to." Jack turned and lasered the canyon wall, bringing molten rock down in front of them, sealing off the tiny vale forever.

They gasped and Mist let out a sound of anguish that pierced

Jack, but he did not stop. He scarcely waited until the last rock had cooled, then proceeded to lean over and tear the rock wall down with his gauntlets, until he stood, swallowed up by boulders. He reached down and tossed an immense rock into the air, blasting it into dust and splinters. Then he took the remainder and sealed them into the mountain again, the side nearly inviolate, except for the obsidian seam, like a scar, down its side.

Except for a second boulder. Jack took it, like a soccer ball, and proceeded to do an exercise from Basic, running, somersaulting, tumbling, and vaulting, all the time bouncing the rock from one gauntlet to another as easily and gingerly as if it had been an egg. Laser fire and projectile fire crackled over, above and about it. When he stopped, panting, the sweat running off him, he took his helmet off in triumph and turned to his audience. He hadn't drilled like that in twenty-three years, yet his heart pounded for only a moment and he knew a certain sadness that, if he hadn't slept for seventeen of those years, he couldn't have done what he'd just done now. The drill needed a young man's body.

Three of the Elders had fainted. Mist swayed upon Skal's arm. Jack felt a moment of shame until the Fisher stammered, "We had no idea. All . . . all that you have done you've been toying with us, when you could have crushed us like . . . like the lowest slug."

"But we don't war like that. We push back just enough to try to get you to stop pushing on your own. We . . . we try to—" Jack paused, his throat dry at the grief of the beings he faced. "There's worse things. . . ." But he didn't tell them. He didn't go on about artillery and bombs and chemicals. It seemed more than enough that they'd seen *him.* "We show mercy whenever we can.

Mist clenched her jaw. "Is it mercy to toy with us? Is it mercy to let us think that we can, that we might possibly, be able to fight with you? What choice have we now, when we know that we cannot stop, that we must carry on with our efforts, even though you have shown us that it is totally hopeless and that we will be crushed to our last cubling. *Is that merciful?"* she said, and gave a piercing cry.

Chapter Twenty-One

"And then what happened?" Dragon said, leaning intently over the edge of the desk, all humor fled from his eyes, leaving them a dark and dangerous brown. He ran his hand through his silvery hair, ruffling it.

"Then I was drugged and brought back to the inn. I reported to you and headed back as soon as I found that the grain silos were, indeed, empty, and, from all evidence, had been that way for several days." Jack answered evenly, thinking of what a few pulls on that pipe of Skal's had done to his senses. He stared at the Dragon, remembering what Mist had said to him. *Born of sand and tempered by flame . . . do not forget your duty.* Or had it been destiny? He dared to think of the Dragon what he'd never dared to think before. Dragon was a survivor like himself—so why didn't they share the same enemies?

"So what do you think was the purpose of the intelligence we received, warning us of pending riots?"

"They wanted to see the suit."

"And did they?"

"I was wearing it when taken," Jack replied. "And I demonstrated it to a council of Elder Fishers."

The Dragon rubbed his right eyebrow wearily. "And what was their reaction?"

"They were crushed. But—I think they intend to continue."

"The same Elders who think they can make it rain." His supervisor sighed and sat back abruptly in his chair. He turned away from Jack and drummed the desktop with an angry staccato, as he looked to the map screen. Overhead, rain pelted the building relentlessly.

Unconsciously, Jack looked up. Skal's last words to him had been vague. He'd said only, "Remember the dam." Why? What should he remember about the dam?

He got up out of his chair and went to the map. Dragon asked heavily, "Trying to retrace the route?"

"No. I was blindfolded, as I told you, both ways. But. . . ." Jack paused, letting the lie sink in as he examined the topography. "I got the distinct impression talking to these Elders that the Fishers are splintered into a number of groups. Shining Fur-grinning tooth can't possibly represent their views."

As he talked, his back to the Dragon, Jack examined the topography. He found the block marks of the newly-built dam and, around the continent, saw the symbols for several more. Jack shifted, eying the four other major land masses . . . and dam construction headed the list of new projects for all of them. This was a marshworld. Water reigned supreme.

Shining Fur-grinning tooth's strategy became crystal clear to him. He was damming up the water rights of every major river he could, forcing the factions to side with him or be driven out of their marshes. And now he could see the sense in Skal's ominous hints. Only the fools didn't know what they were about—but he, with this topographical map and his inside knowledge, could see.

"'He doesn't.'"

"What?" Jack turned, bringing his attention back to the Dragon, forgetting for a moment what he'd said.

"The Fisher emperor doesn't represent a tenth of the population he claims to."

"Then what are we doing working for him?"

"We're not . . . we're working for a private employer. Jack, if you're having problems with this assignment, I have to consider terminating you." The Dragon stood, tension etched in every fiber of his lean body.

Jack shook his head. "I can't believe you would—any more than I can believe you'd work without knowing what was happening here. When you sent for me, you said you wanted a man of conscience. Well, it takes a man of very little conscience to figure out what's happening."

They considered each other.

Then the Dragon said, very quietly. "It's much easier to defeat Poonum working with him than against."

Those words took Jack's breath away. He found himself frozen in place as he considered what the Dragon was saying to him. Then he broke the silence. "Shit. Shit and damn. Amber's right. I'm a gullible son of a bitch. And all this time, I thought you were tweaking Poonum's tail because you thought he was an idiot!"

The Dragon grinned. "And if you'll sit down and listen, Jack, I'll give you an idea of what our employer is really up to."

The rain overhead became even harder.

Jack went to the map screen. "We're out of time, then, if government sabotage is our game. Look here." The Dragon followed, looking over his shoulder. "Shining Fur-grinning tooth has built dams here, and here, and there's work in progress here, here, and there."

The Dragon nodded slowly.

Jack said impatiently, "Don't you see? He's ruining his own people, just to get them to toe the line. He's using water rights to build his empire."

"But if they can make it rain . . . why bother?"

"But they're not making it rain downriver. Just here." And Jack stabbed a finger at the map.

Dragon's eyebrows arched. "They're trying to overflow the dam!"

"Exactly. And if it were a lower technology dam, they'd have done it. But we built it."

The Dragon didn't seem entirely convinced. "And when we built it, we took this minor tributary here into consideration. That's where the floodgates are directed."

"Right. So their efforts are futile. Their lands stay parched, the dam stays operational, and the quasi-emperor stays in power. Unless. . . ." Jack paused.

"Unless what?"

"Unless I blow the dam."

Dragon let out a whistling breath. "You do that and you'll wipe out Shining fur-grinning tooth's capital city, as well as flooding the flatlands."

"But only because of the diversion, which he insisted be built, so that his own city profit from it."

"Killed by his own weapon," the Dragon said slowly. He stood back, considering the map. "What about Skal and the downriver faction?"

"Most of them have already moved up into these hills, where the snow runoffs provide water and springs. Their lands will be inundated, but that will pass in a season."

The Dragon scratched his chin. The humorous brown eyes regained their twinkle. "I can't back you in this. I'll have to be with Poonum and a delegation, trying to convince Shining Fur-grinning tooth of the error of his ways, in light of this new information."

They looked at one another. Jack said slowly, "Can you get out in time?"

"If a pro is doing the job. We'll be on a tight timetable."

"And where," said Amber, with an edge to her voice, "am I supposed to be while you're doing all this brave crap?"

"Wherever Dragon takes you. We're upriver, but there could be some backwash. The main thing is to have you out of the way so that the Fishers can't retaliate."

She looked up at him. "You do care about me, then?" Her eyes shone strangely bright in the electric lighting.

"Of course I do!"

Amber looked away, presenting him with the profile of an attractive young woman, whose ash brown hair fell in soft waves over her shoulders. "I thought—I thought maybe you were mad you'd brought me, because I got in the way and everything. Because I argue with you."

He didn't ask why she'd thought that. He sat there, torn by the desire to hug her comfortingly, and by the knowledge that if he did that, he wouldn't be hugging the urchin kid sister he'd thought of her as, for so long. He sat across the room from a woman who attracted him, and whom he didn't dare touch. "When we get back—" he started, then stopped.

"Back where?" she asked quickly.

"Back to Malthen. I thought maybe you'd like to go back to school."

"School?" Her brows knotted in puzzlement. Her complexion had cleared, her face filled out slightly from its bony triangular shape, but she was still Amber. Her golden brown eyes watched him, and a faint flush colored her cheeks. But it wasn't a demure flush, Jack discovered, as soon as she opened her mouth. "What is this? I used to be just fine as I was. Aren't I smart enough for you?"

"Those are street smarts, and in that area, you're smart enough for anybody. I just thought—"

"You thought! I don't have to know how to build a god-damn starship just to take a ride in one! I'm fine just as I am, and it's time you realized that, Jack Storm! It's time you appreciated me."

Jack said nothing. She'd gotten to her feet. Amber glared down at him for a moment and his ears began to ring. He put his hand up to them, saying, "Amber. You're hurting."

She paled immediately. "Oh, damn." She put her trembling hands over her face. "Damn. I'm out of control again."

"You didn't mean to hurt me." He sensed that she had begun crying silently, behind her mask of slender fingers.

"It isn't that! Rolf had exercises he used to make me do. I never understood why . . . only now I do. It's like . . . like I have to know how to rein myself in." Amber sniffled. "Why can't I be like everybody else?"

"I didn't fall in love with everybody else," Jack said, and the silence fell on his unexpected words as the two of them stared, astonished, at each other. He began to clear his throat when a commanding knock on the door interrupted him.

Skal came in, his pelt dappled dark with rain. He grinned. "A lover's quarrel?" he asked in Fisher amusement as Amber's face turned red again and she fled from the room.

"You have great timing," Jack answered wryly. "Ready to go?"

"As soon as you and the suit are."

Jack stood up. He hesitated, then called out, "Get packed, Amber. The Dragon's sending someone by tomorrow morning. And if he doesn't, steal a skimmer and get to high ground by yourself. I'm depending on you to do that for me."

Amber came to the doorway of her bedroom. "All right," she said softly. She watched him leave.

"Who's in the raiding party?" Jack asked, as he settled the battle armor in the rear seat. This time, Skal had the roof up, though Jack doubted the vinyl covering could withstand the torrential downpour. "And I thought this stuff was supposed to stop?"

"Nobody in the Elders except Mist—we had to wrestle One-arm to convince him his disability would hamper us. And, yes, the rain will stop after this squall. We don't want to give away our change in strategies, do we?"

But Jack didn't like the news that Mist was coming. He said as much.

Skal looked at him. His whiskers and ears flattened, then pricked forward again. "Mist-off-the-waters can call down the lightning," he said flatly. "Or did you wish to go in without a diversion?"

"I didn't wish to jeopardize her."

"Our world is not like yours, my friend. Our mates share equally in everything we say or do.

"And what does yours say?" In that brief silence that followed, Jack knew he shouldn't have asked.

Then Skal said, "Shining Fur-grinning tooth had her killed, to avoid further confusion in the bloodlines of leadership."

"I'm sorry," Jack said. "And I shouldn't have asked."

Skal looked at him again, his dark eyes shining. "No," he disagreed. "You have the right to know. And what is your stake in this?"

"Mine?" Jack thought. "I'm not sure really. Maybe it rests in what Mist said to me."

They finished the trip to the sanctuary hills in silence, and it took Jack quite a long time to realize the rain had stopped before the skimmer landed.

"This is Hooker." Skal indicated a massive, sable-colored Fisher, his shoulders bowed with muscle and fat. Hooker wore a dark jump-suit, taking advantage of its many pockets for storage—of what, Jack couldn't hazard a guess. Food perhaps, or hand weapons. Hooker didn't appear to have a tail, either inside or outside the suit. Hooker gave him a brusque nod and rocked back and forth impatiently on his bare feet.

"Mist, you already know." The ivory Fisher gave him a pleased smile. She, too, had opted for a dark colored jumpsuit, though hers was as sleek as her own pelt.

"We call this feller Songbird, because he rarely has anything to say." Skal nudged the lanky being on his right. Songbird gave Jack a look through eyes narrowed in suspicion. He was a mottled brown, and wore only shorts, with a weapons belt. However, he balanced on his forearm a wicked looking, bastardized laser rifle. Jack gave it a second look.

"And for our lucky sixth, Little Fish here. Even for one of us, she's very quick and supple."

Jack smiled at the small and lithe Fisher. She was a light brown, almost the color of Amber's hair. Instead of reaching out to shake his hand, she did a cartwheel in place, then looked at him, whiskers twitching.

"You're aptly named," he told her.

"So are you," she giggled.

"What?" Jack asked, turning around, as Skal snorted and Mist frowned at the young female. "Do I have a Fisher name and nobody told me?"

Skal shrugged then. "Only when you're wearing your suit."

"What is it?"

"Little Sun," Mist told him. She pointed a finger at Little Fish. "Get armored and remember, young one, that the future of your people depends on what we do tonight."

Jack looked down at himself. The Flexalinks twinkled in the night. He did, he supposed, look like a sun or a moon. There had been some amusement connected with the nickname, but he figured he was better off not knowing what had triggered Fisher humor.

He pointed at the bundles of Enduro bracers he and Skal had lifted from the operations warehouse. "I'm fully armored, but I won't take you in unless you're protected, too. There is enough equipment for all of you. Then we'll pass out weapons."

"I don't use any," Mist said quickly, echoed by Songbird who grunted, "Got my own."

The familiar tension began to run up Jack's spine as Hooker and Little Fish leaned over and eagerly began pawing through the equipment. It had begun, once again.

* * *

Amber woke at the pounding on the front door. She frowned in the darkness and then remembered. She'd gone to sleep dressed, just in case. A look at her watch told her it was nearly dawn, though the sky was overcast and still dark. She swung out of her bed, grabbed her duffel, and went to answer the door.

The men standing outside wore slicks. They stood hunched over in the rain, but Amber said, "I'm all ready to go." She shut the door behind them and followed them to the massive skimmer tied up at the veranda, hovering just above the high water.

She twisted back a second, saying a mental good-bye to the nicest home she'd ever had, wondering if it would withstand what Jack had planned. They were upriver, though. Maybe it would. Maybe she'd be back, briefly.

The gull wing doors of the skimmer opened. One of the her escort grabbed her by the elbow, guiding her to the back seat. As she leaned in, and froze, the man said, "She was expecting someone. She was no trouble at all."

Amber doubled over as the stunner blast hit her in the chest, losing her wind and most of her bile. She had the satisfaction of seeing it spew in the face of the man who reached for her even as she passed out, thinking that he'd had to come to the end of the galaxy to find her—and he'd done it.

Rolf pulled the limp girl over his lap and slammed the door shut against the wind and the rain. "Let's get her out of here," he snapped, and the skimmer took off, bucking against the air pockets.

* * *

They ran across the top of the dam. Jack felt the concrete vibrate with the weight of the water against it, and the roar of the turbines below. He made an effort not to look to his right, where the fall to the valley and the river bed was immense. Songbird led the way, his bastardized rifle gripped tightly in his hands.

Overhead, the sky lashed out in a predawn storm. Lightning crackled, sheets of it, ripping the night apart. But no rain. Just sound and fury.

Songbird came to an abrupt halt as a flood gate worker loomed ahead. The Fishers stood, nose to nose, the worker's hackles raised in surprise.

"We've weapons and you've none. Leave now, while you can," Hooker growled, as Songbird quietly drew a bead.

The worker hesitated. He looked at the six of them, his stare boring into Jack as though he could see into his faceplate by sheer determination.

He turned and bolted. Songbird's laser shot missed, and the supple Fisher dove headfirst down the ladder leading into the interior works of the massive dam.

Little Fish dove after him, but came up empty-handed.

Skal sucked his sharp white teeth. "That'll do it," he said. "He'll bring more out after us."

"Then we'd better set the charges." Jack waved Hooker over and gave him the plastique and detonators. Not the most sophisticated of explosives, but ample for this job.

Mist touched Jack. He could feel her concern even through the suit. "We agreed to try to get the workers out."

"So we did and so we will, unless they come after our hides." Jack handed another charge to little Fish, admonishing her, "Now you be careful with that."

"I will! Where do you want it?"

"On the wall where we talked about. You'll have to go over with a rope."

She nodded. Some of the more dangerous placements had been assigned to her on her insistence. She had, after all, the natural ability to be able to handle them. Jack watched her skipping off.

He gave a charge and detonator to Songbird. "You've got the speed. We need this just above the last floodgate."

Songbird shook his head. "No. Guard door." He pointed his laser rifle at the portal where the worker had disappeared.

"No. If they come, they come. I'll handle them. We need this charge planted and Hooker's too heavy to run the distance."

Songbird hesitated. Then, with a snarl across his lean face, he took the explosives and ran off. Jack watched him go, wondering what fires of hatred burned in the Fisher's soul, then turned back. Mist said, "They're coming. I can feel them."

As used as he was to Amber's flashes of intuition, Jack shivered. He pointed across the way they'd come. "Go back, to high ground."

"No," she protested.

Skal made a grunt and his whiskers flattened. "You must go. You're an Elder, and Jack is right. Hurry!"

The slim, cream female hesitated, then turned and raced off into the graying edge of the storm. Lightning sizzled and thunder cracked above them as she left.

Just before dawn, the contingent of workers boiled out of the portal, armed and shielded to the teeth. Skal let out a curse as Jack cocked his fist, left with no choice but to fight. His heartbeat quickened.

They were caught in a cross fire between him, Skal, Hooker and Songbird. They climbed up and fell, their bodies pushed aside by their teammates coming up from below, like ants boiling out of a hill. Jack laid down a spray of fire, orange against the midnight blue of the storm, and tried not to hear the mourning cries of the Fishers as they killed their fellows.

But it was a cork that couldn't be put back in the bottle. The shields came up, and the fire deflected. Hooker died first, with a snarl snapped off in mid-cry. His heavy form thudded to the concrete dam.

Jack vaulted, landing in front of Skal. "Use me for a shield," he ordered. "Back off after Mist. Then run like hell and don't stop."

"No."

"Get out of here, dammit."

"The cause is not lost yet."

Songbird let out a warbling cry as his laser charge ran out. In a frenzy, he ran headfirst into the attackers. Four of them collided with him, and they rolled off the high side of the dam, into foaming waters that sucked them down. Jack looked, briefly, thanking the gods that were, for not letting them fall down the long drop.

His rearview camera caught sight of Little Fish clinging to that long drop. She peered up over the edge cautiously. The last charge had been set, then.

"Get out of here, Skal," Jack repeated. "Get little Fish and go!"

"What?"

"The charges are set. Now get out!" Jack picked Skal up by the scruff of his neck and threw him down the length of the dam, where Little Fish caught his barreling body. The two of them staggered to their feet in astonishment, then turned and ran, laser fire banked at Jack's chest, a ball of fire exploding off the Flexalinks.

Jack stepped back, out of the wash. He felt a reflection of the heat. He fired back.

Then a reeling lash of pain pierced him. He lost control of the armor and went to his knees. The shields went down. Jack rolled in pain.

Pain. Pain. Kill.

Dimly, Jack heard the voice as he twisted to his side. Bogie! Amber's control was gone. But why would Bogie feel the pain?

"No, Bogie. No pain. You don't have to feel the pain," Jack got out. He spied the Fishers gathering up nerve for a rush. Enough bodies, and he'd go over the edge. He fought for control over the suit's movements. What had happened to Amber? Bloodlust roiled in him.

All right, Boss. No pain. We fight today.

Jack stood up. He cocked the gauntlet. The wall of sleek-pelted beings faced him, their eyes gleaming with excitement and fear. More of them boiled out of the dam's interior. He was the enemy. And more than that he was their predator.

Jack/Bogie felt a hunger for their blood. To hear their death agonies as nerves seared and bones cracked and souls fled. He swallowed, bile at the back of his throat. "No! I won't kill today!" he grated out. Jack hesitated, then laid down a spray of fire at their feet, driving them back. He had the transmitter. The charges were set . . . his job here was done. He could retreat and trigger the detonators.

As he looked at their faces, he knew that they wouldn't let him go easily . . . nor did he want to draw them after Mist, Skal and Little Fish.

He took a step forward. The suit fought him, resulting in a shuddering, lumbering, movement that took him close to the edge of the dam.

"Let go, Bogie."

The Fishers straightened. They raised their shields and lasers, preparing to charge.

"Now, Bogie. Let me have charge now."

*Live, die, live . . . * The suit gyrated in confusion, then, with a *snap*, Jack found himself in control.

He chinned the amplifiers on and charged, letting out a war cry meant to curdle the blood of the listening Fishers. The ones who didn't break and run immediately got laser hotfeet that convinced them to join the pack. Screaming at the top of his lungs and letting out staccato bursts of fire, Jack drove them off the dam to safety.

As he ran, he wondered what had happened to Amber. What could have happened?

He reeled to a stop as Bogie answered his unasked question, answered it with a spear of pain, anger, and bloodlust. His mind, no longer his own, exploded. The suit ground to a halt and stood, convulsing, in the center of the dam. Jack fought to regain control of himself.

He hit the transmitter.

Lightning forked the dawn sky, still velvet black with storm. Thunder boomed, echoed by the explosions. The concrete trembled under his feet. He had but a second as the dam opened up, shards of concrete and tons of water crashing into him.

With a scream, Jack plunged down the long fall of the dam, riding the crest of the breaking water.

Chapter Twenty-Two

Amber woke. Her teeth and tongue were furred and she swallowed the acrid burn of bile in her throat. She stirred, cautiously, pins and needles in her wrists and ankles, before her thoughts began to focus. Then she stiffened. Rolf! Rolf had her!

Her eyes fluttered open. How long had she been out? She lay face down on vomit-stained upholstery. Her hair fanned out lankly about her head. She felt a bucking movement, then realized she still rode in the limo compartment of a skimmer. Amber turned her face, and saw the man sitting in the seat opposite her.

"Like your friend, eh? Never out for long. Long enough though, girl. I have you this time. And while you're awake. I warn you . . . kill me and your friend will follow me soon after."

Amber glared. She struggled to sit up, awkwardly, since her hands were bound behind her back. Rolf lounged opposite her, as elegant as ever in a Shakra tigersilk shirt and circulation-pinching black leather pants. He was handsome in a brutish way. Amber thought, and ducked her chin down, afraid of Rolf reading her thoughts in the old way he always used to seem to have. She preferred sandy blond hair, washed-out blue eyes, high cheekbones, a plain but honest face.

But she faced Rolf again. She had to, if only to keep a watchful eye on him. The man took a long drag of his smoke, and she smelled the drug in it faintly, and watched the blue-gray smoke curl out of his flared nostrils.

Lightning crackled. Its white light pierced the tinted screening on the windows of the luxury skimmer. Amber jerked to attention, remembering the dam and Jack's intentions.

"Where are you taking me?"

"I have a luxury suite reserved for us. The emperor of this world, a nice little beast, is very hospitable. We'll be in a wing of the International Hotel, as his guests."

In the capital, where Jack had estimated the brunt of the water would flood. Amber struggled. "No, you can't. Not there."

Rolf let an eyebrow peak. "And why not, my dear? Surely even a gutter tart like you should realize the hazards of refusing a barbaric ruler. Besides, this place looks promising. I might extend my field of operations somewhat."

Amber bit her lip. She looked out the window and saw the boil of water down below . . . white, angry water, rushing in a tide down the riverbed, and knew she was already too late to affect the blowing of the dam. But old Shining Fur-grinning tooth was still going to be in for the shock of his life unless Rolf transmitted ahead and warned him.

She looked back to Rolf, knowing that she might be diving head-first into a drowning tide, and smiled. "Just get me out of here," she lied. "The sooner the better. I'm beginning to mildew."

Rolf smiled widely. "It's been a long year, my dear—but I'm beginning to appreciate it. Jack Storm has taken some of the edges off you, hasn't he? Yes. I'm beginning to appreciate it."

Amber held his gaze levelly, praying that the driver and Rolf wouldn't be able to tell the thunder of the gathering rainclouds from the rumble of the deathwall of water.

* * *

Jack fell. He nearly lost the contents in his stomach tumbling in midair. He pulled his arms out of the sleeves, hit the pressurization switch, and then wrapped his arms about his head, praying he wouldn't smash when he hit the rocks. The water roared all around him, carrying him, and when he hit, his neck popped, but held.

He saw the water roar over him. The flood carried him willy-nilly, slamming him this way and that, buffeting him wildly. Too scared to know if he were upside down or inside out, he held out, his fingers laced together at the back of his neck.

Bogie whimpered. *Cold.*

Cold was death to the alien presence.

"Me, too," Jack said. He felt a childlike nudging inside his thoughts. Jack took pity on the sentience even as he pitched forward in the dark, churning waters. The suit's lighting winked unsteadily, then went out, as they slammed into a wall—of earth? Or the river bottom? He didn't know. The collision slowed their slide a moment. Jack took a deep breath.

He was helpless until he knew which way was up and out. If the power vault would even work under the weight of the flood-tide. He smacked headfirst into an obstacle. His neck crackled in agony. Then his right leg pinched. Jack whirled around, held by whatever gripped his leg, slowly, but surely, crushing the Flexalinks. Another few seconds, and the integrity of the suit would give way.

Jack opened his mouth in agony as his leg snapped, the bone crushed. Then, suddenly, the weight gave way and they were borne away again. Pain squeezed tears out of his eyes.

Hurt, boss.

Jack couldn't respond coherently to that. Then, suddenly, his leg felt warm and damp. Oh, shit, he told himself. A compound fracture. He was going to bleed to death inside the suit.

The alien nudging shifted suddenly. It left the cavity of Jack's thoughts. Jack panicked as his knee tickled, even as his leg throbbed in agony. Then, he felt nothing. Below the knee, he was stone numb. Jack dropped his chin, fighting to look down inside the suit, to see. "What have you done!" he screamed. "What the frack have you done to my leg!"

The berserker climbed back into his thoughts, sated. *Fixed it, boss. It's growing.*

Cautiously, Jack flexed his toes. Then tightened his calf muscles and let them go slack quickly, as he awakened a tender pain. Growing? Healing, maybe. And he'd thought the bastard had eaten his leg off.

He had little time to think further, as the suit spun him around, and then they dropped through the air again. When they hit, the impact knocked all thought out of Jack, and his mind grew dark. Bogie whimpered and held on a little tighter.

* * *

Mist clung to Skal, even as the three of them clung to the rocks. The very ground shuddered under the fury of the water. They watched as the shining sun of Jack's suit fell into blackness far below them. Skal shuddered, and his tail twitched in agony.

"A hero's death," he said to Mist, in Fisher talk.

But Mist saw the pearly suit bounce back up and shoot along the crest of the wall of water. "No," she whispered back. "He lives. You must follow him, my son, in the stranger's flying machine. He lives yet."

Skal straightened. He did not question the female's wisdom. She knew many things that he would never know.

As he climbed toward where the skimmer was still precariously perched, Mist-off-the-waters and Little Fish stared up at him.

"I will send to you," Mist said, "if I feel that we have lost him."

Skal nodded. He gave a bark of farewell and the skimmer shot into the new dawn.

* * *

The Dragon lowered his sighting glasses. From the high plateau, he had a splendid view of the destruction roaring down on Shining Fur-grinning tooth. His employer would be very pleased. Even if the Fisher emperor survived, he would be greatly humbled and devoid of authority. Mission accomplished. He heaved a sigh.

"You're sure that was Jack who went over when the dam wall blew out?"

"He's the only one out here with a suit besides you."

The Dragon shook his head. Nobody could have survived the fall, even in a suit. And with the tons of water falling on him . . . He turned to his aide. "What about the girl?" The least he could do was make sure Amber was safe and would receive Jack's death benefits.

"She wasn't there, sir, when we went to pick her up."

"What? Why wasn't I told?"

The man shrugged. "We were told not to delay your leaving the palace."

Dragon swore. He swore long and loud and obscenely, his voice lashing into the pure mountain air of a newborn world, tearing into the pink-toned sunrise until even his aide's ears burned red. Then the Dragon stopped. "Any idea where she's gone?"

The aide shoved a note into his hand.

Dragon grasped the situation immediately, if not entirely accurately. This Rolf was an enemy of Jack's; he had Amber, he wanted Jack. It was an age-old scenario.

He read through the note again, without surprise. He'd never met a mercenary without a checkered past; Jack was no exception. He folded the demand and put it in his breast pocket. If Jack couldn't be found, he'd have to deal with this himself. Provided of course, this Rolf survived the flooding himself.

"Get me a skimmer," Dragon ordered. "I want to recon the area."

* * *

Bogie worried at him, wouldn't let him sleep. *Boss? Boss? You're too cold.*

Jack groaned. Even that minor effort cut through him like a knife. The suit had collapsed on him, he could hardly breathe. With a great strain, he managed to get his right arm back in his sleeve and tried to wipe his face plate clean.

Silt. He was buried under a wall of silt. With God knows how many tons of water on top of that.

The good news was that at long last, he'd come to rest.

Bogie nudged at him again. *Too cold, Boss.* The inner voice sounded sluggish.

Jack ignored it. He decided he was face up in the silt, since all the weight seemed to be on top of him. He could try to claw his way out. Jack took a moment to reflect. Was it dying on him, now, after all this? Or sickening? Or regressing? Why? The sentience fed off him, that much Jack knew for sure. It could only grow when Jack was in the suit. And as afraid as he was of the berserker it might possess him into becoming, he did not deny the strength it had given him in the past. Jack sighed. "We're alive, Bogie. And where there's life, there's hope." Jack moved inside the armor.

The nudging became remote.

"Bogie? Come on now. I need you to help me run the suit, if we're to get out of here alive."

?

"Well, because while I do one thing, you can do another. Right? You've triggered the suit's functions before."

(hatching) Bogie said.

Hatching? Jack wondered. Or something like it. He shivered. It was cold inside the battle armor. Some of the functions lost. Chips jarred loose by the fall or connections severed. He had no way of telling. He took a deep breath, and found it stale.

"Then I'll do it myself," Jack said, suddenly panicked. If the refreshing pump was out, he was in for a very rough time of it. He had no desire to suffocate at the bottom of the world.

Every movement through the ooze was painstaking. His right leg, still a little numbed, responded fitfully to the requests he made of it. Jack squirmed, swam, shivered and resettled. He had only his senses inside the armor, baffled and faulty and easily fooled as they were, to tell him if he was making headway. But the silt seemed to give way.

He worked for what seemed hours, until his face was flushed, and the sweat trickled all over him. Bogie trilled happily. Body heat, Jack realized. And maybe the sweat. Both of them seemed vital for Bogie's growth.

Jack paused as he also realized that the catch bag wasn't hooked up and he could no longer bear to hold his water. With a sigh, Jack let down, and his boots filled. The suit fought to filter the excess out and he was left with the faint apple cider smell of urine. Plus he squished a little as he began to swim upward again.

The ooze and silt seemed interminable. Then Jack struck something with his gauntlet. He reached out carefully, grasping whatever it was he'd touched. He fumbled through the mud until he touched it again. A branch! And a fairly stout one, sucked down with him. Jack grasped the branch and pulled it to him.

Then another followed, as he blindly felt along it, the second entangled in the first. If he could break them and tie them together into a kind of mat—he'd have some purchase to stand on. Then he'd be fairly sure he was making headway.

Hands trembling inside the gauntlets, afraid of crushing the branches with his power, Jack wove them into a very rough raft. He swam until he could stand on top of the mat. He pushed down. The mat pushed back, very gently. It wouldn't take much—but it held.

Using the mat as a reference point, Jack began swimming again. His air grew too hot and too stale. He gasped and sweat and clawed. His thoughts swam until Bogie said *I fix it.* and then the air became a little sweeter.

Ouch said Bogie.

Jack grinned, as he realized the sentience had just fixed a short in the circulatory pump.

He crawled away from the mat slowly but surely. His heart began to pound. He stopped. Bogie sighed. Something in the adrenaline, too, Jack thought. Something he shed as waste, with the hormone in it. He thrust the realization aside. Unless he got out of here, he'd never have to worry about what made either of them tick.

Suddenly, the helmet broke into water. Dark, murky, but liquid. Jack let out a yell. He felt its echo inside. As the face plate washed relatively clean, Jack chinned on outside lights. The illumination bounced back at him, giving him only a few inches of sight, but he saw the splintered trunk of an immense tree close to him. Jack reached out and grasped it, using it to lever himself out of the mire.

Now he was clear. He took a deep, shivery breath. He kicked vigorously in an attempt to wash the silt out of the boot jets. With any luck, the power vault would work. If not, it could back up and blow him to kingdom come. He hesitated only a second, looking up, into the flatness of muddy waters, knowing that somewhere above him would eventually be the sky.

He triggered the vault.

* * *

Skal stood uneasily beside the skimmer, watching the waters churning, as trees and shrubs and dead bodies floated past him. Mist had sent him to wait there, but he could see no sign of Jack. A second skimmer circled him once, then settled down beside him, and the commander he knew only as the Owner of the Dragon got out with a grace even the Fishers would admire.

Dragon looked at Skal and put out his hand in that peculiar way the strangers had. "Seen anything?"

Skal shook his head. "No. An Elder of my people has instructed me to wait here, though."

"Is that right?" The human with silvery hair and a metallic blue jumpsuit lounged back against his skimmer. "Would that be one of the Elders who makes rain?"

"It might," Skal said shortly.

"Then I'll wait here, too, if you don't mind."

Secretly, Skal did, but he did not say as much. He watched the dark waters alertly.

The Owner of the Dragon crossed his arms over his chest.

"Not much left of Shining Fur-grinning tooth's city," he said conversationally.

Skal ducked his head, hiding his emotions except for an electric twitch at the end of his tail and the flattening of his whiskers. "Did the emperor survive?"

"I'm told he did. However, he has called for a council to replace him, and to coordinate aid all over the world. He has retired his title."

Skal let his teeth show in pleasure. He said nothing.

The Dragon cleared his throat. "You were a friend of Jack's?"

The Fisher considered that, then said. "Yes. I think so."

"I may need your help, then, if Jack is lost. There is an enemy of Jack's who has taken Amber. . . ."

Skal turned then, his glance flicking away from the flood. "An enemy of Jack's is an enemy of mine. Where is she held?"

"In the capital, at one of the evacuation centers. We may have to fight for her," Dragon warned.

The Fisher tail lashed. "I'm ready," Skal said solemnly. Just then, he heard a bubbling in the waters. Water already churned brown began to thrash white, and he saw the being rise, just as Mist had named him, like a small sun, glowing from the flood.

Jack saw the two skimmers and the two figures waiting for him. He gasped with surprise and the suit collapsed on the bank under him, its energy spent. It wasn't until he'd hit the open air that he realized the damage he'd taken . . . and lived. Dragon sprinted forward and wrenched the helmet off. Jack lay gasping for fresh air.

Skal leaned over him and grinned. "I think Mist would better have named you Fish-out-of-water," the Fisher said.

Jack choked, then got out, "You're safe? All of you?"

"Yes." Dragon knelt by him compassionately, opening up the

seams of the battle armor and helping him out. Jack let the man bear his weight as they stood together.

"And that's the good news," Dragon said.

Jack turned wearily to him, his heart sinking. "And what's the bad?"

"Rolf has Amber."

Chapter Twenty-Three

"You're not getting back in that suit," Dragon argued. "Take mine."

"Yours is antiquated. Besides, I want to use my own equipment."

Skal lashed his tail. "And you won't go alone. I'll go with you."

Jack stopped short. Bogie was braced up against the Dragon's skimmer, and, hands trembling, Jack was working on it as well as he could. Despite the healing Bogie had begun on his right ankle, Dragon had crude splints strapped to it. He stood lopsided, trying to keep his weight off it. Dragon had draped a light shirt over Jack's bare torso, which was already showing huge black and blue bruises from the battering he'd taken.

Jack shook his head. "This is my fight, Skal. Rolf will be expecting a small army. Even if he's in an evacuation center, I'm ready to guarantee he has it cordoned off. Alone, I might be able to make it in unnoticed. But even if he does see me coming, he's going to let me through. The man has a score to settle and I'm willing to bet he wants to blow my head off personally."

Skal stroked his whiskers flat. He said nothing, but his large eyes narrowed a little.

Jack reached out and took him by the shoulder. "We've shared the knife, my friend, and I know you want to help. But this is my fight." He dropped his hand and hobbled back to the suit. It was crimped and dented and silt had worked its way into the Flexalinks everywhere.

Dragon handed him a crescent wrench and a probe. He wrinkled his nose. "That thing needs to be dry docked and flushed out."

"I know. But it'll work for me."

"Look . . . let me contact this guy. Our employer is arriving this afternoon. He's been apprised of the job you've done and he's very pleased. I know he'll foot the ransom for you as part of your bonus."

Jack paused. He looked at his friend. Dragon had gotten a streak of mud worked into his silver hair, but his expression was earnest. "It won't work," Jack told him. "Rolf has what he wants—he wants Amber. All he wants from me is revenge. If he doesn't get it, then he'll still have Amber. He'll bolt and run if we try to delay, and he'll know we're setting up something. He wants a four o'clock meet and I have to give it to him."

"Then what do we do?"

"Stand by to get Amber out, no matter what happens to me."

Skal and Dragon both nodded solemnly. "We'll do our best."

Jack hesitated a moment, then reapplied himself to repairing Bogie as best he could. Dragon helped, before he commented, "It'll never be the same."

"Yes, it will."

"Better to get a new one, Jack, later."

Jack laughed shortly. "Only the emperor's guards have the new ones."

"I'll put in a good word for you."

"Right." Jack reached for the wire strippers, thinking that had been one of his goals. Now he had only one thing on his mind and that was the rescue of Amber. Once she was delivered, then he would think of the future.

A wire spat at him. He found the short and bypassed it, thinking that he and the suit were a lot alike . . . weapons, both. Just point them in the right direction and fire.

He was tired of being pointed in the wrong direction.

The back of his hand brushed across the chamois to get to the circulatory pump. Bogie seemed to have done a good repair job there. The microcircuitry responded well to the probe. Behind his back, Skal and Dragon exchanged brief looks.

Dragon's radio beeped. He climbed into the skimmer to answer it. Meanwhile, Skal shifted uneasily. "Mist calls to me," he said, finally.

Jack sensed a final parting. He put his tools aside, wiped his hands on his hips. "You've been a worthy adversary," he said, "and an even better friend."

Skal's whiskers twitched in embarrassment. The dark brown hide with the golden mottles shivered. He put the ivory-handled knife into one of the pockets of the clean pants Dragon had loaned Jack. He snapped the pocket shut. "I want you to keep the ceremonial knife," he said, "though it is customary to return it when the battle is ended, regardless of the outcome."

"If it's customary—" Jack began, but Skal held up a hand. "Mist-off-the-waters, One-arm, and I agree," he said firmly. "Because of our fighting here, we have long to wait before being accepted into the Dominion, I'm told."

"There has to be a unified government," Jack agreed.

Skal showed his teeth in mock humor. "That may never happen among Fishers. But keep the knife, and show it, and tell of us—that we may never be forgotten, regardless of our foolishness."

"Being a part of the Dominion doesn't give immortality."

Skal shrugged. Jack watched his sinuous body ripple with the movement. "Among the stars, who knows what immortality is, Little Sun." They touched hands, briefly.

"Good fishing," Jack wished.

Skal nodded. "Still waters," he returned, then, with a flick of his tail, was in his beat-up, primer-colored skimmer, and gone.

Dragon leaned out of his. "That was Holcombe. He says that Rolf is holed up on the penthouse floor of the International."

"Then the best way to get in is from the top," Jack said, tearing his attention away from the disappearing skimmer. He slapped his suit: "Time to do some climbing."

Sarge always told them the suits could do anything. Anything, except, perhaps, rappel down the side of a twenty-story building. Jack hung by his lines, feet swinging, rope caught on the nearly imperceptible edge of the scales of the Flexalinks, crimped open along one of his many dents. His throat went dry. The more he swung, the more those links would saw away at the rope, until sooner or later, the suit and the rope would part ways. He looked down again.

There was no way he and the battle armor would survive another drop, even though a watery surface reflected back at him. Flood waters had receded only a fraction.

Dragon manned the winch on the rooftop. His voice filtered in over the com line. "What's wrong, Jack?"

Jack was glad he'd left the helmet on. "I'm snagged," he said. "Any ideas?"

"You've got enough rope to swing on. What have you got to lose? Otherwise, I'll have to crank you back up here."

Going back up meant they'd have to go down the stairwells. There was no problem there, except intelligence had told Jack that the wells were guarded by a small army of mercenaries. Jack had lost his taste for blood.

Hi, Boss.

"Hi, Bogie. Just wake up?"

Hatching (regeneration) Bogie responded. Jack reflected again that talking to the sentience was like talking to an idiot. Sometimes it made sense and sometimes it didn't.

He stared at the sun-screened windows reflecting the suit back at him. The glare wiped out any sense of being able to see inside. For all he knew, Rolf and a small army were staring back at him.

"Bogie, can you operate my left glove?"

Which left?

"Ah, this one," Jack answered, and flexed, in spite of being dropped another breath-taking foot by the maneuver. The gauntlet began to open, even though Jack's hand wasn't moving. "That's it." Jack said, stopping the eerie sensation. "Only I want you to hold on tight. Clench it."

Clench?

Jack projected a bloodthirsty image of strangling a foe by the neck.

His hand clenched firmly.

"That's it. Now keep it that way even if my hand slackens. Okay?"

Yes.

Now Jack could turn all his attention to his right hand, controlling the rope sling, and his basic weaponry. Once he swung in through the glass, all hell was going to break loose, and he wanted his full attention on returning fire.

"Jack, what's up?"

"I'm going to try to swing in and kick my way through the windows," Jack told Dragon.

"All right then. Good luck."

"Right." Jack took a deep breath and began to swing.

★ ★ ★

Amber sat uncomfortably by the windows, watching Rolf pass across the promenade. They were watching the stairwells, he and a small army of mercenaries, rifles ready, waiting for Jack to show up. She tried to roll her shoulders and ease the tense muscles, her hands still bound behind her back. She glared at Rolf. If he hadn't put some kind of psychic muffler on her, she'd consider blasting him anyway. Now, drugged, considering was all she could do.

She squinted. White sunlight glared off the heavily tinted windows. It was the brightest she'd ever seen the sun since she'd come to this marshworld. But then, it had been raining almost constantly. Fuzzily, she thought of looking for rainbows. Amber turned her head, eyes narrowed against the glare. The opalescent sun swung closer, coming right at her bedazzled eyes.

Amber let out a scream of joy, as the windows shattered, and Jack swung through feet first, gauntlet firing. He let go of the rope sling and straightened, the battle armor shining in all its glory.

Tears slid down Amber's cheeks as she got to her feet. Killing Jack Storm in his full battle armor was like trying to kill the sun itself.

"Amber! Get down!"

She dropped to the floor as told, and lay there, cheek down among the glass shards, sobbing in fear and happiness.

Jack laid down a sheet of laser fire that bounced off the flooring. A curtain of fire roared upward, cutting off a bank of mercenaries from Amber. He did a somersault over the curtain, firing as he went. He tried to cock his left fist, his ears roaring with the heightened pulse of the bloodsong Bogie sang.

The room was filled with mercenaries. Jack had a split second in which to wonder where Rolf got the clout to hire like this, then whirled, as a man stood, readying to throw a percussion grenade. Left-handed, he shot. The grenade went flying and came to rest at the edge of the stair well.

He clipped off a second projectile shot, sending it over. Yells cut short told him he'd stopped a second band of men in their tracks.

The gauges showed a red field. Jack pumped his knees and did a somersault, carrying him and the line of fire away from Amber. As he landed, he laid down another spray of fire. The mercenaries tumbled over one another to stay out of range.

A grenade splattered on his armor, knocking him back. He stumbled and righted himself, and took the attacker's head off so neatly, the laser cauterized him at the neck.

But with a red field, he couldn't go on like this much longer. He chinned the mike.

"I don't want you," Jack broadcast. "Just Rolf." He turned, and pointed the left gauntlet at the far bank of windows. He flexed his fingers, triggering the laser cannon. The wall blew out and the wind whistled freely. He turned back around to view the psychological effect of his mayhem.

The mercenaries looked at one another. Their faces were pinched. Jack could read their thoughts as if they'd been spoken. Why should they face him for a few credits, just to save Rolf's hide? Like miraculous waters of old, they parted, and their employer stood crouched in the middle.

Rolf weighed his options. He eyed Jack, then straightened up from behind his shield. It clattered to the hotel ballroom floor. "Take the suit off and fight man to man," he challenged. "You win . . . I let you walk out of here with Amber. I win. . . ." The man grinned evilly. "I have what I came for."

"Jack, no!" Amber, struggling to her knees, begged him.

The suit was nearly out of power, anyhow. Jack didn't have a lot of options left. He reached up and took his helmet off. "You heard him," he told the watching men. Weapons were holstered at his words.

Don't leave me. Berserker joy ebbed. Jack felt suddenly, dismally, alone.

"I'll be back," Jack said quietly. "If not . . . get to Amber, somehow. Okay?"

?. Then, reluctantly, as Jack beamed a mental picture of Amber climbing into the suit and escaping with the power remaining, *Fight free.*

* * *

Jack peeled the suit off. He stood it up on its own, Flexalinks locked into position. He looked at Amber. She was in the process of discreetly sawing loose her ropes with one of the glass shards. She looked back, wide-eyed and innocent. He looked to the suit, trying to communicate with her, then turned his back, desperately hoping she understood.

Rolf approached. He left his shield rocking on the floor. Suddenly, he leapt, bright metal shining in his hand.

Amber yelped. "He's got a knife!"

Jack dodged, but not in time. The man hit him in the shoulder, a shoulder already mottled purple with the beating he'd taken that morning. Jack reeled back. The knife opened up a nasty weal along his ribs. The point stuttered on a bone and twisted away as Jack gasped and went down.

Bare torsoed, as he always was when he wore the suit, Jack was at an extreme disadvantage. As he rolled over to escape a second lunge from Rolf, something hard dug at his thigh. He left a crimson streak on the floor. Then he remembered the ceremonial Fisher knife. He feinted clutching his side as he got to his feet, instead pulling the knife from his pants pocket.

He turned, weight forward on the balls of his feet, ready, his knife glittering in his hand. Surprise flashed across Rolf's face. His knife was slender, a switchblade of honed ceramic, made so as not to set off metal sensors. Jack's was a hunting knife, tempered metal, jagged edge, a wicked killing blade, compared to the epee-thin switchblade.

Rolf lifted his knife and gave a tiny salute. Then he settled into his crouch and they circled one another cautiously. "You can't last long," Rolf said. "That's a nasty cut. And you look like shit. Someone's already beat the crap out of you today."

Jack ignored the pain. He felt the knife hilt warm in his hand. "Don't have to last long. Just long enough to face you."

Footsteps echoed down the stairwell. Jack flinched, his attention going to the noise. He saw Dragon coming down, with a contingent of their own fighters. He looked back to Rolf. Too late. The knife came at his face. Jack parried, but the heavier and healthier Rolf held him in a deadly embrace.

Rolf's flint dark, soulless eyes glittered. "You're about to die. And for what? Gutter slag like Amber? You know what she is? Do you?"

Breathing heavily, Jack fought to break the other's hold. They circled locked in a sinister dance.

"I'll tell you what she is, since she hasn't. She's an assassin. Got that? She's got powers . . . has she shown them to you yet? Let's hope she doesn't. She can kill with her mind." Rolf's lips pulled away from his teeth. A vein pulsed in his temple as he inexorably wrestled the knife closer to Jack's throat. "I've got her trained. She doesn't even know it. But her targets are already locked in. Subliminal like. I say the right buzz word and off she goes. Boom! Like a time bomb."

Amber made a faint sound at Jack's back. But he couldn't afford to listen to her. "No," he said, in her defense. He couldn't say more as he struggled just to breathe.

"That's right. Subliminal. She doesn't even know who to stay away from, but she's a killer. Jack. Remember that. Now you don't want to keep me from walking away with her. I'm the one who programmed her. I'm the only one who can deprogram her." Rolf took a deep breath. "So long, sucker."

Rolf brought the blade down and shifted his hold. Jack took a deep breath as the blade bit into his throat, but Rolf's new hold slipped on his bloody torso, and the blade turned wrong. Fiery pain sliced across Jack's throat as he twisted out from under the knife.

Rolf hit the floor with a thud. He let out a grunt as Jack slammed on top of him and grabbed a handful of greasy, brown curls. He tilted Rolf's head back and brought the ceremonial knife down.

"Just tell me who bankrolled you, Rolf. Who told you where to find us and gave you the money to go chasing us."

Rolf made a hissing noise. Then he got out, "Gilgenbush." He tried to shrug loose. "You've got some real enemies, whoever you are."

Jack pressed on the knife blade. "Are you sure?" He wanted to hear the name Winton—oh, how he wanted to hear that name, even though it meant that Winton now knew who his enemy was and how to reach him. But Jack wanted even more desperately to be able to reach Winton.

For the Sand Wars. For Claron. For his dimly remembered home. His vision blurred with pain and dampness. "Are you very sure?"

"Hell, I'm sure! It's Gilgenbush, the rogue general."

Jack thought of Skal, his friend and honorable enemy, and began to draw the blade across Rolf's swelling throat. The skin parted at the point and the first few crimson drops welled up.

"Hold!" Dragon's voice rang out authoritatively. "Hold in the name of Pepys, Emperor of the Dominion."

Breathing gustily, sweat obscuring his eyesight, Jack looked up and squinted. He saw the small, compact man moving down the stairwell. He stayed straddling Rolf and left the blade resting on the skin of his throat. "I would suggest," Jack said huskily, "not moving until we find out what's going on."

Rolf stayed very still.

"Jack," Amber said, her voice quavering. "It's him. It really is."

Jack felt the blood seeping out, from his side and from his neck. He fought to keep thinking coherently. He wiped the back of his left hand across his face and eyes, keeping the other with knife steady at Rolf's neck.

The Dragon and the emperor stopped in front of Jack. Pepys was a wiry, compact man, with frizzy red hair, already terribly thinned, and electric green eyes that smiled at him almost before the rest of his curious face did.

"Let him go, Storm," the emperor said, kindly. "Dragon here has filled me in on the situation. But, I may remind you, Rolf is a guest of the ex-ruler of this world, and diplomatic courtesy requires that we let him go unharmed."

Dragon said tersely, "You need medical attention, Jack. Amber's safe now." He leaned over. "And he's our employer."

Employer? Jack blinked. He felt very cold.

The emperor nodded. "You've done a good job here. Discretion is the word, of course. The sooner you let him up, young man, the sooner we can discuss your joining my elite guard. Dragon has recommended you very highly. I think it's safe to say that you'll be going places—if you live."

". . . answers," said Jack faintly. "I need some answers."

Pepys reached for the knife. "Then I suggest we make sure you stay alive to ask the questions."

With great effort, Jack unclenched his hand from the knife, letting the emperor take it. In a swoop of blackness, he heard Amber scream, very faintly.

* * *

Amber rubbed her bare shoulders. In the late night breeze, her evening gown ruffled and billowed, carrying an echo of the glow from the rose obsidite palace. She went to the parapet and looked down over the cities. "I keep wishing it would rain," she said. "To clear the air."

"We can go back someday," Jack answered.

"Skal and Mist would like that." She smiled wistfully. "I'm sorry about Claron."

He shrugged. "The project's not hopeless. At least terra-forming is workable there. On Dorman's Stand—it's not." He paused, both of them thinking of the planet lost forever behind a Thrakian curtain of sand.

Good fighting, Bogie interjected. Amber reached out and patted the suit sleeve. She looked up at Jack, who stood, helmetless beside her. The scar at his neckline was barely noticeable. "I'm glad you kept the suit."

"Get rid of Bogie? I couldn't think of it. Besides, he's good as new." And, somehow, in the last few weeks, Jack had won obedience from the demon-driven fighter presence within. He felt an uneasy rapport with the warrior spirit.

"He?" Amber grinned.

Jack shrugged. "Feels like a he."

"Maybe it's a she." Amber tossed her head. Her light ash brown hair flowed back over her shoulders, with a subtle scent of perfume. "What about it, Bogie?"

"Questions," Jack said. "We all have questions." He reached out and put an arm around Amber, drawing her close to the suit. Bogie put feeling into the Flexalinks, and it was like hugging her to his bare skin. Amber flushed demurely. "Tomorrow I'll start working on the answers."

She looked up at him, her golden brown eyes shining. "I always wondered what it would be like to kiss you," she said suddenly, boldly.

"Well, maybe not all the answers tomorrow," Jack returned, bending down to her. "That one I can handle tonight."

www.ingramcontent.com/pod-product-compliance
Lightning Source LLC
Chambersburg PA
CBHW020410180626
46812CB00003B/906